GRAVE MAGIC

DARK URBAN FANTASY
THEA ATKINSON

THEA ATKINSON, AUTHOR

Have you got your free ebook yet?

Be sure to visit http://theaatkinson.com to get your freebie.

CHAPTER 1

I WASN'T DEAD. THAT was the thing that hit me as I climbed up from unconsciousness and scented the tang of antiseptic and old blood. The only thing that kept the panic at bay was knowing that if I was dead, I probably wouldn't smell the antiseptic. Blood, maybe, but not antiseptic. Neither of that helped, though, because some part of my lizard brain whispered to me that I should be afraid. Very afraid.

Then I wished I was dead because at least I'd be past fear.

I struggled to open my eyes against the glue of tears and dried fluid that held them together. Swallowing became an issue. Weariness wore me like an old rag.

A cough rattled my throat and caught midway from my voice box to my uvula. That was when everything else came riding in like a storm of hornets. Magic. I smelled magic. And magic was bad. Magic had tried to kill me.

Tried and failed, my brain rasped against its synapses. I'd beaten it back. But it had cost me. It may still be lurking nearby, waiting for its chance to strike. Lurking. The way it had at the hotel when I'd thought I was safe. When I least expected it.

A scream tore its way up my throat, and that too got stuck. The gurgling, wet sound of it filled my ears. So at least my hearing was still functioning if my voice wasn't. The hammer and anvil inside beat its little drum in time with my ragged breathing, shallow and growing faster by the second.

Other sounds leeched into my ears and consciousness: the distant sound of a P.A. calling for a doctor. A clock ticking. The sound of vegan leather creaking from somewhere close. Conversation chattered away nearby like plastic teeth muffled by walls and plaster.

I was in a hospital then. My head thrashed back and forth on a pillow with very little give as I tried to wake up fully, and the sound of movement rustled in my ears like plastic wrap. A hospital was about as safe as a hotel room in my experience. Neither had proven truly safe.

Terror bit at the edges of my awareness. I wanted to wake the hell up for real, but I wasn't sure yet why I felt such panic.

Someone—a nurse, probably—laid a hand on my forehead and whispered that everything was going to be alright. I was going to be fine.

Fuck that, I wanted to say. Being fine was going to take more than a cool hand and a soothing voice. Even I knew that, and I was climbing out of the hole of near-death.

But my tongue wouldn't obey. It took several struggles up that mountain of awareness before I realized I was drugged and therefore unable to do more than blink in and out of consciousness. It took several more Sisyphean ascents before I remembered why.

I'd fought the coven. I'd fought the coven and I'd lost. They weren't broken or defeated. They'd managed to get away and in doing so, left me in tatters.

Each time that memory came to me, something inside cringed and whimpered and shrank down into a

pathetic ball and I dropped back out of consciousness again. The cycle repeated itself too many times,
enough that I started to wince when I knew awareness
was pushing back the fog of sleep again.

"Water," I said when I crawled out of the hole far
enough to feel my tongue in my mouth as it worried my
back teeth. "Thirsty."

I tried to lift my hand to indicate I wanted a drink
because I was pretty sure that the words that slipped
through the slackness of my lips sounded like gibber-
ish. I had to swat at my chin twice before I was able to
mime holding a glass.

The nurse swore. "Fucking Christ on a cracker," she
said. "You're thirsty. Fuck. Jesus what is wrong with
me?"

The leather chair creaked again and a moment later
the rim of a Styrofoam cup crinkled against my bottom
lip as a strong hand cupped the back of my head.

Ice chips eddied onto my tongue with a sort of frigid
taste of chlorine, but I gobbled them down anyway.
They numbed the rawness of my throat. The fire inside
was quenched for ten blessed seconds.

Then my synapses fired off other memories of Styrofoam. Cups with steaming coffee being drank outside
my shop by a pack of strange men as I waited to go in,
being pressed into my hands as I stood on the pier with
a dozen police officers scurrying around a crime scene.

I shoved the cup away. The nurse cussed again as it
fell with a thwack to the floor.

"Thank fuck this isn't my day job," she said. "Much
easier dealing with the dead."

Not a nurse. Parrish. I should have known long before this. The strong hand. The language. The smoky
voice.

"Owen," I said and tried to lift my head. I had to warn her. I had to tell her something about him. Something important.

"He's already on it," she said. "He's got Layne guarding that little fledgling, trying to get some answers out of her about the alpha. Don't you worry, Brie. We got your back."

Tears spilled over the rims of my eyes. I chased the thread of memory the way a hound did a crafty rabbit, but it got away from me, and I could feel myself falling asleep again.

I dreamed of puppies and old musty books. The smell of cinnamon and licorice wafted around me as I stooped to pick up a length of scarlet ribbon and followed it to a mossy cave with a black earth floor and a pinprick of light at the end shaped like a crown.

Teeth flashed in the dark. I gasped. Scrabbled for purchase along the walls with nails that were bitten to the quick.

I had to find my way out. I had to run. I had to—

"Brie!"

Soft fingers trailed my cheek. "You're having a nightmare."

I choked as I tried to swallow. Parrish let go of a frustrated but sympathetic sigh. "Here. Drink this."

Not Styrofoam this time. Plastic. And not just water and ice but watermelon and strawberries. I gulped the cool liquid down. Then seconds later my stomach heaved it back up in wracking spasms that left me feeling as strong as a cup of dishwater tea.

Liquid pooled in the space between my chin and shoulder.

Parrish groaned out loud. "What in the bright blue hell was I thinking? I should have fucking known. God, Brie. You and your stomach."

This time, I managed to crack an eyelid. She was coming at me with a white hospital terry cloth. She wasn't rough as she hoisted me onto my side and rolled me over, but she was firm. My back rested against the flat of her palm as she fiddled with something beneath me. Cleaning up the mattress, I supposed.

The sheets peeled against my bare legs with the determination of a soldier shaking out his bedroll.

She let me back down against the plastic protector.

"I'm going for the nurse," she said and squinted down at me, her gaze soft but scolding. "Don't puke again."

I nodded my response and I was pretty sure she hesitated, that her gaze flicked to my neck, but then she spun on her heel and left me alone.

The next time I woke, the smell of vomit was gone. The sheets had been changed. I wore a fresh hospital gown. A strange weight pinned my legs to the mattress. I might have panicked if I'd been a bit more coherent. As it was, I felt soggy and thick. Like a wet cotton ball.

Drugs. They'd pumped me with drugs again. No doubt they were on a schedule. I supposed I could find solace in that. They dulled more than just pain. My mind needed to be combed through just to clear it of the tangles and knots.

Parrish was snoring. The full-throated noise of it must have been what woke me. I hefted my head from the pillow and sent a bleary gaze over my torso to see her right arm flung over my legs. Her head lay just next to me.

Judging by the ache in my legs, she'd been there a while. I scooted sideways, trying to move. Dizziness swirled through me like water down a drain.

"Parrish," I said and was surprised to hear how coherent it sounded even if it came out as no more than a whisper. "Parrish, wake up."

She bolted awake, jumping to her feet and holding her arms out at her sides as though she expected to be attacked. In the shadows of the room, she looked very much like a predator. Her eyes glowed yellow then blinked back to normal when they swept over me.

"Brie," she said, and the relief in her voice was palpable. She approached the bed on cat feet, quiet and swift. Her hand brushed over my forehead. "Thank the sweet little baby cheesey. You're not so hot anymore. I'll go get Zach."

"Owen," I said, and when my eyebrows knit together, I couldn't remember why I'd said his name.

"No. I'm not going for that prick, but I wish I could," she said patiently. "Alas, it's Doctor No Good for you. He said to wake him if you woke." She canted her head at me. "That almost sounds punny."

A jolt of fear raced through my chest. "Don't leave me," I said. I clawed for the buzzer, feeling panic cresting like a tsunami despite the haze of drugs.

She reached for my hand and met my fingers with hers. Squeezed. "You are fine, Brie. No one is going to hurt you."

"Hospital," I said in a trembling voice.

She nodded. "I know. Believe me, I know. But it's not some lackey watching over you this time. It's me." She slammed her chest with her fist. "And they'll have to fucking dismember me to get to you."

I tried to swallow and couldn't. She pulled the sheets up with her free hand and tucked it beneath my chin. "He's at the desk. I won't be just three minutes. We disconnected the buzzer because we didn't want you ringing for a nurse. Zacharia is tending you personally."

She pulled her hand from mine and curled my fingers into my palm before patting it. "You're at the end of the hall in a private room. Anyone coming in has to come all the way down the hall past Zach. They'll have to pass me in the hall when I leave, and I won't let anyone past me."

I nodded.

"You trust me?"

It took a moment, but I nodded again and she smiled. "Good girl."

She halted at the doorway and looked back at me. "Count to a hundred."

I knew what she was doing. Misdirection and distraction. Keep the crazy panic attack lady quiet. I let her go and whispered out the numbers to myself, fighting the drowsiness that threatened to pull me back under.

It took some minutes before I heard voices again. They were arguing and apparently had been for some time judging by the raised voices. One of them was Parrish, evidenced by the almost gratuitous lacing of cuss words interspersed throughout her conversation.

The other had to be the good doctor. He was the one with the hum of thin patience in his voice.

"You can't keep glowering at anyone that walks by," he said. "People come to the hospital all the time."

"That's your problem, Zachariah," she said. "You don't glower enough and that's what got her nearly ripped up in here the last time."

His laughter came out forced. "I doubt very much she'd have been ripped asunder, Bea."

"Don't. You. Fucking. Call. Me. That. I told you a hundred times already. Beatrice is dead. That's a dead name. You of all people should know how much it matters to me that the name stay dead."

I tried to lift my hand to interject myself into the argument. It felt like a lead weight with an oil tanker on it. It took several seconds to realize Zach was sitting on my hand. No. Had fallen onto my hand. Cancel that. Had been shoved backward and landed on his ass on my bed right where my hand lay.

Parrish had shoved him, based on what she said next.

"Layne paid you well to watch over her," she said, all the vitriol in her voice dripping with a sweetness that didn't sound like her at all. "He paid you in advance. And you let her down. That bastard wolf and that bitch," this last said with a shrill note that indicated she had probably sprayed a little saliva at the same time. "That bitch tried to kill her. All on your watch."

He sighed and lifted a butt cheek so he could plumb beneath and extract my hand from beneath him. I tried to squeeze his fingers, but he evidently felt nothing because he laid my hand gently on my abdomen. It felt very much like someone else's hand except for the pins and needles that had started to prickle through the fingers.

I tried to lift my head and blackness swelled over the back of my eyelids. The voices died and rose again, and I guessed I'd passed out for a second or two. The skip in the argument, like a bubble in an old vinyl record made me feel like I'd lost time.

"Third," he said, and I had the feeling he'd held up his hand because she snorted before he had a chance to continue. Whatever the first and second items were had got lost in the fog of coma.

"Third: I'd stop calling you by your dead name if you'd stop treating me like you hate me."

"I do hate you."

I managed to peel open one eyelid and, for an instant, the elation of victory seared a path along my mind. The doctor raked a hand through his hair, but my eyelid shuttered down again before his fingers made it all the way to the back of his skull. I tried again and failed. Left to just lie there and listen to them argue, I groaned deep in my throat.

They paused at the sound. I guessed they were both looking me over, seeing if I could respond any further. My mouth worked around the words that tried to escape. Strong hands adjusted the sheet, tucking it in around my shoulders and making me feel like a mummy.

I wanted to cry at the futility of it. And when Zach smoothed out the sheets and continued talking to Parrish as though nothing had happened, my eyes burned with tears.

"I want to respect you, Parrish. I really do. But no matter how much I try, you just hold onto that grudge like a dog with a bone. What recourse do I have except to fight back?"

"Fight with something else," she said. "

"A warrior goes for the jugular, Parrish. You should know that. You want me to respect the death of that name, you start treating me with respect."

"Go fuck yourself."

The mattress shifted as he pushed off the bed. Pins and needles spread to my forearm.

"I want you out of here," he said. "I've already let you stay too long."

"You can't do that. She has no one to look out for her except me."

"She has me. She is safe here." He must have set something down on the side table because a clipped sort of thud sounded. "We've taken all the precautions we can. You're making people nervous. Anyone so much as steps foot in the hallway, and you're on them like red on blood. And that's just when you step out of the room. God forbid the maintenance staff try to come in and clean the room or the nurses check on her."

"She has you. She doesn't need a nurse. And the janitors can go fuck themselves too. I'll change her sheets."

"You can be very scary, Parrish. Even when people don't know your past, they can see the monster inside because you are letting her show. Put her to ground or leave. That's your choice."

"Prick," she said, and I had the feeling he shrugged by the noise of fabric rustling. They argued more, their voices rising and falling now very much like the ebb of an old sea, taking me to the heights of the crest and down again, lulling me to sleep, pulling me under.

My eyes burned. A snore slipped out, a sure sign I was on the cusp of awareness but not quite under.

And that's when I saw something on the edge of a shadow, sliding into reality.

CHAPTER 2

DRUGS ARE A STRANGE thing. Some say they dull your senses, but I sometimes think they sharpen some as they soften the hard edges of reality. I'd certainly seen it happen when I'd been using psilocybin to aid my clients in seeing what I needed them to see. I wasn't sure what kinds of drugs Zach had pumped me with, but I knew what I was seeing wasn't of this world.

I sucked in a breath at the sight of the shape morphing into color and form from the darkness of the corner shadows. Parrish must have heard my inhalation because she shot me a sharp glance with her auburn eyebrows lifted half an inch from their regular positions.

Thank god, I thought. Thank God she heard me.

"Owen," I said and this time she responded, halle-freaking-lujah.

"Brie?" she said. "Are you alright?" She shoved past doctor Zach with a brush of movement that sent him reeling back on his heels.

By the time she reached my bedside, she was sniffing, scenting the air as though she could smell something rotten.

"Sulfur," I said.

"Smells like rotten eggs," Parrish said over her shoulder to Zach. "Brie says witches use it before casting to protect themselves." She touched my hand. "Is it magic, Brie? What's happening?"

"Owen," I said again, my eyes glued to the thing that had shivered out of the corner. It didn't look like a werewolf, but it wore his face. Almost as though it was trying to tell me something. It nodded, and I said Layne's father's name again. One long, slow incline of the beast's head and I knew it was trying to communicate with me.

Parrish squeezed my hand. "What's wrong, Brie," she said and looked over her shoulder. "Zach, what's going on over there? What are you doing?"

"Nothing."

"You're doing something because Brie is looking at you and she looks pretty damned terrified." She dropped my hand and spun on her heel to face the doctor. I only had eyes for the creature. It was mouthing something now, slowly, as though I was deaf. I sort of wished I was. Maybe then, I'd have acquired some skill at reading lips.

I strained to make out the words. It looked like the thing was trying to say Owen, but I couldn't be sure. I'd have to get out of bed, pad closer, and lay my ear across its mouth to be sure. I couldn't do more than gawk at it.

"What the fuck?" Parrish said and gripped my arm. "Zach what in the hell did you give her?"

"Just some pain meds. Nothing special."

Parrish scooped for my feet, and I realized I'd slid my legs free of the blankets and nearly touched down to the floor. "PCP would be my bet," she said. "Or cocaine because she shouldn't be able to fight me like this. Fuck. Do you have a nice little sideline going, trying to create your own clientele?"

"Trust me, it would be a hell of a lot more lucrative than doctoring for Layne. He squeezes every bit of metal out of the dime he pays me."

Zach rushed to her aid, and together they had me bundled back beneath the sheets, Zach complaining he'd have to put the intravenous back in. With a numb feeling, I swung my gaze to the arm he was holding onto. Blood had risen on my inner elbow like a rose in bloom.

"Owen," I said to Parrish and tried to point at the creature in the corner. All I managed was to lift my arm an inch before it fell like a sack of dried beans to the mattress again.

Parrish shook her head and peered over her shoulder. She looked straight at the creature. "She's seeing things," she said. "Maybe you should lessen the dose, you quack."

Zach swiped at my arm with a cloth. I swung my gaze to his and back to my arm as a sting raced up my veins. My eyelids felt like they had drawstrings on them and someone was yanking down the shades.

Even as they closed, the creature in the corner began to transform. It had tentacles now. Nine of them. And its three heads were spinning like a top, Owen's facade a distant memory. I had the horrifying sense of falling as I watched the creature. The feeling of deja vu became a spiraling carnival ride that made my guts twist.

When the thing reached out for me with four of those long arms, I screamed. Next I knew, Parrish was sitting next to me with her arms flung over my chest. I blinked. Zach was gone. The shadow creature was gone.

And I felt more lucid.

"Layne?" I said, the name scratching along the inside of my throat as though it was bits of glass.

Parrish lifted her head from the mattress. "Brie? You're awake? Are you alright?"

"I'm thirsty."

She narrowed her gaze at me. "We've done this before. You're not going to puke or see things are you?"

I shook my head and thankfully, nothing rattled inside.

She grunted but pushed herself to her feet. I watched her pluck a water bottle from the side table along with a thick terrycloth square of fabric with hospital branding along its edge. Not taking any chances, I guessed.

I waited for her to return with it, noting how much darker the room looked than the last time I'd been awake.

She put the bottle to my lips and tilted. I drank greedily at first, letting the cool water spill over onto my chest and soak my gown until she yanked the bottle away from me. I motioned for more.

"Be careful," she said. "They had you intubated for a few hours. You're probably just sore."

"Layne," I said again. I had no idea how long I'd been there, but during my conscious moments I hadn't seen him. My heart hurt remembering why that might be. Tears filled my eyes.

Parrish must have noticed them because she swiped the back of her hand across my cheeks. "I haven't let him in," she said. "Remember? It's one of the things you kept muttering when you came to. Keep Layne away."

I'd said that? I had no recollection. Probably because of the curse. He was cursed, wasn't he? That's what Owen had said. That a witch would be the death of him.

I was a witch. I was *that* witch.

I nodded at her. The pain in my chest didn't go away, but at least I knew it was of my own making.

"He's with that fledgling," she said. "I didn't tell him you're here, Brie. I didn't think I'd be able to keep him away if I told him."

She hung her head and the grease in her roots showed she'd not washed it in a few days. "I'm not strong enough for that, so I had to improvise. There's no way I could lie. Seemed easier just not to tell him you were here."

So he didn't know. At least I could still fool myself into thinking he still cared. Although how could he? I'd hurt him so badly to protect him. I both wanted him to barge into the room and declare his undying love for me and wanted him to hate me at the same time.

I tried to smile for her but my lips stuck to my teeth.

She lifted the bottle to my lips again. "Here. Have another drink, then I'll put some more balm on your lips. They look like frayed paper."

I took another swallow and when she slid a greasy bit of fragrant balm over my lips, I felt a bit better. Not great, but better. "It's OK," I told her. "I understand."

"I don't," she said. "I mean, I know you two had a fight, but he would want to know you're in the hospital. He would want to know what happened."

"It's better this way," I said. "I'm still a little fuzzy on the details too."

"You nearly died is the details," Parrish said. "Not sure I need more than that."

I pressed my lips together, smearing the grease as I ran one lip over the other. "You'll have a hard time keeping it from him when Zach sends his bill."

"Layne isn't paying Doctor-Good-for-Nothing. I am."

I blinked at her. "Parrish, that's a hell of a lot of money."

She shrugged. "Money well spent as far as I'm concerned. Plus, he's cutting me a deal. I call him Doctor Zach instead of whatever else pops into my mind—at least to his face—and he bills me for your meds only."

My eyebrows climbed high enough to make my skin hurt, and she gave me a sheepish smile because I'd been party to her verbal recitations of his skills or lack thereof.

"He's the best, Brie," she said. "No matter how much swamp water is under the bridge we dance upon when we see each other, even I had to concede that."

I recalled their argument I'd overhead as I lay drugged and immobile. No doubt the deal had cost her a lot more than just money. Pride is a pretty valuable thing, and Parrish took great pride in hating the man.

"At least you didn't have to lie to Layne," I said, feeling the pang of loss once more. "I know how hard that would be." A sigh of longing slipped out of me as I thought of Layne and that powerful alpha energy, so potent it even affected me. It would be nearly impossible for her to lie to him and make it convincing.

I shifted on the mattress, feeling as though my butt had gone numb. "How long have I been here anyway?"

"Three days."

I closed my eyes at the words. Three days gone from my life. But at least I had a life, I reminded myself. Things were coming back in blips like on a radar screen. There one second and gone the next but I had the feeling from those millisecond blasts that I was damn lucky to be alive.

"I'll pay you back," I told her.

She patted my hand. "No worries. I've got coin to spare. Been around the block a few generations. That tends to rack up a bit of savings."

"Even so. I want to pay it back." I thought of the thick wad of bills an earlier client had paid me for exorcising a death mask. "As soon as I get out of here, we can go back to my apartment. I have a bit of savings there. Not sure if it'll be enough, but it's a start."

I lifted my right hand that was still attached to an I.V. "I'm guessing now that I'm conscious, Zach will unhook me and let me go."

"Suit yourself. Far be it for me to rob a gal of her independence. Sometimes we just gotta stand up on our own two feet."

A pang went through my chest at her words. A flash of memory tripped through my mind's eye like a Russian dancer stomping through with hard-soled boots. In it, Scarlett stood before me, an ethereal wisp emerging from the darkness. She was whispering something. Tentacles reached out from behind her to grapple for my limbs.

A gasp escaped me, startling Parrish.

"What's wrong? What is it? Should I get Zach?"

Not Doctor-good-for-nothing. Not Doctor Quack. Zach. She was worried, that was plain.

I waved her away as she hovered over me. "No. I'm fine. Just a memory, that's all." I squinted up at her pinched face. "At least I think it was a memory." I waited till she pulled up the plastic chair, its feet scraping the floor noisily.

"Scarlett," I said. "I saw Scarlett."

She made a thoughtful sound. "I didn't want to bring it up," she said. "You being so fresh out of your coma and all, but you told me something interesting about her when I found you."

I held up my hand because just talking about it was wrestling recollections from the mud of my memory.

"She told me who I was," I whispered and swung my gaze to hers. "That's it, right?"

I held her green eyes with mine a long time before she nodded. "You said your mother was lost, is what you said. You didn't indicate you were anyone other than Brie."

I noted she was being very careful, the way you were with a person suffering from dementia. She didn't want to upset me, it seemed. Probably thought I was unstable.

"I am Brie," I said, just as careful. "But it's who my mother is that changes who I am." I closed my eyes, trying to catch the tail end of the thread as it sailed back into the darkness. "Hecate. She's my mother. The coven broke her."

"I remember," Parrish said. "That's exactly what you said when I found you, which I might add, we will have major discussions about when you are well, and part of that will be you finding a way to patch up the crater in my nerves that you dug out."

"It's not my fault," I said.

"No, it's that damn dog of yours that's to blame. It should have been Layne she dragged to your near-dead body. Fuck." She ran a hand through her hair and bits of it stuck up around her temples. "Do you know what that did to me?"

Her index fingers moved to her eyelids, and she peeled them down, showing how red her eyes were. "These peepers are as crimson as my pubic hair for Pete's sake. I haven't slept decent in three days. My wolf was so upset I had to force her into a corner in case she decided to go on a rampage. And trust me. We both wanted to go on a rampage."

She shuddered. "Zach calmed her down. Fuck him. Now I owe him more than money." She glared at me with a wet softness in her eye.

"I'm sorry."

"You should be. Do you know how much I hate that Doctor Quack is one of only two shifters who can soothe the beast?"

"I imagine."

She made a humming sound as though she didn't think I could imagine. "He'll never let me live it down, either. If I could have gone to Layne..."

I reached for her hand. "Thank you," I said. "You're a good friend."

She glowered at me. "You need Layne," she said. "When he finds out I kept this from him, my ass is so much grass I'll be churning out cuds."

"We can't," I said. "And I don't think he'll even care."

"Of course he'll care. He loves you."

I turned away from her because my eyes were stinging. "I can't, Parrish. What's done is done, and it's best it stays that way."

"What in the hell did he do to you?"

"It's not what he did to me. It's what I'll do to him."

I explained it all, then. The curse that Layne had hanging over his head, the one that meant a witch who didn't understand her own power would cause his death.

"So that's why Owen was so dead set on witches," she mused aloud. "Forgive the bad pun. But he's been bitching about them for a hundred years or more. I always thought it was because he'd had such a hard time breaking our pack away from the witches we guarded."

Just like that, the memory flooded in, and I remembered what Owen had done to me.

Chapter 3

THREE IMAGES FLASHED THROUGH my mind, and each of them sent shivers down my back in waves that had me curling over my stomach protectively.

The first was Owen telling me I would end up killing Layne because of his curse. The cell memory of that moment was one that I felt in my marrow, and it was quickly replaced with the image of Owen phoning his driver to take me to a hotel of his choosing so I wouldn't have to go home to a house that might be staked out by the coven.

The third was the one when his fledgling wolf pulled me into the hotel room where the black coven was waiting for me.

He'd not only set me up, he'd made certain Layne wouldn't look for me after the coven had their way with me. I was beginning to doubt there even was a curse. I'd been foolish. I prided myself on reading people, and he'd completely duped me.

I might have whimpered at the thought because Parrish grappled for my shoulders, a note of worry in her voice.

"What's wrong," she said. "What is it?"

I peered up at her as I sat on the bed so curled into my core that I felt my boobs on my belly. "Owen," I said. "He's working for the coven."

She drew back as though I'd slapped her. When she shook her head in disbelief, her mouth hung open. "No."

My fists balled against my stomach. "Think about it. Who knew where I was when I was taken from the lingerie shops Who paid for the hotel room? Whose driver took me straight to them?"

Her head waggled back and forth as she fought the words she knew were true. "You're clutching at straws, Brie. Because you're sick and afraid and you're angry at him for putting a wedge between you and Layne."

"I wish I was," I said.

She was shuffling backward toward the door, shaking her head. The creamy complexion went so white the auburn eyebrows looked like little flames that flicked out toward her temples. I knew she had pieced together all the things in that moment that had taken me a near-death experience to puzzle out.

She might not have fitted each puzzle piece together, but she had enough of the picture to see the grand, sweeping theme of it.

"You're wrong, Brie," she said. "He's a bastard, but he wouldn't do something so heinous. He wouldn't have stood by and let all those people get murdered. He wouldn't have participated in it." She stomped her booted foot so hard on the tiles the impact put a pinched look on her face. "Fuck."

I hugged myself because I wanted so badly to embrace her and soothe away the shock but I was attached to the damn I.V., and I couldn't reach her.

I had to speak through tight lips because I really didn't want to have to admit the truth of it. "Honey told me. When she had me trapped in her circle. She told me Owen belonged to the coven. I know it's true. So do you."

Her lip curled back as she regarded me. In the moment, a flash of rage ran through her gaze, one so intense it turned her eyes yellow. The hairs on the back of my neck shot up in reaction. I was weak and vulnerable in the presence of a predator at that moment and my entire body knew it.

Her voice when it came was a mere rasp filled with threat. "What you're saying would tear the pack apart."

I didn't need her to explain what would happen to me, to our relationship, if I was wrong.

"I know," I murmured. "I know how bad it is. Do you really think I'd sling this accusation if I didn't know it for a fact?"

Her arms went round her midriff in echo of my own posture. She swallowed several times. The backs of her thighs butted up against the door handle of the private bathroom. With a growl, she spun on the door and kicked it. The resounding crack that shot through the room told me she'd broken the locking mechanism.

When it flew open and struck the wall on the other side, I wondered if she'd broken the hinges too. As if that one act had broken something within her, she fell against the frame, her hand clutching at the wood in a way that told me she wasn't sure of her own footing.

I felt for her, I wanted to help her, but I knew she'd have to process it all on her own. Like Scarlett, she'd have to stand on her feet and face down the worst of her fears.

We waited together for that moment, she with white knuckles and tense shoulders, facing away from me as she hung into the bathroom, and me tense on the bed, gripping my torso as though the hold was the sole thing that could keep me erect.

The clock's ticking was the only sound in the room for several moments until I heard a long, heavy sigh slip from her. The white-knuckled hand clutching the door wood slid down the frame and fell to her side before curling into a fist. The nail with the violet polish stroked along her index finger twice and then stopped.

I thought it best to wait for her to speak, to turn back to me and become the rational Parrish I'd come to know, but my anxiety wouldn't let me wait. I was afraid of what she might do if I didn't try to pull her back into the moment with me, to ground her again to our voices. Plus, I was damn terrified in general.

"I can tell you the rest," I said. "If you want to hear it. I can tell you all about the things I remember from that room where they held me. But if you don't want to hear it, I understand."

She spun to face me. The deadpan look on her face, I knew, was a conscious effort to keep herself calm. The wolf in her eyes stared back at me, and I grew acutely aware that I was bound to the bed by the tubing and equipment.

I remembered the moments weeks earlier when I'd confronted Sherry, one of my new clients who suffered a bad trip under the special brew of tea I used to employ as an authenticity tactic.

I instinctively pulled the memory to me and used it to put a soothing tone in my voice instead of the terrified note I knew would drip from me if I wasn't careful. That terror was bad enough I was pretty sure she could smell my fear, I couldn't compound it with sounding afraid too.

"The dog—Abbi—she knew they were in there," I said in a hushed voice. "She knew they were waiting for me and tried to warn me, but I was too trusting of Owen. Too busy trying to figure out what horrible thing the dog's appearance was portending to think for one second the danger might come from someone close to me."

Parrish's chest moved in deep, rhythmic inhalations and exhalations. In through her nose noisily. I swallowed and kept going, the tone just as important as the words. I'd had long days to work it through as my subconscious crawled over the events and circumstances.

Whatever she'd done while she sat with me for those days, she couldn't have gone over the things I knew because she hadn't been privy to them. She'd probably ran through a hundred scenarios, but not this one. Not the knowledge that her pack alpha was one of my biggest threats.

That bit of explanation should wait, however. It was too close to her sensibilities. I wasn't sure I'd keep the wolf at bay if I leaped right into discrediting a man she thought had pack interests topmost in his priorities.

No. I'd hooked her with the shock of his involvement, but now I needed to backtrack and give her a chance to process it before I returned to his deeds. Back story was important now. Enough to help her regain control. Enough to let me weave it for myself aloud.

"I think the dog wanted me to understand what waited for me, but she still wanted me to enter," I said. "I didn't know it then and certainly not right away, but Abbi knew I'd have to face them. She knew they'd call to Hecate and that once the goddess came, she could enter with me."

Parrish's expression loosened a little from the tight contortion of fury. The yellow in her eyes dimmed. Confusion crested over her brow, and I realized I had to back up even further.

"She's my mother, you see. The goddess. The coven did something to her. I don't know what, but they drained her. Maybe they are still draining her. It's what Scarlett told me. What I needed to remember. I'm the daughter of a goddess. Her blood is in my body. Like the other things are, the dog and John Smith."

Parrish swallowed, probably to oil the growl out of her voice when she said, "That's what you meant when you said we needed to put her back together. She's split. Not herself."

"Right. Whatever the coven wants from her, they must have messed up. They need me to complete their spell, but Hecate came. We...we fought them. She and I. She used the magic inside my blood to hold them back and help me resist them."

"And the dog was sent to fetch me."

"I think so."

I explained the rest as well. I started from the time I'd been pulled into the hotel room by the homeless youth turned werewolf, omitting for the moment, that Owen had been his sire. I told her about the candles, the circle of power.

When I relayed the story of that young werewolf's self-sacrifice under Honey's spell, she snarled, and I kept on despite the hatred in her expression for the thing he'd been forced to do.

I repeated the entire story, including the young wolf's sacrifice to initiate the spell, and the way the coven had been angry at Honey for bringing Hecate to the circle. The ones who died beneath the magic and the way

Honey nearly won but ran instead, taking my mother's amulet and grimoire with her. The sound of rage and regret in John Smith's voice when he knew the objects had been lost to her care.

I finished with the web of light that I thought heralded my death and let her piece the last together for me, taking up the story and explaining how she'd found the door partially open and how the dog had pushed her over the threshold and then just disappeared as she fell at my side and called 911.

"I haven't seen that stupid mutt since she abandoned me with you." She took a step toward me and I cringed at the unexpectedness of it. A look crossed her face, of regret and shame and she folded her arms over her chest as she stopped short of the bed.

"And Owen?" she asked in a low tone that sounded very much like a growl. "You're sure he's in league with them."

The way she said it made it sound so comic book evil, but we both knew it was more serious than that. She hadn't phrased the comment as a question either, because I sensed she was beginning to believe it. She was a smart woman. She'd see the hallmarks of betrayal for what they were.

"I don't know why," I said. "But Honey made it sound as though the coven felt he and his minions were no better than dirt under their nails."

"Honey," she spat out the name, and her lips peeled back from her teeth. "Bitch needs to get bitch slapped. If she thinks she is superior to a wolf, I'll be happy to show her a proper measuring stick. Stupid stupid bitch."

She pulled up the chair with a scraping noise as it moved along the tiles. When she settled onto it, she propped her elbows on the bed and planted her chin on the tops of her clasped fingers.

"That's just it," I said. "Owen and Layne both told me they were the guardians for the cult way, way back. I have no idea how long ago, but it sounds like perhaps Owen never did break with the coven." I gave her a look, one I knew she'd interpret correctly.

She shook her head at the inference. "Impossible. I'd know if the pack was involved. Because Layne would know."

I chewed my lip, afraid to broach the next question. She saved me the trouble by dropping her forearms to the bed and pushing away. "You can forget that possibility too," she said. "No way Layne is involved. Good guy, remember?"

I wanted to believe it. Thinking Layne might be in league with his father, that I'd trusted him, that I loved him, would be too much to deal with if it was true. But I had to play Devil's advocate. It was what made me good at what I did, so it hurt to follow the line of thought even if it was necessary.

"You're sure? He was off on a research trip, one that took weeks. And that fancy dinner he brought me to. Those other wolves were not just business associates. Owen wanted to show me off."

Again, she shook her head, this time with enough force to shake loose the bandana holding her hair. "I'm telling you, Brie, Layne isn't involved and frankly, I'm hurt you would even consider it."

She caught the bit of fabric as it fell across her shoulder and pulled at it, stretching it between us. "I've known Owen and Layne for over a hundred years. Long before you came into the picture. Owen hates witches.

Layne has told me he's cursed, but if he knows the extent of it, he never told me that."

I sagged against the mattress, sure of her conviction. So there really was a curse. A sigh of relief slipped out of me even though I'd not really believed it of him.

"I just...I just had to ask, you know?"

She pressed her lips together and nodded. "Not that it makes any difference," she said, "but I'd believe in Layne's innocence even if I didn't owe him my life. He's too damned puritan."

There was a long moment of silence when she looked down at her fingers. She ran one along the only nail she painted, the thumb of her left hand, always sporting a bright purple shade so out of character that I often wondered about it.

"Owen broke those kids, didn't he?" she said finally, looking up at me and stowing her hands onto her lap, out of my sight. "Just like he did with Farrel. He's making a new pack. One that can serve the coven without alerting his real pack of what he's doing. Using people he thinks of as expendable."

It hurt her, saying it. I wanted to find some other explanation, but there wasn't one available that could acquit him.

"Looks like that may be the case."

"Bastard," she said. "I didn't want to feel sorry for Farrel but Hell. No wolf should be made to feel expendable. None should be used or exploited. That poor bastard had no chance. It's pretty hard to resist your alpha, harder if he's also your sire. But for Farrel, when Owen was both of those things? Impossible."

She looked away, but I could see her chewing on her lip, thinking. I waited, feeling the electricity of tension as whatever long journeys of her memory she was travailing down took her to places that I couldn't share.

"Parrish," I said, finally. "I have to ask you something delicate."

She turned her attention to me. In her face, I saw the residue of those thoughts that probably haunted her when she was alone, and I saw the dread in her expression as she understood what I was about to ask.

"Don't ask it, Brie."

I fumbled for the hand she had laid onto her lap by grappling for her arm and sliding my fingers down until she pulled away.

"I have to ask," I said. "I'm sorry."

I paused, trying the words in my mind before I released them to sit between us. "Will you have to answer to your alpha if he asks you about me? Will you have to betray me to him?"

"Yes," she said without a trace of guile. "If my alpha asks where I've been these last days, I will tell him. If he asks me under alpha energy if you're still alive, I will have to confess what I know."

My stomach twisted. "I see," I said.

"I told you not to ask."

She reached for my hand then and held it between both of hers. "But all is not lost, you silly bitch. You asked about my alpha. Owen is not my alpha. I walk the thin line of his leadership, bowing where I should and yes siring him when he needs it. But Layne brought me into the pack. Layne is my alpha. When the chips are down, he's the only one I'll subjugate myself to."

She smiled right then, a bright, broad grin that showed her teeth. Her eyes flashed with a cheerful yellow glow. "And I doubt Owen told him anything about what happened to you in that hotel room."

"And what if Layne asks?" I swallowed a hard lump at the words because Layne had every right to hate me and I didn't blame him, but it still hurt to consider it. Even though I knew he wouldn't ask, I had to know what my options were. I had to know who was on my side.

"He's been real busy with that feral wolf chick, so I doubt he'll be scratching around any time soon, but if he does, then I got you covered," she said. "I'll just tell him I thought you died."

Chapter 4

"She did die," said a familiar voice from the doorway.

Zach. He wore a loose green shirt, open to the third button. His stethoscope danced in and out of the gap when he moved. He inclined his head toward me on the bed. "You know that, right?" he said. "You flat-lined."

I'd died. At some point between those moments I'd seen the golden web and the time I'm come to here in the hospital, I'd met my maker. The truth of his words hit home like a bat connecting the sweet spot of a baseball.

Fingers of memory reached for me and turned to smoke at the same moment my mind noticed they were there.

Whatever additional truth waited for me behind the darkness, my mind wasn't ready to know it, but that sense that I'd died should have been something I noticed the moment I'd first come to when I'd realized Parrish and Zach were in the room with me. When I knew I was in the hospital. That ethereal form sliding in from the shadows.

My mouth went dry as I regarded Zach who had slipped into the room and closed the door behind him, bracing his back against the panel. The door was green. Mossy green, much like Parrish's eyes.

"What do you mean I died?" I asked.

He ran his palm down over the front of his white coat, brushing away unseen crumbs or smoothing out nonexistent wrinkles. I'd come to recognize his nervous tick.

"I'd think that would be pretty clear, Brie," he said. "You died. Parrish doesn't have to lie to Layne at all. She can tell him exactly that in about..." he hooked his wrist toward him and peered down at a watchless arm. "Oh, I'd say pretty much right now."

Parrish gripped the arm rest of her chair as though she was going to hurl it at him. Instead, she used it to leverage herself to her feet." Fuck me with a silver spoon," she said. "What are you talking about?"

"I mean, Layne is on his way down the hallway right now. He's got a girl with him, and he looks pretty hot."

Hot, meaning angry or upset, not steamily gorgeous. The thought of him ranging toward us put a bud of urgency in my spine. Layne shouldn't be in the hospital, and he certainly wasn't coming here for me.

"Don't look at me," Parrish said as she eyed the plastic glass of orange juice that sat on my bedside table. "I didn't tell him you were here." Her eyelids shuttered to half-mast as she glared at Zach, and I had the feeling she was about to grab the O.J. and hurl it at him. "Did you tell him?"

A single raised brow over those baby blues indicated he had not.

Layne was here though. After all I'd done to keep him away from me, safe and unmolested despite his father's machinations. He was here.

I nearly leaped from the bed and might have made it all the way over the edge if not for the tubing attached to my arm that tugged on my skin and reminded me it was there.

I flinched at the expected pain and clasped the entry point, holding down the stent, praying I hadn't just done more damage. I didn't know anything about needles and tubing and veins and my eyes sought Zach. When they found him, I grazed his face, looking for evidence of trouble. And not just for myself.

"What's wrong with him?" I said. "Is he hurt? Did someone hurt him? Should we do something? I can't just lie here while he's in trouble. Why aren't you doing something?" I grabbed for Parrish's arm. "Why aren't you going to help him?"

Zach held up his hand to stem the tide of questions. "Hold on," he said, ticking off one finger by curling it into his fist. "He's fine. At least he appears to be at first glance. All piss and vinegar and that's a good indication he's not hurt. I didn't look him over very long. Just caught sight of him coming down the corridor and ducked in here."

He panned Parrish with a knowing glance. "Two, three, and four," he said, ticking the rest of his fingers down into his palm. "You owe me for this," he said. "I'm pretty sure he saw me slip in here."

This time Parrish did heft the chair with both hands from its place on the floor and swung it back like she'd let it go at him. "What the fuck, Zach?"

I had to give her credit. She remembered to use his Christian name the way she'd promised and not some slur she'd made up on the fly. Even if she was threatening to throw a chair at him. But I tended to agree with her. She had the best of points even if they weren't delicately articulated.

I pulled the blankets up to my chin. If Layne was hale and healthy, no good could come from him storming in here and seeing me hooked up to equipment. Not when I wasn't sure how we were going to handle the truth about his father. And not after what I'd done to him.

I wasn't ready to see the hatred lining his expression when he came face to face with the woman he thought had screwed his own father.

Parrish dropped the chair to the floor next to the bed and stormed the few feet to the doctor.

She slammed Zach on the shoulder with a flattened palm. "Get the fuck back out there, you dolt. Take him to the cafeteria or some shit. Just get him out of scenting distance of Brie for fuck's sake."

She ran her hand over the back of her neck as she scanned the room in a gesture that made me think she was looking for a place to hide me. She looked back at him when he didn't budge.

"Well?" she said with a flap of her arms. "What are you waiting for? Get the hell out of here and distract him."

"Sure," he said in a casual tone. "I'll bring him down to the gift shop and buy a little stuffie he can snuggle with tonight. A cup of coffee and a donut. Maybe he'd like a chocolate bar."

"Fuck, Zach," Parrish's voice rose a note before she caught herself and lowered her voice.

I was reaching for the privacy curtain, thinking I could at least hide that way, but the fabric was just out of reach. I caught sight of Parrish trying to shove a very cool and collected doctor backward toward the door.

The good doctor was obviously made of lead beneath that white jacket. As strong as Parrish was, she couldn't move him.

The sound of Layne's voice outside asking for Zach had me ducking beneath the blankets.

"Alright, Zach," Parrish whispered in a frantic voice in the direction of the doctor. "I'm sorry. OK? I shouldn't have called you a dolt. Could you please go distract Layne? Not for me. For Brie. For the good of the pack."

A short humming sound came from Zach followed by a soft tread toward the door, his loafers scuffing in a rhythmic fashion, mumbling something about Layne hearing everything anyway.

A moment later, Parrish was by my side, the sound of the metal rings of the privacy curtain jangling against the bar. When she yanked the sheets back, she wore a panicked expression that scared me. I didn't have time to even process the fact that she had the glass of orange juice in her hand before she dumped the entire thing onto my head.

I gasped and sputtered. Orange juice burned my eyes when I blinked. She clamped her hand down over my mouth and told me to be quiet.

"Rub it on your neck," she said in a hoarse whisper. "Get the pulse points." She sent a pointed look between my legs. "And your crotch," she said. "Don't forget that or we'll all be in a world of hurt." Then she ducked back to the other side of the curtain.

Her footfalls raced to the door, and I traced her ragged breathing across the room. I did what she told me, already feeling sticky and cold but too in tune with her panic to question her orders. There was a long moment of silence in which I deduced she had lain her ear against the door because her cursing grew thick and more creative.

"They're talking about you. Fuck a duck." The next moment, she was behind the curtain with me again. I was in the middle of running a juice-soaked hand over my panties.

"I got to go out there." This in a throaty rasp. "I'll try to lure him away. The last thing we need is for him to find you here right now with you barely over the threshold of hell." She tittered in a most unParrishlike laugh. "And if he corners me, I'm about as screwed as a rusty nut on a 70s spare tire. It's gonna be hard to convince him you're dead if you're lying there with juice all over you." She tracked her gaze along my throat to the wet hospital gown.

I couldn't imagine that it would matter to Layne the way she seemed to think it would, but my throat went dry with anxiety just the same. She was right. Even if Layne didn't care for me anymore, we needed time to consider what to do before we faced him. And I was pretty sure her comment about me being dead was the best option.

"Get up," she said and strained over my midriff to grapple with the IV stand and when she couldn't yank it over the bed, she ripped out the tubing and started shoving me toward the bathroom. "We need to get you into the tub."

We were only a few steps away from the bed when a piercing howl rolled through the hallway to crawl beneath the door. There was only one thing that could make a noise like that, and I knew that somewhere in the hall, a man had lost a loved one. Grief clutched at the lower register of the sound, and the top notes held the shrillness of rage.

Before I had time to process more than that, several loud crashes reverberated from beyond the walls. Whoever it was, he was in a right rage. Even here, in the safety of my own room, my throat tightened in fear and my heart hammered away at my ribs in response. Someone screamed, a nurse probably.

I shot a glance at Parrish, thinking to crack a joke, but she had an odd look on her face as she cocked her head.

"Sweet fucking fuck," she said and just like that, she gave up pushing me to the bathroom. Her hands left my back and instead, she scooped me off my feet. I felt like I was all arms and legs as I tried to recover from the surprise of it. She grunted once, as though I was heavier than she thought, but then she adjusted and carried me under her arm like a bedroll.

The sound of the door being struck by her booted foot was like a crack from a rifle. It had already taken a beating but ended up on the other side of the bathroom in a lopsided slant. I was still scrambling to rearrange my limbs when she slung me into the tub.

I slid down the side into a ball. My hospital gown, soaked with juice, stuck to my knees and my stomach and I shivered at the clamminess.

"Stay down," she hissed. "Whatever the fuck you hear. Stay down."

Then she was gone.

The door to the room clicked closed, and with a shudder, I fell all the way in the bathtub.

I didn't need her to tell me who was suffering beyond the room to know who it was. I felt the truth of it in the way my stomach had begun to twist, the perspiration beaded between my breasts, the way my throat hurt at the thought of swallowing.

It was Layne who had made that noise, who terrified a nurse, who was probably fighting the wolf within and sounded like he was losing.

I fought every instinct to climb from inside the well of porcelain to go to him. Parrish had said to stay down. I had to trust her instincts. She was infinitely more knowledgeable about what was right in the circumstance.

For all I knew, Layne's spying me after I'd hurt him so badly would just make things worse. What if he hurt someone? I didn't want to be responsible for that.

So I stayed down. My breathing filled my ears with a hollow echo each time an exhale burst from me and it sounded like I was pulling in air through a straw each time I sucked a breath in. I shivered from adrenaline and the cold that seeped into my bones from the wet johnny gown.

An eternity seemed to pass with me lying in the tub soaked with orange juice, the liquid drying on my skin in a tacky residue. I curled my knees up to get warm and considered reaching for one of the towels on the stainless steel shelf, but in my mind I heard Parrish's insistent command and stayed where I was.

I wasn't sure I'd be able to clamber out of the tub anyway. My energy reserves were too low and the adrenaline of the moment had soaked through any muscle tissue that had decided to fire. I was left feeling exactly like the sticky surface of the orange juice drying on my skin.

When I heard the hospital room door click and snap back open, I cringed deeper into the tub, afraid of what I might see barging through the door. A few footfalls, a low grumble, and then the bathroom door swung open on its broken hinge. I caught sight of the door frame through the split in the curtain.

My fist went into my mouth instinctively to cut off the scream that did its best to slip past.

But it was Parrish, not Layne or some rabid monster of a wolf hell-bent on killing something. I started to shake in earnest then. My intestines twisted painfully.

My body didn't care that it was safe; it wasn't finished mopping up the puddle of adrenaline.

I peered over the tub edge at her, doing my best to speak past the dryness of my tongue. The look on her face perplexed me. It was so patently un-Parrish, I didn't know what to make of it. The peculiarity of her expression freed me from my paralysis.

"What is it?" I tried to uncurl my knees and unfold from the tight ball, but my legs had gone asleep. I couldn't move at first. My feet felt three sizes larger than normal. "Something's wrong," I said.

She chewed the corner of her lip, and her gaze flicked away from my face to the sink. I dropped my arms over the tub, using the leverage of my armpits to finally free my legs from their awkward position. My foot clunked on the porcelain, drawing her attention.

She eased over to the tub and reached down for me. Silent, still, however. I pulled away from her.

"That you aren't cussing up a storm tells me I'm right. Spit it out."

She straightened up and planted her hands on her hips. "You're dead," she said in a flat tone. "We successfully killed you."

CHAPTER 5

DEAD. AS FAR AS Parrish was concerned, I was dead. The deja vu swam around me, making the soaking of adrenaline a minor thing in comparison.

"What do you mean, I'm dead?" My forehead dropped to the edge of the tub, and I let it lie there. The coolness of the porcelain helped me fight back the faint that prickled at the base of my skull. "That doesn't make sense. I'm here. I—"

I wanted to say I was alive, but I choked on the words as a wave of nausea overcame me. My skin crawled with a thousand fire ants roaming through the fine hairs, lifting each one to strain upward. Terror seized me as I considered her words. I gasped for air.

The truth was, I felt like I was alive, yes. I'd been conversing and breathing and feeling the sensation of touch, but something had reached for me in those moments while I'd been in bed and listened to her and Zach argue. Something I'd felt before, back when I'd contacted Scarlett from beyond. She'd held the entity back from swallowing me whole then.

Zach had said I'd died. Had I lost the battle at that moment and Zach and Parrish had been trying to tell me I was gone, but I just hadn't realized it till this moment. Were they just shades my mind was struggling to put into a reality I understood, basing it on what I'd known when I was alive?

A sob slipped from me. I felt the dreaded blackness from those moments gathering around me, becoming part of me. I couldn't beat it back. It wasn't just dizziness, not just the sense of losing consciousness. It was greater than that. A sense that I was part of it. That maybe I'd never truly gained awareness at all.

I scrabbled for the edge of the tub, panic putting my limbs into motion the way determination couldn't. My breath sounded loud in my ears, like a razor slicing through hard leather.

Warm hands stroked the back of my neck, smoothing down the hairs that reached for heaven.

The blackness receded. My breath came back in a rush.

"It's alright, Brie," Parrish murmured as her fingers met the hump in my shoulders and paused on the vertebrae there. "You're going to be alright. You *are* alright. Just breathe, babe. Just breathe."

She stroked my skin lightly, running her thumb along my hairline. "I just meant Zach told Layne you were dead. That was the howling we heard. At least most of it was him. I'm not sure how much the feral she-wolf understood, but Zach had to stick him with a sedative."

She looked at my face, reading the confusion. "Layne lost it, Brie. He went totally bat-shit feral wolf crazy."

She was angling my body so she could lift me from the tub and I got a good look at her face. The expression said she hadn't expected Zach to break that news about me, and it also made it clear she thought it was a very bad idea. I blinked at her stupidly.

"Yeah, I know," she said, misinterpreting my confusion for disbelief. "Damn good thing I ran out there when I did. I had to hold him down while Zach searched for a syringe. Stupid idiot."

She shook her head as she grunted me out of the tub and waited till I had my feet firmly planted on the tiles before continuing. "You'd think a good doctor would be prepared for emergencies like that. Drugs don't keep the strongest of us down for long, though," she said, "and Zach is going to have a hell of a time explaining to the nurse what she saw, but it has bought us some time."

I waggled my toes on the cold tiles, reveling in the feeling of the way they moved. I was alright. I was alive. I swallowed hard. "Bought us time?" I asked.

She aimed me for the threshold and then over to the closet. "We have to get you out of here."

She let go my shoulder and pulled on the knob. When the door opened, a waft of dust came out, and she muttered something about the cleaning crew that didn't sound precisely fair. She rattled through the hangers and pulled out a coat. Her coat, it looked like. The whole of the closet seemed to contain her clothing: a pair of slippers, a housecoat, a sweatshirt and boots.

She grabbed the sweatshirt with her other hand. "Zach says he'll come to my apartment and check on you, but since you are mobile, it's best if you leave. At least until Layne stops demanding to see your body."

I lifted my arms at her silent bidding, and she pulled the sweatshirt down over my head and over the juice-stained gown.

"Why can't I just move to another floor? He can't search every room in the hospital, every floor, every closet."

She all but rolled her eyes at me. "I thought you knew him better than that, Brie. He's not going to stop. He's not going to just accept that you're dead without getting a good look at your body. He won't stop. He doesn't want to believe you're dead."

I was still processing the thought that Layne cared enough about me after my betrayal to grieve me. Part of me buoyed at the thought and part felt nothing but dread.

The one fact that seemed to matter seemed to also be eluding her. "I'm not dead."

She sighed. "Of course not, but you're the one who suggested it was a good idea to disappear, to die for the time being. For the safety of everyone the coven might decide to sacrifice in its service to killing you for real this time. With you dead, we can track them without them being active. We can root out the bastards without worrying some other poor woman will die because they're trying to get to you. It will make Owen believe you're not a threat anymore, and we can—" she halted there and grabbed a breath. "We can fucking make him pay, the bastard, for what he did to you."

She inhaled, and her nostrils flared. "But we can't do that if Layne knows you're still alive. If he scents you here in the hospital, all that will be gone. Hell, even I can scent you, and you're covered in OJ."

She didn't wait for me to work my way through all that. She just muscled me the way a mother might a child, and I let her pull the sweatshirt down as far as it would go, and then she pulled the coat over top. "Here," she said, bending to retrieve the boots and shoving them in front of my bare feet. "Put these on. We need to high tail it."

"But he saw you," I said. "He'll want to know why you're here."

She gave me a look. "He thinks I identified your body. Zach told him I found you and that the coven had a hand in your death."

I felt wooden and numb, but I held tight to the fact that this was for Layne and that kept me moving. It was for Scarlett and Iris and the other psychics who had fallen beneath the Cult of Blackburn's nefarious plans, and I could do this thing. Parrish was right. We both were. Faking my death might buy us enough time to ruin the coven, and it might in the end be the thing that could turn this whole thing around.

I was holding onto my cell phone, dead though it was, and considering whether or not a dead Brie would leave her phone on the nightstand when Zach burst in through the door again. He panned the room, taking in my appearance in Parrish's oversized sweatshirt and boots with my legs bare and the bottom of the gown flapping with my every movement, and groaned.

"It's not enough," he said to Parrish. "I smell orange juice, but it's not enough."

"Then give him another shot, Zach," Parrish said. "Or have him wheeled off the floor long enough for us to get the hell out of here."

Zach held up a finger, indicating we should wait, and then bolted back out the door again. I exchanged looks of confusion with Parrish, who dropped her head back.

"He's a drama queen, that one. Probably wants to wake the beast just so he can watch the fallout."

"I doubt that's his intent," I said, and with a long sigh, dropped my phone onto the nightstand. If the rest of my clothes had to stay here, then so should it.

Zach returned with an armful of plastic bottles and gauze. "Alcohol," he said.

Parrish's face lit up. "Brilliant," she said and ran to take the bottles from him. A trail of gauze spun out behind her as she ran to the sink and opened a full bottle onto a cushion of gauze. The smell of alcohol rose around me, making my nose twitch.

She squeezed out the gauze and motioned me closer. When I reached her, she and Zach started lining the sweatshirt sleeves with the stuffing. "The alcohol will evaporate eventually, but it will disguise your scent trail as we leave."

So that was what they were doing. Wolves had an amazing sense of smell. It didn't matter if I managed to sneak out without Layne seeing me; his nose was far better at sight than his eyes were. And my scent trail would be one of life, not death and decay. That must have been the point of the orange juice and the nail polish.

"There," Zach said, standing back and waving his hand in front of his nose. "He and that she wolf he brought with him will be waking soon. You best leave. Go the stairs so nothing gets trapped in the elevator. I'll tell him you went home, Parrish." He gave her a long, pointed look. "Make it count."

She nodded. "You know me, Zach. I make everything count."

"That's what I'm afraid of," he said and dug into his doctor's coat, pulling out a bottle of pills. "Antibiotics. "And make sure you pump her with fluids and electrolytes. I won't be able to come to you for a couple of days."

He made a wry face, his mouth screwing up as he jerked his chin in the direction of the door. "I'm sure yon monster will be trailing me for a while, making sure I'm telling the truth."

"Right." Parrish clunked her boot heels together.

He canted his head at her. "What? No flippant comment, no insult. No ridiculous joke?"

She snagged my elbow and used the motion to angle me closer to the wheelchair. "That's what makes you such an idiot, Zacharia," she said with a toss of her head. The red tresses that had come out from beneath her bandanna stuck to her cheeks from the perspiration. "This is not the time for petty jokes. Really. You have no sense of timing or priorities. Probably why you ended up as a doctor and not the warrior your father hoped he was going to get."

When she prodded the chair into the backs of my legs, I sat with relief. The stuffing in my legs had just about got used up, and I was grateful to sit.

She wheeled me past Zach and out into the hallway. I looked back over my shoulder to see the slump of his shoulders as he watched us go. I wasn't sure if it was relief that bowed them or the final retort, but I was pretty sure if her words had meant to be a weapon, they'd hit their mark.

I was beginning to believe we were home free until we got to the door to the stairwell. I'd had a quick glimpse out my room window, and we were several floors up. The wheelchair was not going to go down a single step, let alone a bunch of flights.

"This is where we change cars," Parrish said as her hand went around my wrist. Her free hand scooped beneath my bottom, and she hauled me forward out of the chair to toss me fireman carry style over her shoulder.

She swung slightly to the side so she could grip the door handle, and in that movement, I caught sight of

Zach in the hallway. He was motioning at us to run, his mouth forming the word.

And then a roar that seemed to come from behind him and around him all at once thundered on the air.

"Fucking shit pies," Parrish said and threw herself through the door. "The fucking beast is awake."

CHAPTER 6

SLEEPING LIKE THE DEAD should have been restful, but it was filled with nightmares because evidently, the dead did not rest and they suffered horrible tortures. I woke in a room so dark I thought I was underground at first. The smell of detritus and sulfur and the faint aroma of musty earth wrapped about me like a shroud.

I all but crawled through the dirt, my breath a stagnant thing I kept locked away in my lungs because I didn't dare to breathe and pull in earth into my lungs. I fought my way through the heavy weight, and it took several moments before I realized it was a wool blanket holding me captive.

Not a grave. Not the unending tunnel to Hades.

Even as the thought crept into my mind, I wondered why I'd considered the realm of the dead in that way.

I was alone. With determination, I forced myself to recall where I was. Not the hospital. Not the hotel room where I'd died. Parrish had brought me to her apartment, and she'd tucked me into her own bed while she took the sofa.

We'd arrived long past midnight,and I'd taken only a few minutes to wash off all the sticky juice with a facecloth before dropping into bed, but it was still dark as I peeled open my eyes and stared into the room. I felt like I'd been sleeping too long for it to still be the middle of the night.

As I crawled toward full awareness, I rolled over onto my back and stared upward without seeing anything through the dark. Parrish's apartment was in the basement of a townhouse. We'd walked down a flight instead of up, and the windows were below street level, with wells around them on the outside that anyone could drop into and break in through.

And yet, I felt safe. At least safer than how I'd felt while I'd been sleeping. Nightmares were no stranger to me. I'd had nightmares frequently as a child, brought on by the trauma of my father's death and my mother's spell casting. But these ones were different. They felt visceral. Real. As though I'd traveled somewhere during my sleep.

I thought of my mother. Hecate. The goddess of witchcraft. I'd seen her embodied in John Smith's form and in the eyes of the familiar she'd chosen to guard me. Two parts of the three-faceted goddess. I wondered where that third part resided now and what could be done to reintegrate the goddess since I was pretty sure that would be the only way the coven could be stopped.

That job of reintegration would fall to me now that I wasn't dead, and I had no idea where to start. Mostly because of the fact that I wasn't dead, but to the world at large, I had to be. It would be difficult to parade around and ask questions when you were supposed to be six feet under.

I sat bolt upright in bed at the thought. Parrish and Zach had both indicated that Layne would not give into belief until he'd seen my body for himself. He might not have been given the chance, but he knew who had. Parrish.

It was just a matter of time before he came here to her apartment. And if he did, he'd be in closer quarters to me than the hospital. My smell would be all over the place.

I rolled from the bed, grabbing for the lamp switch at the same time, and ended up knocking it on the floor. It struck the cushy mat with a loud thud and a snap as the light bulb splintered. I froze. Not sure where to place my feet in the dark.

I shouted for Parrish, and before I had spit out the second syllable she burst through the door and the overhead light suffused the room in a bright yellow glow. I had to shield my eyes against the glare.

"What in the holy fuck is going on?" she demanded in a voice that sounded remarkably awake for the time of...

"It's five fucking am, Brie. You scared the cotton out of me." She heaved a sigh that let my shoulders un-pinch.

I pointed at the floor and the winking of several shards of thin glass. "I broke the lamp." I lifted an apologetic eye to hers. "I got scared."

That was when I noticed she was fully dressed. "You've been out," I said with a narrowed gaze.

She stooped to pluck the biggest pieces into her palm and toss them into the bin by the bed. "I've been to your apartment. Well, not in the apartment, more like lurking around the block. It's a shit show of terrifying over there," she said. "That abandoned lot is spooky as shit."

I side stepped her hand as it sought the base of the lamp. "Tell me about it," I said as I recalled the weeks earlier when the reaper had tried to attack me, and Layne and Abbi had stopped him. "What were you doing there?"

She righted the lamp on the bedside table and swept the rest of the glass aside with her boot. "A hunch," she said. "A hunch that turned out to be correct, which means we're not out of the woods yet."

I hitched myself back onto the bed as she prowled to the closet and started rummaging through it. "Someone posted a few guards around your place. They are werewolves, so it seems news of your death is greatly exaggerated."

"You think they are waiting to ambush me."

She paused with her hand deep inside the closet, then sought me out over her shoulder. "I think Owen or the coven are covering their bases and waiting to see if you go home. They think you survived the casting."

"I did."

She hummed deep in her throat. "Yes, but we want them to believe otherwise, right? So we need to steer clear of it until we come up with a plan."

She muttered to herself something about cleaning out her closet, and closing up windows then turned to me. "It's not Layne posting guards; that's all I know. He doesn't want to believe you're dead, but he won't go to your apartment. He'd just come here."

"Because you identified my body."

She cackled. "He knows me well enough to know I didn't answer him for a reason. So yes, he'll want to hear it from my own mouth." She pursed her lips thoughtfully. "My guess is he'll wait for a decent hour in order to catch me unaware."

"If he wanted to catch you unaware, wouldn't he come in the middle of the night?"

She snorted. "That's exactly what I would think, and that's exactly why he won't come until daybreak. He'll let me think I'm in the clear since he didn't start banging on my door in the wee hours. Crafty bastard."

She turned her attention back to what she had in hand, twisting it back and forth in the depths of the closet. "But he doesn't know everything about me."

At that, she pulled out a long black wig with elaborate plaits at the back and tendrils of wispy hair along the sides. It was beautiful.

"Is that made of real hair?" I couldn't stop myself from touching it.

"It needs to be, or it gets too itchy. Plus, I can dye it and strip it and dye it again a few times before I have to buy another."

She passed the wig to me, and I took it, letting the silkiness of the strands run through my fingers. "Reminds me of my mom's hair," I said, then peered up at her. "I'm not sure I want to know."

She chuckled. "Nothing so nefarious. I like to cosplay." She flipped the ends of the hair thoughtfully. "I haven't used this one yet, so it should be fine for you." There was a longing in her voice that urged me to set the wig down on the bed.

"I can't take this."

"Sure you can." She plucked the wig from the bed where I'd placed it. "Layne has no idea about this side of my life. It's not dirty or naughty. Just plain fun. Sometimes I go to comic conventions and dress up and roam around, taking it all in. Once, I went to the convention in semi-shift. Won a prize that year for best costume."

She ran her hand across her brow. "They gave me a ticket for the next year," she said. "I think I wanted to win more than I wanted the ticket. It certainly wasn't worth the week's worth of recovery I suffered through from holding half a shift."

A shudder ran through her, making the wig tremble as she held it out to me. "I bought this one as part of my Madonna outfit, complete with a long black dress from her 90s phase."

I cocked my head at her, imagining Parrish, who was model gorgeous but who also most of the time, wore boots and jeans and flannel shirts.

"What?" she demanded. "You don't think I can pull it off?"

"I didn't say that," I said. "I didn't say anything of the sort. I didn't say anything at all, actually. Besides. I saw you at the charity dinner in that little black dress. I know you're a hotsy totsy beneath all that flannel."

That seemed to mollify her, and she held the wig up to my head and studied me.

"Girl, as fucking steaming hot as I am in this, you're gonna burn the streets down."

I reached up to pluck the wig from my head and held it between us. "And I need to wear this because?"

She sighed as though just thinking about explaining exhausted her, but I knew it was probably because she hadn't slept well. The black smudges beneath her eyes told the entire story.

"I need your help shutting down your shop, and ordering your funeral, and closing up your apartment and burying you and mourning you. I mean, I love you, Brie, but that's a lot of work."

"What do you mean, shut it all down?"

She tapped her knuckles on my temple. "Dead girl walking, remember? Dead chicks don't go to work or live in their apartment. Dead chicks have a funeral and get buried and have gorgeous lesbian chicks bawling their eyes out for the love that might have been."

I snorted. "You aren't in love with me, you idiot."

She cocked her hip sideways. "No, but I do like an air of mystique, don't you? The image it paints is pretty haunting."

I spun around wig in hand, to drop down onto the bed. I hadn't expected just standing there to be so much work. She followed me, taking a seat beside me on the mattress.

"Look," she said. "Layne will expect to see those things happening. You want to make him believe you're dead, right? We need to make it real enough that the coven is screwed and Layne is safe."

I nodded mutely, too miserable about it all to speak.

She patted my hand and let her fingers trail over the back of it to the wig, seeming to enjoy the way it felt. "It's no biggie, Brie. You'll go out and about town with me to take care of shit." She put air quotes around shit and I couldn't help a short grin.

"Smart," I said.

She tapped her temple. "Like a wolf, I am," she said. "And I'll just tell everyone you're my new squeeze, helping out because I'm the first person to make you squee between the sheets and are willing to do anything to keep me happy. "

"Dear God," I said. "Do I have to be so fawning and so—naïve?"

Her auburn brows scuttled down. "Hey," she said. "You told me you wanted to repay me for Zach's work. This is what I want. A smoking hot straight chick who can't get enough of me." She tucked a stray lock of hair behind my ear. "I take my reputation seriously. And it took a hit with Honey."

"You've thought this all out," I said.

She stood and stretched, reaching for the ceiling with waggling fingers. "Never doubt that this wolf is always thinking ahead."

"I suppose you had to do something while I lay there in that coma."

"I had plenty to do what with keeping everyone out and wiping the snot from your nose. Sheesh, Brie, was there any good reason for all that snot?"

"Hot chicks like me just melt everything inside," I quipped.

She sent me a studious look. "Well, try not to be so hot then," she said. "Because that is not the kind of hot I'm looking to show off. Anyway, at least you can get out this way. Not stay stuffed in a room somewhere in hiding. Because that would suck."

"It would suck," I said. "And speaking of hot..." I lifted my arm to sniff my armpit, the sweat of a nightmarish sleep drifting up and reminding me of something far more important.

"I can wear a disguise," I said. "But what about that scent you seem to think Layne will recognize. How are we going to hide that from him?"

When I expected her to answer, something caught her attention from beyond the door. Her attention swiveled to it so quickly that I thought I'd missed a loud thunk coming from the other room.

"What is it?" I said, pushing off the bed with an anxious movement.

She held her hand out to me, keeping me from following her as she headed to the bedroom door.

"Parrish?"

She looked back at me over her shoulder. "I think we're about to find out."

"What do you mean?"
"I mean a wolf is at my front door."

CHAPTER 7

WHAT WAS AT PARRISH'S front door was not a wolf, but a dead mouse. She carried it back into the apartment with a pincer grip on its tail, and found me cowering in the bathtub, reasoning that if it worked once it could work again.

"What in the great green fuck are you doing in there?" she said.

"Layne," I said. "The tub worked before."

She crouched beside the edge of the basin and held the mouse up to my eye level. "It wasn't the tub, Brie. It was all the other scents. The alcohol. The nail polish. Orange juice." Her eyelids went to half-mast, thinking.

She snapped the fingers of her free hand. "That's just how we can disguise you. Essential oils."

My gaze pinned to the mouse that swayed in the air as she moved. "And is dead mouse an essential oil?"

She went cross-eyed as her eyes darted to the mouse. "Oh, right." She leaned sideways to reel off several squares of toilet tissue and bundled the vermin up in the roll before laying it on the sink. Then she shoved her hands beneath my armpits and hoisted me out of the tub. "I was afraid Layne was at the door."

I lifted my leg to step over the side of the tub and when both feet were planted on the tiles, my gaze went to the tidy white package with a thin line of tail sticking out. "You can smell another wolf right through several rooms and the cold outside air? Impressive."

"That would be impressive indeed, but as amazing as I am, I didn't smell him. I heard him."

"Him meaning Layne."

She shrugged. "I heard a big animal. I expected it to be Layne because...well, Layne."

I didn't want to stare at the mouse's tail, but I couldn't help myself. Something about it drew my attention the way a chocolate cake sitting out on the sideboard calls to a sugar addict. "I might be mistaken, and I know women sometimes have issues with size, but that mouse doesn't look like a big animal."

She bent to open the cupboard beneath the vanity and pulled out a pair of pink rubber gloves with spotted fur around the cuffs. She slipped her hands into them one by one, all the while staring me down as though I'd comment on them and she wanted to dare me to say something.

I didn't. I knew better. She plucked the package from the vanity. "This is newly dead," she said. "And the animal that left it is big. Not Layne, but maybe another wolf. I sure as hell smell magic."

She carried it with her to the kitchen, and I followed her. Tired as I was, and weak, but my hands ached to hold that small form. I was worried she'd toss it in the trash, and the confusion about why I cared bothered me.

"This little guy was left there on purpose," she said. "I'm pretty sure it's not a gift for me." She spun on her heel and tossed it at me and I caught it automatically.

I'm not sure how to explain what happened when the little body slipped free of its tissue and connected with my skin. A sizzle might be the best description, or maybe a buzzing. Whatever it was, it surprised me enough that I dropped the mouse and it fell at my bare feet. The strip of tail curled around my big toe.

"You're terrible at hot potato," Parrish said and stooped to pick it back up. "You don't want it? No trouble."

"Don't," I said as she lifted the lid of the compost bin.

She hesitated, eyelids narrowing as she eyed me. "What do you mean, don't?"

I wrapped my arms around my midriff. "I don't know."

"Bat shit crazy," she said as she held the rodent over the bin by the tail. "That's what you are. Dying was not good for you."

I hugged myself tighter. "It burned me," I said, finally, and jerked my chin at the mouse. "Like the grimoire did. Like the amulet."

She canted her head at me then at the mouse, running an assessing gaze over the little thing. "You think it's magic?" She hoisted it higher, holding it up so the light from over the sink played over its fur. "Like the dog? You think it's like Abbi?"

I shook my head. "No. Not like that." I took a step toward her, close enough that I could run the backs of my fingers over the fur. I fully expected the same electric buzz to move through my veins, but nothing happened.

"Huh," I murmured and dropped my hand. "Nothing."

At that, Parrish snorted and made a comment that wasn't too flattering. "Leave it to a witch to see magic where there's nothing but mud."

She lifted the bin lid again and dropped the mouse in. This time, she dropped the lid and pressed it closed. The snapping sound made me jump.

With a close eye on me, she began peeling her gloves off one by one, pulling them inside out as she went, then balling them up the way a doctor would. "Shame about these gloves. They were my favorite pair."

I wanted to ask how many pairs she had, but I'd gotten a glimpse under the sink and there were boxes of latex gloves. I figured it would be best not to bring it up.

"You go shower," she said. "I'll wash up and get us some breakfast. We have a big day ahead of us."

I nodded and headed thankfully to her bathroom. I found unscented shampoo and soap on the shower ledge along with three peach colored razors all with the plastic still covering the blade.

I decided she wouldn't mind me scraping one of the razors beneath my arm and over my legs. After a bunch of days in the hospital, the hair had sprung forth like a mystical forest, and I felt decidedly grimy until my skin was smooth.

I watched the bits of hair swirl around the drain, almost rapt with my attention. In the moment before the last of it went down the drain, I fancied the hair had made a shape of sorts. The instant reminded me of the practice of reading tea leaves, something I offered my clients, using the patterns to tap into universal symbols that I could then infer futures or pasts or whatever it was they were after.

It wasn't until I heard Parrish knocking at the door and shouting at me to please mind the water bill that I realized I'd been standing under the stream for a long time staring at the places the hair had been and was now gone. I reached for the tap to turn it off and a wave of dizziness swam over me.

I called to Parrish then, afraid I'd pass out and crack my head against the porcelain. I dropped to my knees in the tub, the water still streaming over my back. Figuring I wouldn't have as far to fall if I passed out while on my knees, I crouched there as she burst through the door, and I could barely look at her from the side of my vision because moving my head made small black particles prickle at the corner of my vision.

"What is it?" she said and reached in past the shower curtain. Her hands groped around and found the tap. They turned off with a screech and were throttling the pipes when her hands found my shoulder.

"Brie," she said, as her hands roamed my skin, searching for an appropriate place to settle while trying to figure out if there was something wrong. "Are you alright?"

"I need help getting out."

To her credit, she didn't ask why. She shoved the curtain aside and in a swift gesture, had a broad towel in her grasp. She tossed it over my shoulder. "I'm going to pull you toward me," she said. "Do you think you can stand if I help you?"

I nodded and let her ease me to my feet. She wrapped the towel all the way around me and muscled me over the rim of the tub the way a mother would a toddler. I was useless until my feet found the tiled floor. Then, a soft sigh escaped me, one of relief and surprise.

I twisted my fists into the fabric and pulled the bath towel tight. "Weird," I said.

She lifted one eyebrow. "Weird? You freak out in the tub, and all you have to say is weird?"

"You're right," I said, moving to settle onto the toilet seat. "It was fucking weird."

She propped her hip against the vanity. "Care to expand on that statement?"

I lifted my gaze to hers. "I saw my death."

CHAPTER 8

I COULDN'T EXPLAIN WHAT my death looked like or how I knew it for what it was. I just knew in those moments I'd watched the shaved pieces of hair eddy around the drain, they made distinct shapes. I'd held time in my grasp in those moments and those symbols clung to the moment long enough for me to interpret them.

"You're shitting me," Parrish said.

"Judging by how pale your face is," I said, "I don't think you believe for a second I'm shitting you."

She chewed her lip. "That fucking mouse," she growled. "It was Honey. It had to be. She spelled the fucking thing and dropped it here to attack you."

I shook my head. "Were you careful about bringing me here?"

A storm crossed her face. "You know I was."

"Then Honey would have no idea I'm here." I tried to get up and had to reach out for the vanity for leverage. "I don't think it was the mouse at all. I think...I think I had a flash of those moments I was dead."

I eased up, standing slowly and leaning on the vanity just in case I wasn't quite ready to be mobile. She watched me, but I noted she didn't try to help. Shades of Scarlett and the need to stand on your own when you felt the most vulnerable, gaining you strength and confidence to face the worst shit.

With a wink, I stood and her shoulders relaxed. She'd been waiting to see if I needed her. She wanted me to stand on my own, but she wouldn't fail me if I needed her. I plucked a towel from the rack with a trembling hand and wrapped it around me, securing it between my breasts by tucking in the tail.

"If that little bastard vermin did all that to you, then good riddance," she said. "I had considered saving it for my wolf, but she prefers pussy, so..."

I wasn't going to touch that one. Instead, I sucked in a deep breath. "Maybe it was my imagination," I said. "I've not been feeling quite myself."

"Good," she said. "No better time to be someone else." She tossed me the wig that had somehow made it into the bathroom with her. "What should your name be? Raven?"

I snorted. "Too cliche. I'm surprised at your lack of imagination.

"You want imagination," she said and grabbed me by the shoulders to spin me facing the mirror. "Watch and learn," she said.

Watch and learn I did as she pulled open a drawer filled with cosmetics and colored contacts and all manner of hair nets and scalp glue. At least twenty minutes in, I barely recognized myself. Half an hour, dressed in a skin-tight black leather pants and a low-cut purple lace tank top, and I was a new person.

She stepped back and whistled. "You know I might just change my mind about wooing the pants off you. You're even hotter than I hoped." She sent me the kind of look I supposed could be called lecherous if she hadn't added a mocking kissy mouth along with it.

I spun in front of the mirror. I had to admit, I did look pretty damn good. The green contacts made my eyes look almost turquoise and the black hair against my milky skin contrasted in a striking way. I wasn't sure about the pants or all the cleavage I was showing, but I also knew no one would recognize me even up close.

"Desirée," I said as I stared at my reflection. "My new name is Desirée."

She let go a squeal that was most unlike her. "It's perfect. Are you ready to go bury yourself six feet under, Desirée?" she said.

I nodded. "Let's get this thing done."

I'd say we piled into her car, but I had a hard time bending and moving my legs to get in on the passenger side, wearing the tight pants. She eyed me from what I supposed was her idea of pretending not to watch, then tapped the roof four times absently before rounding the vehicle to push behind the wheel.

I had to suck in my stomach in order to gain enough slack in the pants to reach for the door. I yanked it closed with a grunt.

"You should have greased me up before you made me wear this outfit," I complained.

She gave me a side eye that examined me more astutely than should have been possible. "Don't think I didn't consider it, but I wasn't sure we'd get anything done."

She chuckled, then revved the engine. One thing was certain: driving with Parrish was like drinking five shots of espresso. Except for the few moments when we'd pulled into a drive through to grab a coffee and a bagel, I pretty much had my eyes closed for most of the ride, so I was surprised to find she'd pulled up to the curb outside my house and not my store.

"We need your keys to the shop," she said, explaining why we were parked in front of my house. "I have your house keys because I took them from your pockets when the paramedics came to the hotel room. But I'm not sure where your shop keys are."

"If you have my house keys, you have my shop keys." I held my hand out across the cabin of the car. "But since we're here, I might want to pick up a few things."

She dug through her jacket pockets and came out with a ring with three keys on it, all hanging from a stress figure of a duck, whose eyes popped out when you squeezed it. I started to take them from her when she yanked them back, catching them in her fist.

"My lover wouldn't be unlocking the door," she said. "I would be. I'm Brie's friend. Not you. You don't even know her for Pete's sake."

My jaw clenched. "Right. I'm incognito."

"It's easy to forget," she said. "But you're not just incognito. You are Desirée."

I stared down at the scuff in the leather at the knee. Not new pants. Someone had worn them before, but not Parrish. She was too tall for them. "Brie is dead," I said in a flat voice that somehow managed to make me feel forlorn.

She sent me a pitying look. "I'm sorry, Desirée. It's just the way it needs to be for now. I told you there were other wolves watching the house. We need to make it real."

She stuck her nail into the corner of her mouth and chewed for a moment. All sympathy disappeared as she leaned across the cabin, a glint of yellow in her eye. "Don't be shocked when I treat you like my lover. OK? I don't know who might be watching, and that social media post we sent might not have gone the rounds yet."

Right. The social media post she'd sent as the medical examiner answering a fake question about the death of the Satanic cult leader who had murdered the psychics during the summer. It was a ruse to ferret out Honey since she had blasted my picture out to the Internet when she'd met me.

It had the effect of blowing up my email for three days, and I had to assure my clients that I wasn't some Satan worshiper. Most of them believed me. Most.

I held her eye, mustering all the courage I had in me. "I understand. Do what you need to. Let's just make it look real enough that we don't have to keep doing it."

She touched my cheek with her fingers. "For Layne," she whispered. "And for that bitch, Honey." Then she kissed me.

I wasn't ready for it. I froze as she held my mouth with hers and slipped her hand beneath the wig of hair to cup my neck. I think I even held my breath as the shock took me, but she didn't close her eyes, nor did she do more than rest her lips on mine. Those bright green eyes held mine, and she shifted slightly so that she turned enough to speak against my mouth.

"I won't ever take advantage of you," she said. "This is for show. That's all. But for fuck's sake, could you at least not look like I'm assaulting you?"

I didn't dare nod. Instead, I forced my arms to lift to her shoulders. I pulled her as close to me as I could over the cupholder and gear shift.

"For Layne," I said. "And for that bitch Honey may she get torn to shreds in Hell."

We held each other, our lips touching, our hands cupping each other's necks for several moments—make it look good, I thought. Then we parted. Slowly, with just the right about of staring into each other's faces for anyone looking to think we were starved for each other.

"You're a good actress, Desirée," Parrish said in a breathless voice. "I just might forget my promises if you keep that up."

"I just might have to curse you with a black spell if you step over the line," I said, and she barked out a laugh, waving her hand at me as she did.

"Straight chicks," she said, still laughing as she threw the handle on her door. "You crack me up."

She slung her arm over my shoulder and walked me to the door. I did my best to melt against her, telling myself even best buds weren't afraid of a little personal contact, so there should be no problem with me letting her hold me the way she did.

By the time we made it up to my stoop, I felt more natural and was even getting into the act a little. A smile played with my lips, and I was beginning to relax.

Until I saw the small, shriveled body of a baby owl lying in front of my door.

Parrish sucked in a sharp breath at the sight. "Fuck," she said. "Fuckity fuck fuck."

She pulled her arm from my shoulder and fumbled with the keys. "Are you sure you need to get inside? I mean, really, really sure?"

"My mother's will," I said. "And other things. If we're going to do this, I need those documents."

"Christ on a cheese cracker," she said as she tried to jam the key into the lock. Her fingers shook enough that I noticed. The key slid off the lock and gouged the plate.

I tried to keep my voice even, but seeing her startled unnerved me. "That's the shop key," I said in a bland voice.

She glared at me, the yellow of her wolf's eye high in her gaze. "You might have fucking told me that when I took out the fucking key in the first fucking place."

I lifted one eyebrow in pique. "Is this how you treat all your girlfriends?"

She exhaled a long, grumbling sigh. "I'm sorry," she said as she pointed to the little form at our feet by way of explanation. "Owls. Not a good sign. Plus, you did say you were going to curse me."

I nudged the baby owl with my toe. "I think I'd need more time than a few seconds from car to door to get a curse like that revved up."

She jumped backward when the owl, propelled by my foot, scooted toward her. "Watch it, witch," she said, and then hopped another foot sideways for good measure.

"Superstitious much?" I said with a grin. I knew owls were supposed to be harbingers of death but this was a bit ridiculous, especially for Parrish. "It's just a dead owl."

She passed me the keys. "Fuck it," she said. "You open the door if it's nothing." She hugged herself, then, as if she realized how it might look, squared her shoulders and stepped around the dead owl to my other side. With an arm slung around my waist for optics, she waited for the door to swing open.

For one second, the smell of familiarity wafted out at me and brought with it a sense of home and belonging. The vanilla candle I left in the entry way to catch the warmth of any sun coming in the window emitted a homey fragrance.

The aroma of my soap and shampoo permeated the air as we stepped inside and with it, my shoulders let go the knots that had fisted between the blades ever since I'd awoke.

Then, I remembered this visit might be the last time I'd step inside my home for a long time. Anxiety and grief clawed at my throat as I wondered how long it would be before my life could resume its normal course. Maybe it would never be normal again.

I couldn't speak around the nerves as Parrish pushed past me and asked me how long I thought it would take to find the papers.

She picked up the candle from its spot in front of the entryway sidelight and gave it a sniff and sneezed. "Too girly," she said as she put it back down. "Well?"

I clutched at the newell post that sat atop the stairwell, a thick column with a carved gargoyle crouched, facing the door.

"Not long, I don't think," I said, fighting the urge to bolt up the stairs and sink into the bed of the spare room where I stored all the things from my mother that I didn't want to have to look at every day. I knew exactly where the pile of papers were. Deep in the closet of that room, inside a banker's box.

"Hop to it, then," she said and leaned to peer out the sidelight window. She didn't have to say she was looking for the owl or for the sentries we both suspected who hid somewhere in her plain sight. "The faster we blow this pop stand the better."

I nodded silently. The pop stand was my home, one I wouldn't see for God knew how long. When I bolted up the stairs, I ignored the bed no matter how weak my knees had grown from the exertion, and headed to the closet.

The box was there, of course. I lifted the lid and pulled out the blue accordion folder the lawyer had given me when I'd arrived in the city. She'd been gone for a while by then, and I had no intentions of doing more than setting up shop and settling into my home. I hadn't questioned him beyond the basics. I didn't even know where she was buried.

Now, of course, looking at the folder, I considered it might be time to look her up. She wasn't a typical mother anymore. She was a goddess, broken by a coven of witches for some purpose I didn't understand. Perhaps the first step was finding her resting place.

The coven might have broken her spirit and splintered her magic, but the woman had to be buried somewhere. After all, the lawyer had given me all her things.

I slipped the folder beneath my arm and dragged out several more, moldy smelling things. The ephemera had grown damp in its box and stank of dust and neglect. These, I shoved inside the blue folder and pulled the elastic band around the lot. It snapped audibly when I let go.

With a sigh, I retreated back down the stairs to find Parrish looking out the window.

"They're there, all right," she said.

"I didn't see anyone."

She waved me over and pointed to the side of the property, where a black sedan idled quietly. Two men inside argued behind the windshield. "Frick and Frack," she said. "Twins from the 80s. Newly turned. They get shit duty usually."

"Thanks for the vote of confidence."

She rolled her eyes. "You're dead, remember? Watching a dead chick's house is akin to watching water boil without all the excitement." She twisted the doorknob and held the door open for me. "Don't forget to kiss me, sweetie."

I groaned and touched the edges of my wig to make sure it wasn't askew before stepping out into the air. I waited by the side of the door while she made a big show of locking up.

She swiped her cheek with the back of her hand and with hunched shoulders took the papers from me as though they were a terrible burden to carry. Then she pulled me to her side. I tried to look consoling.

"Count to three," she said. "Give them a nice look, then follow me to the car. We'll go to the shop and do the same fucking thing for the fuckers that are there."

The thought of doing it all again exhausted me but I did as she bid. We reached the shop in silence, both of us deep in thought, and probably for different reasons.

The windows were dark and cold looking, and without the sandwich signs, the facade had a dreariness that put me in mind of abandonment. Uninviting, that's the word I would have used. It made me shiver to see my store front looking like it was in mourning.

"I'm guessing we're here to put a sign on the door?" I turned to her as she kicked open her door.

"Seeing how it's Sunday," she said, "it's a good time to do it without worrying about customers. Plus. You're going to want to gather a few things."

I followed her to the door, panning the sidewalk because I felt too visible even in the disguise. We were several feet away before I noticed the ball of fur lying in front of the door. I rushed it without thinking. I recognized the tom cat I'd been feeding for the last three years.

"Oh no," I said because I knew what I was looking at. "No one put out any food for him for...it must be a week or more." I dropped to my knees and was about to pick the body up off the cement when Parrish stopped me.

"Don't," she said.

I looked up at her to find she wore a peculiar expression. "What's wrong?"

"He's not newly dead." She toed it aside with her boot. "And he didn't starve to death."

"What are you saying?"

"I'm saying someone killed him."

CHAPTER 9

SOMEONE HAD KILLED THIS cat and put it on my doorstep intentionally. Whoever did it, wanted me to see it.

She didn't say that, exactly, but that's why her mouth was twisted in a line that showed every thought running through her mind.

Parrish nudged the body with her boot. "He doesn't have the smell of poison on him, but I'd say arsenic."

I dropped my gaze to the orange tabby. "Who would do such a thing?" I sat back on my haunches, not caring about the distinct sound of material threatening meant I'd probably torn the ass out of the leather pants. "Honey," I said in a bald voice. "That bitch."

I'd fed that stray for months before it would even let me catch a glimpse of him. He'd sired a dozen kittens before I live trapped him and had him neutered so he could go on living without making a nuisance of himself to the neighbors.

He'd never let me so much as touch him, but he waited eagerly for his daily kibble. At times, I drank my coffee outside with him while he scarfed down the food, gave me a quick look of appreciation, and then scooted back into the alley until the next morning.

He wasn't a pet, but I'd grown accustomed to him and he, me. Now, staring down at his lifeless body, I wanted to strangle Honey. My nails bit into my palms before I realized I'd clenched my hands into fists. I was about to scoop his body up into my arms when Parrish hooked my elbow, holding me back.

"Not a good idea," she said. "Can't you smell it?"

I furrowed my brow in query.

"Magic," she said. "He reeks of it."

Magic. So it was Honey after all, the nasty, rotten, bitch of a witch. Tears stung my eyes, and I swiped at my cheeks with my sleeve where hot water had begun to run. Parrish used her grasp on my elbow to yank me to my feet.

"Careful, Brie. Anyone watching might think you cared about that mangy carcass."

I lifted my gaze to hers, knowing the magnetic lashes she'd applied to my lids were probably askew from the quick swipe of palm I'd run over my eyes. She was right. No doubt someone stood watching from some safe place, ready to report it all to Honey and the coven.

She'd probably done the same thing with the owl, with the mouse. Testing me. Testing for proof of life or sending a message that she wasn't done with me, not by a long shot.

"He's not mangy," I said, swallowing the clump that kept growing in my throat.

"No, he's not," Parrish said softly, and I forced myself to stand with her. It was difficult. My legs still tired easily after being in bed for the few days I'd been immobile in the hospital bed. I wasn't entirely sure that the trembling wasn't from exertion.

The pity that rode Parrish's face steeled my spine, helped me realize what was at stake if I let my weakness show.

I swallowed and lifted my chin, gathering the courage to say what had to be said, loud enough for anyone in range to hear.

"Scrape that disgusting thing up and throw it in the trash." I hugged myself as I peered down at it with what I hoped was a convincing look of disgust. At least I didn't have to fake a shiver. "It's gross. I'm not taking one step into that shop until that's gone." I curled my lip back for effect and jerked my chin toward the tom.

Parrish let slip an approving murmur and tugged me aside, the way she might if she was my doting lover. Her arm slung over my shoulder as she steered me toward the back door, saying she'd take care of it while I had a cup of tea inside.

I wasn't sure all the acting was necessary, but my nerves were on high alert, and the faster I could get inside my shop, where I knew every inch and every smell and sight, the better for my anxiety. I could already feel the prickling along my arm, and seeing the tom had made my chest tighten up.

And I had the feeling I was about to burst into tears and I would rather have someone rake out my eyes than let those bastards see me cry.

I pointed out the shop's back key to Parrish so she could open the door for me, remembering that a stranger would not have the familiarity with the deceased Brie to unlock her store's back door. I waited, arms wrapped around my midriff, while she fiddled with the fussy lock until it gave way beneath her manipulations.

"Did you just break my door?" I asked.

One auburn eyebrow lifted half an inch. "Someone should really come look at that lock," she said. "Damn thing broke the key right in half." She lifted the key to show me.

I didn't have the heart to complain that she'd got frustrated and just used her brawn to get in. I was just grateful we were in.

I pushed past her, not caring at that point who might see me flee into the depths of the shadowed back room. Every shape within the gloom of the shop wore a familiar cast.

I could have found my way in complete darkness. A stash of Earl Grey tea waited for me in the back room. There was probably half a lemon in the bar fridge, and if I was lucky, there might be a mickey of Canadian rum too.

"Right," Parrish said from behind me. "Leave me to find the light switch. Bravo warrior queen."

I tossed a gesture over my shoulder. "It's on the wall next to Napoleon," I said and headed for the storage closet where the fridge and a basket of teabags waited.

I stopped short long before she came up behind me after flooding the room with light.

"Fuck," she said from over my shoulder.

I didn't bother to turn around.

"You have a knack for nailing a sentiment in one word, Parrish," I said. "But at least, I'm glad you see it too."

My mother's familiar, the dog I'd named Abbi on the night Scarlett and I had found her in the back alley wounded and nearly dead, now lay behind the counter in my shop proper. She was a large beast, black as liquid tar, with eyes that penetrated you when they turned on you.

At least, that was how she normally looked. Now, a mere ghost of the creature sagged against the floor.

Gray and filmy, she lay panting on the wooden boards in front of my beautiful Nova Scotian artisan counter. The very place where she'd helped take down the reaper the coven had sent to collect me.

I didn't think she had heard us enter, or if she had, she didn't have the energy to lift her head.

I should have rushed to her side, but I found I couldn't move my feet. Dread climbed my spine the way a kid navigated monkey bars. Fast and without consideration for what might happen if it all came tumbling down in one instant.

Parrish's hand brushed mine as she moved closer to me, protective, I thought. Maybe she was afraid I'd decide to go to Abbi's aid and she wanted to be close enough to me to hold me back.

"It didn't look like that last time I saw it."

"She," I said. "And no. She looks very different. Sick."

"Dying," Parrish said, correcting me with a subtle glance at the dog.

I twisted to look at her. "Do you have to be so astute every single damn time?"

She shrugged. "It's what I do." She patted her chest with the flat of her palm, drawing my attention. "Coroner, remember? I know the look of death."

That got my feet moving, finally. She might know the look of death, but it wasn't going to be this beast who had saved me time and again, dying there in my shop. My mother's beast. The goddess's familiar. Imbued with life, if I was to believe Scarlett's shade, by the dozens of dogs and puppies my mother had sacrificed to bring her into creation.

They lived on in that creature, and I'd be damned if I'd let them expire now because I couldn't bother to help the beast who housed them.

I didn't even know if death was the right word for what would happen to the creature, but I rushed her anyway, despite Parrish hollering to me that I needed to be careful.

I dropped to my knees beside the dog. The last time I'd knelt beside her when Scarlett and I had found her injured in the back alley, she'd been marked with what looked like burn marks or gouges in her flesh. Those same wounds scored her skin and fur now, except she was paler.

Fear of what the dog might do to me, kept me from touching her, but I wanted to probe her body, investigate the wounds. Not like I knew what I was doing, but even without medical knowledge, the desire to touch her was strong. Parrish must have felt it too.

She crouched next to me, her hand hovering over the dog's ribs where a pinkish area the size of her palm showed through the fur.

"Looks like she's disintegrating or something," she said.

"I'll be damned."

Parrish looked askance at me, pulling her hand away and tucking it beneath her armpit. "You think so too?"

I nodded. "I wouldn't have come up with that description, but it looks right."

The dog's eye rolled toward Parrish, and she laid her palms on the floor, all the better to peer into the dog's eyes.

"You are one hell of a bitch," she said. "Hang in there. We'll find a way to make you right."

I nudged Parrish with my elbow. "I'm not so sure we can."

With a roll onto her hip, Parrish eyed me. "What do you mean? It's your dog. Your magic. Surely you can fix her."

I shrugged my shoulders back. "That's just it. She's not my dog. She's my mother's. Hecate's, I mean." I ran my gaze over the dog's hindquarters, where the tail swished once against the floor. "The magic isn't mine. I didn't do anything to conjure her. Whatever, however, she got here, it was my mother's doing."

"You mean—"

"I mean, if she's dying, I don't know what to do to help her."

"But she came to you," Parrish said. "She came here. She must think you can help." She crouched down low, muzzle to nose and stared into the big dog's face as she spoke. "She came to me, found me, when the coven had you, so I could find you and save you."

"She did more than that," I said, recalling how the dog had broken into the circle and provided Smith with the magic he needed to hold back Honey's black spell. If not for the dog, the goddess within Smith wouldn't have been able to break the coven's magic and help me fight them back.

A thought struck me at the remembrance. "Oh my God," I said. "That's it."

Parrish straightened up and I grabbed her by the arm in my excitement. "It's magic," I said. "She needs magic."

I tried to get up but dizziness washed over me. Parrish had to hold on to me while the blackness receded from behind my eyelids, but when it did, I climbed to my feet and pushed myself up, using her shoulder as leverage.

"You remember," I said, sweeping the dog with an assessing glance. "She attacked Farrel," I said. "She consumed his magic somehow. Transferred it to Smith. They're connected, you see. Like Horcruxes from Harry Potter."

Parrish stood, leaning away from the dog and edging sideways, finicky or afraid, I wasn't sure.

"You think your mother stored her soul in this dog and in John Smith."

I decided to ignore the fact that she obviously had read the series, putting it aside as one more bit of information on a woman who was an enigma, and stuck with the issue at hand.

"Hecate is a tri-faceted goddess," I said. "She would need three of them, I'm guessing." I peered down at the creature lying on the floor. "Abbi is one, I'm pretty sure."

The dog's tail twitched against the floor and then lay flat. My heart hurt at the way her eyes rolled before the lids closed.

I caught Parrish's eye, and with a jerk of my head, I gestured at her to follow me to the front of the store, out of earshot of the dog. I wasn't sure if the dog could hear or understand, but she had seemed pretty sentient before.

"I think it took all the dog's power to come to you when she did, when I was in the hotel with the coven. And I think when she used up her store of magic fighting the coven, she must have begun to fade."

I thought of all the magic the beast had probably used up trying to keep me safe all these weeks. The wounds on her outside my shop that I'd thought had been inflicted by the coven or Kenny, might easily have been caused by the leeching of magic.

Parrish nodded mutely, catching on to the fact that I didn't want the dog to hear.

"Maybe being here in this shop, close to my mother's things: her pictures, maybe they're a sort of power station."

Parrish stuffed her hands in her pockets and rocked back on her heels. "Or maybe it's you, Brie. Maybe you're the powerhouse."

I thought about that. It was possible the connection to my mother's blood, running in my DNA might be enough to help. Maybe that was why the dog had come here.

"Home base," I said thoughtfully and leaned against the wall for support as my legs began to tire.

Parrish noticed and tugged on my elbow, guiding me to one of the chairs. She pulled up a stool and sat, her elbows propped on her thighs. "I always thought the grimoire was the thing that powered that dog up, I mean, based on what you told me."

I snapped my fingers in realization. "The grimoire. That's it. That's why she's fading. Honey has the grimoire. And she has the amulet. They were both in the circle with me. The coven must have needed them, need them, for their spell."

"Fucking bitch," Parrish said. "I ever get my hands on her, she will die very slowly and with my name carved all over her body with my claws."

I leveled her with a look. "She needs to go to jail, Parrish. She and the entire nasty coven. They need to rot in prison."

She mumbled something beneath her breath and I had the sense that even if Layne was able to find and pin them with the murders, they would somehow not make it to trial.

"So Smith, then?" Parrish whispered, as though she was worried the dog would hear. "The same thing must be happening to him."

I nodded unhappily, not wanting to think the same fate of the man who had called me daughter, who had saved me from Farrel and used my magic to fight back the coven when they would have killed me.

"He used the magic in my blood to protect me too." I'd told her as much as I could about my time in the hotel room, and although some of it was fuzzy, I remembered that much.

He'd needed magic. Honey had mocked him for not having enough, and the entire coven had been afraid of him until they realized he wasn't as strong as they were. At least, until he'd used my magic to blast them back.

My fingers tapped my chest in recollection. I'd cut myself in the hotel room, when I knew I had to use the magic in my blood, the ritual I'd been calling to unknown, to do what I could to break the coven's power. Smith had planted his palm over my solar plexus and created a web of magic that held Honey and her coven's black spells at bay. I'd nearly died.

Correction. I had died from the blood loss and the draining of energy. But we'd won.

"Smith is the second, I'm sure of it," I said, leaning toward her. "He was able to tap into my mother's blood—my blood—and fight back."

"Smith?" she said, and I could see her trying to put it all together as her brow furrowed in contemplation. "You keep saying he when you refer to Smith, so is he just some lackey or is he your mother? I'm fucking confused."

I blinked at her, the question raising an unexpected thought. "They're all my mother," I said. "Smith called me daughter. Honey referred to him as 'she'. The coven thought he was the goddess herself."

She ran a hand over her hair, scrubbing the scalp at the back of her head. "So your mother is trans, bi, pansexual?" She whistled softly. "Way to go, Hecate."

"Kate," I said, correcting her, and as I said my mother's name, I sagged backward into the chair with a sigh of comprehension.

"Fuck. Kate. My mother's name was Kate. Not exactly a perfect shortening of the goddess's name, but it's close enough. I can't believe I didn't piece it together sooner." I flung my arms over the sides of the chair in mock irritation of my stupidity.

"We all have ninny moments, Brie," she said. "But shit. You're so right. Things are starting to make so much sense now." She squirreled her face up as though she meant the complete opposite, and it made me chuckle.

"There's a third vessel, though," I mused aloud. "There has to be. Whatever that is, it must be fading too. Maybe that's what Scarlett meant when she said my mother was broken. That we needed to piece her back together."

"Like Humpty Dumpty."

My hands went to my chest automatically at her words, feeling for the rune tattoos I knew marked my skin. She'd said the same thing to me when she'd found me on the floor of the hotel room.

I'd scored myself across the chest with Honey's knife, slicing across the marks no one could see but me. Marks that burned me nearly very time I contacted magic of some sort.

I had yet to figure out their true purpose or why they had appeared weeks earlier when I'd touched the Hecate symbol drawn in blood on a murder scene wall.

All I knew was they gave me access to power I hadn't had before all this began.

"Honey said Farrel was too new to offer much power. She didn't think it would be enough to fight off the magic of the coven, and she was right. Smith's magic didn't last long. He wavered and needed my blood."

I felt as though we were closer than ever before. Hope bloomed inside me. I couldn't stop smiling.

Then I looked at Parrish's expression, and the smile froze on my face.

"Don't move, Desirée," she said, using the moniker we'd decided on instead of my name the way she'd been doing since we got inside the shop. I knew something was wrong the moment she did.

I just didn't realize how wrong until I turned around and saw the wolf shifter at my door.

CHAPTER 10

"DON'T FREAK OUT, DESIRéE," Parrish said beneath her breath. "Just sit there like a good little lover, all innocent like." Her hand landed on my thigh and squeezed in warning. "He doesn't know you, remember?"

I dropped my gaze back to her face because looking across the shop to the door made my breath feel like it was clawing its way out of my lungs. In the exhale, a shrill note sounded, one that indicated my throat was clinging to the breath as it tightened up.

"But he'll know me, Parrish," I said with another flick of my eyes to the door to where Owen stood. He held the tom in both hands, oblivious to the mangy fur falling out from its body and dropping like rain drops to the sidewalk.

It was too late to hold the panic at bay. It was blooming beneath my breastbone with every breath. I had the nearly irresistible urge to scratch at the scabs that had begun to form over the cuts I'd made in my skin.

Parrish made a big show of dropping her head back in annoyance and groaning loud enough in irritation that Owen would have to hear her. I thought she might be doing it to disguise the ragged breathing hiccuping from me.

She sent me a sharp glance. "Have you met Mr. Garder before, Desirée?" she said loudly enough that a shifter's ear should be able to hear, and with one more warning squeeze on my thigh to console me. "He's a pretty randy old gent with tons of money. It's not unheard of for him to woo younger women."

She pushed herself to her feet, keeping her eyes on my face and I read in her expression the things she didn't want to say. Be careful. He can hear. Don't blow it. All the while I was more worried he'd scent me the way she'd mentioned earlier.

I needn't have worried. Parrish was far cagier than I'd given her credit for.

She pulled me to my feet along with her and pulled me close against her chest. Only my determination to fool Owen moved my arms to encircle her neck and let her run her palms over my clothes, marking me.

I trembled next to her, the adrenaline and fear taking over the autonomic things I couldn't disguise.

She took great care—what might look like seduction to the casual eye—in cupping her hand behind my neck and stroking the skin so that she touched every inch that was bare. Her fingers dipped into my bodice and flicked across my chest. I swallowed down a clump of nerves as I held her eye.

"For fuck sake, Desirée," she whispered. "The least you could do is kiss me."

In other words, put on the show. Make him believe I was her lover. I knew better than most how important sleight of hand was, how critical distraction is to per-ception.

So I let her fill every inch of my skin and clothing with her scent. Enough to throw him off for a few moments. The unique miasma of patchouli and some unname-able pheromone that was Parrish swirled around me.

"Make it quick," I said in what I hoped was a throaty voice in case Owen could hear us, but meaning the same thing she did. That we needed to get rid of Owen before I totally lost my shit and he ferreted out the real scent beneath all the cover.

My only hope was that he didn't know me enough for him to see through the disguise.

The door rattled behind us from the pounding Owen put on the glass. Most undignified for the alpha of the pack. A grin tugged at Parrish's lip. She was enjoying this.

Parrish spun me around so that I was facing Owen, but had a better line of escape, then she dipped her head, claiming my mouth with hers.

Like before, the kiss was not intimate, just skin on skin, but she took her time, her eyes wide open, gazing into mine as though to say, "give that bastard a good show." And I did my best. Despite the shaking of my knees and the trembling in my chest, I did my best.

When she broke off, she rubbed her cheek against mine and buried her face in my neck.

"Once I let him in, you head for the bathroom and run the water over the soap. Good and hot, you get it? It would never fool Layne, but it might throw off his dad."

I nodded, and she released me. I caught sight of the hard jaw line and stiff shoulders that indicated the leader of the Garder pack was most horrifically annoyed. With the ringing of the bell as Parrish let him in, I forced my legs to move, backing up toward the bathroom.

After what he'd done to me, I wanted to both claw his eyes out and tear off to some place safe at the same time.

"Jesus H Christ," he growled as he stooped to lay the cat at the threshold. "You keep me waiting out there in the cold while you make out with some trollop?"

My eyebrow lifted at the word and I had to bite down on my tongue to keep the retort inside my mouth where it belonged. Parrish's mouth twitched, and I had the feeling she wanted to do the same.

Luckily, we both managed to clamp down on the reprimand. One didn't scold an alpha. At least, not one that had tried to kill me just a week earlier.

He pushed passed Parrish, a rough shove that did nothing to move her out of the way. She was stone with a column of rock that went deep beneath the surface. He looked her over thoughtfully, and she stepped aside and dropped her gaze.

I wasn't sure if Owen knew it, but I was sure she'd done it out of respect for keeping our ruse and not because she felt submissive to him. I recalled her saying Layne was her alpha. She'd demure to him only. So Parrish was a dominant wolf. One more bit of info to squirrel away for another day.

While it wasn't a surprise, I did find it interesting that I'd not caught it sooner.

As she moved aside to let him pass, he swung around to take in the shop. He'd been there before, of course, the day he'd found me heaving my guts up in the bathroom.

That had been the same day he'd come onto me and sent me to the lingerie shop to buy something to please him, assuming, like most women he met, that I could be bought.

Arrogant, cocky bastard to assume I would fall at his feet.

And he looked no different now. His presence in the shop created an electricity that told me he believed he owned the space. The shudders that went through me transformed from nervous energy to rage. My hands fisted at my sides as I tried to keep from storming him and punching him in the revoltingly handsome face.

His eye took me in and flickered over me in one second before it returned to Parrish. Apparently, whatever he saw, it wasn't his type. His dismissal might have hurt if I'd cared what he thought at all. As it was, I just wanted to rake his eyes out for delivering me to the coven.

That he didn't like Parrish was obvious. That he obviously needed her help and hated to ask for it, was something she hadn't noticed yet. She couldn't see it in his body language, the way he pointed his toes toward her, the way he rocked back and forth on his heels, shushing himself the way a mother might a colicky baby.

That he resented having to come to her for help was clear in the way he wouldn't give her the dignity of speaking to her face when the words did tumble out.

"Send her away," he said with a gesture in my direction. "We have to talk."

His agitation was uncharacteristic, even for the short amount of time I knew him. Parrish's gaze went to half mast as she considered his words.

"Desirée knows what I am," she said.

He didn't bother to look in my direction, just swore under his breath. "I'll deal with that later," he said. "For now, I need you to find Layne."

Parrish's fists clenched. "Find Layne? What do you mean?"

He shoved his hands in his trouser pockets, a nice gabardine that had to cost a fortune. "Have you seen him?"

Careful, that Owen. So damn careful. He wasn't about to give anything away, but I sensed the worry in his voice. My solar plexus felt it. I had to bite down on the inside of my cheek to keep from demanding he say what was wrong with Layne.

It took an eternity for Parrish to ask what she should have asked straight away.

"What's wrong?"

He shot a glance my way and she said in an irritated tone that sent a dark look across his face, "She's fine, but if you must have her out of earshot, she'll go wash up in the bathroom." She jerked her thumb in the direction of the dead cat. "No telling how long that thing has been dead."

She sent me a meaningful glance and I took a step back. She wanted me to leave. She'd tell me everything later.

But I didn't want to go. Something was off with Layne. Owen's presence here confirmed it.

"How did you find me here?" Parrish asked.

"Zach."

She nodded slowly. "You've been to see Zach and he told you about Brie."

My heart lurched when she said my name. I was afraid his hearing it might make things click in his mind over the woman who stood there frozen wearing a black wig and fake eyelashes, but I should have known he'd not given me much of a glance.

"He told me, yes."

"You were worried about her?"

Oh, Parrish, how rich. How well played. Not a trace of guile anywhere in the tone. Brava, girl. Brava.

He sighed. "My son loves her," he said. "And I was sad to hear of her passing." He paused as though expecting some sort of freaking ovation for the obvious drama, and I all but choked on my own spit. Parrish slid a look of warning my way and I dropped my gaze.

If Owen noticed the moment of tension, he said nothing about it. Merely continued on. "Be that as it may, it's what else Zach told me that sent me here, looking for you. And when I do arrive, it's to discover you necking with some stranger in the middle of her shop."

"She's grieving, you bastard," I said, forgetting that I was supposed to be high-tailing it to the bathroom.

Parrish glowered at me. My voice. He'd recognize my voice at least. I clamped my mouth closed.

"I've seen grieving," Owen said, deigning to show me a short moment of attention, before letting his eye trail back to Parrish, looking at her directly finally. "If that's grief, then maybe I've been grieving far too much."

She shrugged, nonplussed, or at least acting as though it didn't matter to her what he thought. "Don't tell me you wouldn't get a little hot in the crotch with a woman like this embracing you."

She canted her head in my direction, letting an expression of longing slide over her features. I had to give it to her. She was good. I almost believed she fancied me.

My admiration for her acting skills died as he turned that assessing gaze back on me, a most unwanted attention in the moment. "She does have a certain something," he said as his eyes narrowed. "But is it enough to give dignity to a dead friend's memory?"

I did choke at that, but Parrish merely plucked a candle from the shelf and examined the bottom, giving the impression she didn't care what he thought.

"Don't tell me you haven't sought out similar comforts over the centuries, Owen," she said.

He glowered at her but she didn't back down and I was beginning to see why he hated her so much.

"You haven't told me how you found me here," she said, and I knew she was pressing him to admit to having my properties watched. It was a clear accusation for a man who was guilty the way he was, and he showed himself so when he spun on his heel and headed for the door.

"I am sorry," he said. "I have made a mistake."

I couldn't let him go. Parrish may not have figured out something was wrong, too intent on one-upping him, but I knew. I knew something was wrong. If he didn't know where Layne was, it had to be.

"I'll leave," I said, and he froze. I spoke to his back as I gestured wildly at Parrish to put aside her anger at him and find out what he wanted. "I touched that damn cat and I have to wash up anyway. I can leave you two to your business."

He turned around then, his eyes narrowing as his gaze landed on my face a little too intensely to be just a glance. Parrish must have realized he was suspicious because she stepped between us, putting her back to me.

"What do you need, Owen?" she said flatly. "You found me here because you were looking for me." She put a hand up to her head. "I owe it to Brie to close up her shop and her apartment, but you know this or you wouldn't have found me here."

It wasn't quite the truth, but she was giving him an out. Act normal, she'd said. Well, she was doing her best.

He nodded silently as he pulled his hand from his pockets and motioned toward the chair. "I don't know what you've heard from Zach," he said.

Parrish perched on the edge of the seat and I found my hands moving to my chest. I wanted to retreat to the bathroom like she'd said, but my feet wouldn't move. If Parrish felt the need to sit down, then she must have realized something awful was coming.

Dread danced along my spine. I didn't have the same acuity of hearing as Parrish, so I left the bathroom door slightly ajar as I ran water into the sink. I didn't doubt Parrish would tell me what the issue was after Owen left, but I still couldn't bring myself to close the door. I couldn't bear to wait.

I angled myself near the gap in the door, with my ear straining to drown out the sound of the running water. As if Parrish knew what I was doing, she got up and moved closer to the bathroom, drawing Owen along with her.

"What is it, Owen?" she said. "What is it about Layne that you couldn't say in front of my partner?"

"Maybe you should sit down again," he said.

"I'm not so weak," was her answer and he grunted.

"I'm not weak either, but the news near took the knees out from under me."

"You said you needed me to find Layne." She pressed him and he groaned and sighed all in one breath.

"You know him better than anyone," he said. "And it's going to take a hell of a good friend to find him now."

"I've got things to do," she said in a voice laced with cautious and intentional ennui. "What could I do that his own father can't? If he doesn't want you to find him, what makes you think he wants me to? He deserves some peace if he's grieving."

"That's just it," Owen said. "It's not just that he's grieving. Zach told me word of Brie's death made him go completely rabid."

CHAPTER 11

RABID. PARRISH HAD USED the term masher about the young girl Owen had turned in order to cleave her to him in an attempt to create a new pack ignorant of his nefarious work with the coven. The word struck horror in my gut even though I didn't fully understand what it meant.

If this was the reason Owen couldn't speak of Layne's condition in front of me, it had to be bad. I inched closer to the door, terrified I'd show myself to Owen's peripheral vision, but unable to stop myself.

I strained to hear more, but the silence in the room beyond was so laced with tension that part of me cringed away at the same time.

It took a long time for Parrish to speak, and when she did, her voice sounded broken.

"Zach didn't tell me this." Not an accusation, but very close to it.

"Zach was under orders to keep it quiet. I don't want the pack to know."

She snorted. "They'll know soon enough." Her head hung and she shuffled her foot back and forth on the floor. "Soon as bodies start turning up, they'll know it's a wolf."

"That's where I need you," he said and her face jerked up.

"I can't hide that many bodies," she said. "I can't fake that many death certificates."

On my side of the door, my knees went to water and I had to feel for the wall to ease myself down onto the floor. Some vague thought reminded me the water was still running and Owen would realize I wasn't still washing my hands, but I reasoned he wouldn't care so long as I wasn't interfering with his tete a tete.

I sat with my back against the wall beside the door and tried to control the breath that had started coming in gasps. Layne was going to hurt people. Badly.

"Layne told me a bit about your condition," Owen said, stressing the word as though he found it distasteful. "I'm to gather you understand a bit about that sort of grief that can send the wolf into a fugue frenzy."

"It's not the same," she said in a dull voice, one filled with pain and dare I think recollection? "Violet wasn't the same as Brie. Brie died in a hospital after losing too much blood. She went peacefully."

No mention of the horror that would have put me in the hospital, and I guessed the omission was a calculated thing on her part. Even so, the words shivered through me and my head fell back beneath the weight of them.

Owen murmured something I couldn't hear, then said, "Be that as it may, he is beyond grief. Maybe you can understand better than anyone else what he's going through. Maybe you can find him. Maybe you can save him."

His voice broke on the words and it was such a gut punch to hear the pain in his voice that I dared peer around the sill of the door. He wasn't facing me anymore. Instead, he was turned slightly to the right so that he could plant his palm on Parrish's shoulder.

She shrugged it off with distaste and that was when he grabbed her by both shoulders. A bit too rough for my liking. She looked frail and weak in that moment and I hated seeing that happen to her.

Trouble was, the defeated look wasn't from Owen's aggression; it was from something entirely different. Something that went beyond her worry for Layne, and maybe something that heightened her worry for Layne.

I'd seen that look before in a few clients. Those were usually haunted by something in their past that they couldn't forgive themselves for. I'd felt it myself in what I thought was the betrayal of my mother. The hardest absolution comes from within. Those who felt the depth of guilt and shame were the sternest judge.

It took everything I had within not to crawl out from the bathroom and go to her, and not just because I knew she might be the key to helping Layne and saving all those would-be victims of his. Owen's voice helped.

It kept me cringing inside because the situation just seemed to get worse and worse the more he spoke.

"Zach managed to sedate him for a while," he said. "It took three shots to put him down, but when Zach went on rounds, Layne just disappeared. Took that little stray with him."

"That's why he didn't come to my apartment," Parrish murmured and when Owen asked what she meant, she shook her head. "I expected him to come talk to me at least. But I never saw him after the hospital."

Owen shoved his hands in his pockets again. "Someone has to track him, Parrish," he said. "I can't have him killing civilians. Not now. Even as pack alpha, I can only do so much if that happens. I'll have to send the enforcers after him."

Parrish ran her hand through her hair. "Fucking Jesus Christmas. This is so not a good time."

Owen canted his head at her. "You got something else on your plate more important than my son's life?"

She snarled at him, the growl coming from deep in her chest and I thought I saw him wince for an instant before he gathered himself together.

"You are part of my pack, Parrish. I didn't invite you, but you are a member just the same, and as such I expect you to act as though you are. If you want to go rogue, you'll be hunted the same as Layne will be if he isn't contained. I suggest you find him. And quick."

"So what you're saying is you're sending in one masher after another because if he hurts me you'll be out a problem wolf. If I end up bringing him out of it, then you have your son back. You win either way."

He held her immobile for a long moment with a raking gaze, and she dropped her eyes, dipping her head toward the floor. I didn't think it was an act. She really had submitted to him. Only when he was sure of her subservience did he speak again, but at least there was a note of pity in his voice, sincerity.

"I lose either way," he said, and his hand went to his heart, where it lay as he looked at her. "Pack is pack. I would grieve you as I would any other member. Don't make me grieve, Parrish. I have enough to do."

It wasn't a loving statement, but she lifted her gaze to his, and with a quick swipe of her fingers over her cheek, she nodded.

I was so confused. I knew authenticity when I heard it. He hadn't brought her into the pack, and he might not like her, but she was his to protect, and his tone evidenced clear intention to do both. If I hadn't known he'd made three expendable werewolves outside the pack, I might have believed him.

I waited for him to spin on his heel and head for the door before I crept out from the bathroom. Parrish had sunk back into the chair when I found her. She lifted her head from where it hung between her knees.

"Thought I was going to faint for a second," she said and leaned back, flinging her legs out in front of her, heels digging into the floorboards.

"I heard," I said, and she nodded. "How bad is it?"

"Bad enough to make me want to pass out, I suspect," she said in a wry tone. She dropped her head forward and rubbed at her forehead with the heel of her hand. "Do you believe all that bullshit?"

"You might have to be more specific."

She waved away the comment and pushed herself to her feet. With a long look in my direction, she said, "I don't think I can help you any more, Brie. At least until I can find Layne. He needs me more."

My hand snaked out and grabbed for hers before she could get too far, and I'd lose my nerve.

"You don't have to help me," I said. "I'll help you. Whatever you need. Whatever Layne needs."

A flash of something moved through her eyes as her throat worked visibly to contain what I knew was the urge to cry.

"He'll be alright," I said to give her time to gather herself. Honey and the coven could wait. If they all thought I was dead, then it was possible their activities would slow down. Maybe we didn't have this critical crisis waiting to drop a shoe on us. "I know you won't let him down. He can count on you. On us. We won't leave him hanging."

She squeezed my hand hard enough to make me want to wince, but I wouldn't let it show on my face.

"You can help me best right now by doing what we set out to do." She nodded in the door's direction. "He'll probably assume I've left the task to you anyway while I hunt Layne."

A heavy sigh escaped her, but at least her voice was level. That was a good sign that she was back in the driver's seat and out of the tailspin of emotion, and I had the feeling she worked best that way.

"Start with the death certificate and arranging a plot to bury yourself, and go from there. I have a feeling Owen will have you followed now. I didn't like the look in his eye when he heard your voice. He's not going to let go quite so easily. So do what we talked about and I'll keep you updated as I can."

She let go of my hand and went for the door, then backtracked and pressed a set of keys in my grip.

"You can't go home. I wouldn't let a lover into Brie's apartment without me, but I would let her stay at my place even if I'm not there."

A sound from behind the counter caught our attention, and she slapped the top of her head. "Sweet cheese and crackers, it's a damn good thing he didn't catch sight of your familiar."

Indeed. Far better to keep the recollection of that night in the hotel and all the various bits and bobs of it out of his mind.

"She'll need to stay here," she said of the dog. "I don't know that we can get her out of here without any of his sentinels seeing her."

"She came here for a reason," I said with a nod.

She ran her hand along her leg, fingers tapping her thigh. "I'll try to look in on her for you, but I can't promise anything."

"And when I'm finished all those little tasks? What then? How do I find you?"

I had the dreaded sense that I was saying goodbye, and my eyes stung. This wasn't easy. I'd been alone for dozens of years, but now that I'd found people to care about, who cared about me, I didn't want to just let go. Not without a fight. And I felt like the fight was avoiding me.

"I'm not going to war, Brie," she said quietly. "I'll text you. If you can help, you can be sure, I'll ask for it."

I walked her to the door, and she hugged me tight. Her heart hammered against my chest so hard I knew she was feeling the same dread. Out of instinct, my palms cupped each side of her face.

"Whatever haunts you from your past, it may serve you now. Embrace it. That thing that wounds you from within can be a balm for another if you let it."

She shifted her face just enough to kiss my left palm and whispered against the skin. "If it doesn't kill me first, Layne can have it. I'm fucking tired of carrying it."

She dipped into her pocket and extracted a phone—my phone, she'd obviously taken from the hospital room. She passed it to me with a grin. Then she stepped out into the sunshine and left me alone in the shop.

It took me five full minutes to hunt a placard and pen that I could write on and tack to the front door. STORE CLOSED DUE TO DEATH seemed about the least final while still alerting those who might be watching that Brie McAllister was dead. Every now and then, the phone blipped with a notice of someone responding to Parrish's social media troll. None of it was flattering, and I'd grown numb to the sound of it ringing and trying to distract me.

It buzzed a few times while I worked on the sign, and I shoved it atop a stack of papers to smother the sound, then shook out the broad sign and held it up to my eye.

"Good enough," I murmured aloud and headed to the front of the shop. I had taped it to the door, right in the center, and was heading back into the shop proper when the toe of Parrish's tramp boots that I was wearing nudged the dead cat.

I stared down at the animal for a moment, working out what bothered me the most about the whole affair. The cat didn't smell dead. As Parrish had suggested, it had a strange scent that wafted up at me in subtle waves.

Magic, she'd said and I was inclined to agree. I crouched next to it, mindful of the tear in the seat of the pants that I'd forgotten in the rush of Owen's visit and Parrish's departure.

With my hands over my knees, I forced myself to study the tom more clinically. Dead long enough to be stiff, his fur had lost its luster, and his face had frozen in a snarl, as though he had fought whatever came for him.

I let the tears run for the poor thing, thinking of the time when he'd scared the bejesus out of me, and I'd called Layne—at the time, I only knew him as Officer Garder—to come to the shop because I thought the killer was inside.

My throat grew tighter as the memories played out in my mind. Layne hadn't argued with me at the time. He just came. Now, he was the monster in the corner, and

I hoped desperately that Parrish could find him before he did anything he would regret.

As I squatted there, a hum lit up behind my ears, like the sound of a swarm of mosquitoes on an early spring night. I checked over my shoulder. Nothing. I cocked my head, and closed my eyes to concentrate better. Yes. It was surely there, but not behind my ears or inside my head.

I held my hand out over the cat, letting it hover in the air above him. The hum became a sensation, and it moved from that place of auditory sense to something more physical. Like a strange bit of synesthesia, my palms buzzed; static moved between the tom and my hand.

I lowered my palm. The prickling on my palm moved to the base of my spine and climbed my vertebrae like a ladder to the spot just behind my occipital bone.

And when it struck my skull and slammed through the bone to the space behind my eyes, it lit up the room with a blinding light.

CHAPTER 12

I BROKE THROUGH THE veil of awareness some time later to find myself lying on the floor on my side. The shop was in shadow, but not completely dark. My first thought, was shit, not again. I'd unintentionally called to my magic and ended up unconscious and badly hurt.

I did a tentative mental check, roaming over my body in a swift assessment. No sore head to indicate I'd whacked it when I'd fallen and given myself a concussion. No broken bones. No pain anywhere.

Admittedly, the distance to the floor from my knees was short, thankfully. Otherwise, I might have done some wicked harm.

So what had I done, then? I'd not cut myself or touched my runes the way I'd called to the magic before. This time, something was different.

Then I remembered the cat. I scrambled to my knees, sweeping the floor with my palm so I wouldn't accidentally shove my chin in the dead cat's fur when I tried to get up.

I needn't have worried. By the time I got to my hands and knees, I knew the thing was gone. There was no sign of it anywhere within my reach. I sat back on my haunches and stared at the space it had been. No sign of blood or fur or anything from the animal to indicate it had even been there.

I ran my palm over the floor boards where it had been, almost to test the veracity of my senses that told me the dead cat had disappeared.

Stunned, I thought, or spelled, because a dead cat did not simply get up and walk away. Even in the world I now lived in, where magic and ritual and werewolves thrived in the shadows, creatures did not re-animate. Ghosts and spirits and goddesses, maybe, but not mortal creatures.

I should have felt relief that the poor tom was alive, but somehow the thought that it was spelled was more chilling because it meant that the coven was probably involved. It might even mean Honey lurked somewhere nearby watching the whole damn ordeal.

I touched my wig, afraid all of a sudden that it had come off when I'd collapsed. If she was skulking outside, watching, then the disguise really needed to be impenetrable to keep my life hidden. I didn't dare look around, but my whole body tingled with the sensation of residual magic.

Or was that the feeling of suspicious eyes on my back?

A shiver moved through me, and I strained to catch any sound of movement in my shop. I had no idea how long I'd been out, and anything—anyone—could have broken in.

After a moment, I did hear a sound. A groan of sorts. I jerked my head in the direction of the counter where Parrish and I had left Abbi, my mother's familiar. We'd left her there behind the counter, thinking her safest there.

Out of sight, she might go unnoticed by the pack and the coven until we could find a way to help her.

Now, she lay several feet away from me and where Owen had dropped the tom--in front of the counter and not behind it.

I pushed myself to my feet, and with a lingering glance at the empty part of the floor where the cat had been, I crossed the room.

The dog lay on her side. When we'd left her to deal with Owen, pieces of her bare flesh had shown through in patches. Hours had passed since then, and I imagined she'd grown worse in that time, tried to find a way out the way dogs do when they're about to die.

I inched to her, thinking the worst. Dread shivered through me at the thought that she might have tried to help me when I passed out. She'd proven a protector as well as a warning to me in the past. If she'd tried to get to me in her state, she might have done worse to herself.

I dropped to my knees next to her. "I don't know what to do for you, girl."

Her eye rolled in my direction, and she moved just the slightest bit toward me, her head lifting and swinging closer before it dropped back to the floor. I didn't need her to be able to speak to tell me what was happening.

It was clear that whatever Honey and her coven had done in the hotel room where Smith had used my magic to fight the coven, had tapped into my mother's stores.

She was broken, Scarlett had said. Now I knew what she meant when I hadn't before.

But as I roamed the tips of her fur with my gaze and considered each spot that looked so horrendous earlier, I realized her eyes weren't so rheumy. The fur wasn't as mangy and dull-looking as before. Some luster had crept back in during the hours I'd been unconscious.

Even more surprising, the bare patches where her flesh showed through had begun to close up.

Just like they had before when Scarlett and I had seen it do so right before our eyes.

There could only be one explanation, as improbable as it seemed.

"Sweet Jesus," I said out loud, surprising myself enough to drop my palms to the floor beside Abbi's head. I leaned in. "Did I do this to you?" I asked her.

The magic inside me had done other things I didn't understand when it dropped me out of reality and into some other realm I didn't remember. To me, it seemed like I was sleeping without REM. But there were times, like when I'd contacted Scarlett, that the realm was all too clear.

Had I tapped into it and healed the dog?

She had been suffering before, evaporating, the way I expected as each part of Hecate that my mother had stored in various places came apart, the magic spent and no longer able to hold her vessels together.

With my mother's mortal body long gone, those vessels spelled to hold her spirit were breaking apart. I imagined that with each piece that disappeared, the goddess herself evaporated.

Those things had protected me without me knowing. No wonder my mother had instructed her lawyer to make sure I received her things, her apartment, the building that I turned into a good livelihood. She knew the coven would come for me, the daughter of Hecate, a conduit to the goddess they had broken.

If I couldn't find a way to restore her, then this dog, and Smith and the third unknown vessel would cease to exist. Hecate would cease to exist.

That was one realization that floated to mind when I looked down at Abbi. The other was that I'd fallen unconscious after feeling the electricity of magic coursing through me. I'd felt that before. It always ended badly.

But it also always brought with it some magical change.

"It's me, isn't it?" I asked again. "I healed you somehow."

This time when the dog rolled her eyes, it looked nothing like agreement. The expression would have been sarcasm on a human face.

This dog knew what was going on. She was incapable of telling me, but she was trying.

Or perhaps the coven would own her power. Maybe that was what this was about. Maybe they'd been trying to steal it all along. The phone calls after my dad died. The treks to the graveyard to collect grave dirt so she could use it to power her spells. The yelling into the phone that they'd have to kill her before she gave them what they wanted.

It had terrified me as a child enough to run away countless times. The last time, I'd informed social services that my mother was insane. I'd told them about the late night treks to the graveyard, the incantations and sacrifices in the basement.

When my mother gave me up, she told me it was better for me anyway. Safer. And when the lawyer called me to tell me she'd died, I'd told him to pack it all up and leave it in her attic. I'd come home when I was damn good and ready.

Too many painful memories ran through the rooms of our house. I wasn't sure what had called me home

I ran my hand over the dog's fur, and it shuddered beneath my fingers. I wondered what would have happened if I'd not come home, if the lawyer hadn't tracked me down and told me I had to acquit him of my mother's inheritance.

"I'd thought him a bastard," I said to the dog, and she thumped her tail once on the floor as though to agree with me. "He had zero social skills. Said he'd put the blasted boxes in the attic but I'd need to come to close up the house for myself unless he wanted me to cough up a few more K."

With forearms slung over my knees, I regarded the creature with a critical eye as I let the memory roam the corridors of my mind. The sleekness of the fur had dulled, and in places, the sheen of jet was more like a smudge of ash.

Smith had said something back in that hotel room that had escaped me till just now. I'd been on the cusp of understanding when Owen had shown up at the door and distracted us.

But with Parrish gone, and with Owen out of the shop, with just the dog and I sitting there together, the truth started to scratch through.

Smith had used my magic to power when his had waned. Honey used the feral wolf's to amp up her own. The dog had attacked Farrel.

I sat back on my haunches, thinking it over, letting my eye run from one end of the dog's hind quarters to the tip of her nose.

That was when I noticed the blood on her snout. I leaned in closer, my fingers reaching for her nose.

A low growl rumbled through her, and I pulled my hand back thoughtfully. She wasn't warning me, not angry, but telling me something.

I looked back over my shoulder at the spot where the tomcat had lain. My attention drew itself as if by magnet to the blood on the dog's nose.

"Oh my God," I said. "You ate my cat." Revulsion raced through me as I considered the truth of it. "You ate my fucking cat."

The dog's tail thumped twice, and she licked her lips. The tongue ran over the stain on her nose, leaving it clean and glistening.

My hand went to my chest automatically as I considered, really considered, what had gone on while I'd been out.

"It's the magic," I murmured as the thought struck me. "You need it." I swung around, my arms to the sides to keep me from stumbling as I took in the entire shop and let the air whistle over my skin. It wasn't me at all. The cat held residual magic. It hadn't been merely stunned and leaped to its feet by some miracle when I passed out.

No. It had been consumed.

I spun on my heel and regarded the dog once more. "You magnificent beast," I said. "You eat magic."

It was clear now, where it hadn't been before. My hand reached out for her nose. The velvet of it had been dry and cracked earlier. Now, she looked back at me with clear eyes, not rheumy.

"You ate Farrel's magic," I said to her.

Her lip curled back in a semi smile. Sentient, for sure. A dog built of the spirits of all those puppies and imbued with Hecate's power. Her familiar.

"That's it, isn't it?" I asked. "You need to be fed magic."

I fell back against the counter and stretched my legs out to uncurl the knots in them from squatting too long. Smith used my magic when his had waned. Honey used the feral wolf's magic to power her spell. Not just blood.

If there was any sort of hierarchy to power, and death magic was stronger than blood magic, then what of the power of pure magic. Not contrived and gathered from natural sources by witches with an affinity for energy. Real, pure magic.

Like the magic that came from a goddess.

I pulled out my phone and messaged Parrish. I know how we can save Abbi. She eats magic. Like with Farrel.

The reply came back almost instantly, indicating she wasn't yet hard underground, searching for Layne, or caught in the throes of taming him. I didn't know how I felt about either one, so I just squirreled away the emotions and read her message.

"She's not the kind of bitch I let eat me, but I'm sure we can find some other poor wretch to do the job."

I ignored the joke although I was sure Parrish would have liked me to acknowledge it. Instead, I zeroed in on the idea within the comment. "Like a witch," I muttered to myself, thinking if I found Honey I would feed her to the dog without reservation. "If we can find someone with magic, then we can heal her."

"Don't go thinking what I'm thinking you're thinking," Parrish texted back. "We don't know any witches, Desirée. The last witch I knew is dead now."

The warning was clear. She wasn't sure if someone might be listening in and wanted them to keep believing Brie was dead. I needed to remember that if we were to keep up the ruse. She needn't have worried.

But looking at Abbi, I wondered if there was another way. I didn't want to say it out loud to Parrish, but I wasn't about to offer myself up to the cause. Smith's tap into whatever magic lay in my blood left me in the hospital near death.

I still suffered bouts of weakness, and my muscles didn't obey me as fast as I wanted. Unless I could figure out how to call to the magic without doing considerable harm to myself, there was no freaking way I was going to even think about trying to help by offering up my magic to the dog.

Because while she'd regained some power from the stray tom, she needed more.

I scoured the shop with a roaming eye. I needed to find more magic. A consumable one that could power a goddess's familiar, but that wouldn't hurt me.

And that's when I noticed a pair of eyes looking in the window at me.

I knew the eyes. I knew the face. He didn't look much like himself anymore, but it was Layne. And he was looking straight at me.

A tremor ran through my chest as I held his gaze. It was him. All six feet four inches of him.

I'd passed out long before I turned on the lights, so I was in shadow in the shop, so with the night creeping over the city outside, he probably couldn't see clearly or well into the interior.

But there was a street lamp nearby, and it cast a pale glow over his form. The fairy lights of the window lit up his features, and I was so thirsty for them, my gaze drank him in from the days' old scruff on his chin to the buzz cut that had grown past its stage of manicured and roamed into scraggly territory.

He was incredible.

If I closed my eyes, I knew I'd catch a whiff of his scent, of mint and musk. I wanted it so badly I must have made a sound because Abbi's tail thumped against my calf, demanding attention.

I skirted a look over her to be sure she was alright, tearing my eyes from Layne's for just a moment. Abbi growled low in her throat. She tried to get up and fell again.

My hand went automatically to her neck, my fingers burrowing into her fur.

"Shh," I said to her. "He's a friend. You know he is."

I turned back to the shop door, both terrified he'd know me and afraid he wouldn't. He still stood there. In the few seconds my head had been turned, he'd put his hands up on the glass, shielding his eyes as he tried to see inside.

In that instant, I saw what my excitement had glossed over. He looked haggard. The circles under his eyes had a purple hue so dark, it was clearly visible all this distance apart. His cheeks were hollowed in. The feral look in his gaze bore into me and sent a shiver of fear up my spine.

He did not recognize me in the disguise, or if he did, he was too far gone to care.

With extreme caution and painfully slow movements, I pulled my phone out again. I tapped the numbers to Parrish's phone.

It took forever for her to answer, and in that time, Layne had begun to shuffle back and forth and side to side. His arms crossed his chest, and his mouth was moving as though he were talking.

"What in the devil's fuzzy slippers is so important you have to call me twice, Desirée?"

"He's here," I said, and because I knew someone was probably listening, I added, "At least it looks like the man you're supposed to be looking for."

My gaze flitted over Layne's face, searching for something I could use that wouldn't reveal how well I knew him but would tell any eavesdroppers I had the right guy.

"His eyes are glowing," I said. And it was true. The longer he stood there, the more yellow his eyes got. By now, they were almost akin to predator's eyes in the dark.

The line went dead without a sound.

CHAPTER 13

THE WAY MY HEART hammered in my chest, I was terrified Layne would be able to hear it even through several feet of shop floor and a few panes of glass. I swallowed hard and minced my way onto my feet.

The tear in the back of the pants let in a draft of air that ran down the back of my thigh. I couldn't have felt more exposed if I'd been naked, not with him looking in at me.

When I stood, he leaned away from the window. A peculiar expression crossed his face for an instant. The yellow in his eyes blazed. He leaned back in with a smirk and placed his full palm on the window, fingers splayed.

I had expected him to be in wolf form, but this was far more terrifying. I had to remind myself I was in disguise. He couldn't scent me, he couldn't see me, he couldn't hear me.

He couldn't know it was me.

And yet, that smirk spoke volumes in the fleeting seconds it played on his mouth. If he knew me, he didn't care about me. If he recognized a woman he loved beneath all the black and leather, the false eyelashes, the putty Parrish had applied here and there to change the shape of my cheekbones, he certainly didn't love her anymore.

I reeled backward, feeling for a chair or the counter, forgetting to mind my steps where I could trip over Abbi. My hand came down on the counter top right where the reaper had torn into the surface with his scythe.

But I did not trip on Abbi. With a sweeping glance, I ran my eye over the floor where she should have lain.

She was gone.

"Not again," I said aloud and thought I could see Layne cant his head sideways. "You can't hear me," I whispered. "You can't fucking hear me from there."

As though to argue the point, he struck the window with the ball of his fist. Instead of pulling it back, it stayed there, the heel of it smearing the glass as he leaned in again.

With that same smirk, he pressed his forehead onto the glass, next to his fist. The condensation of his breath clouded his features, obliterating everything from view except those eyes.

It took one more slam of his fist on the glass, this time harder, louder, to free my feet from their paralysis. Without taking my eyes from his, I backed up to the counter, thinking I'd edge my way out of view.

Then I caught sight of something else, or rather, someone else, over his shoulder. The young wolf Owen had turned, who'd come to my shop after he'd bitten her. Trish, her name was.

Layne was supposed to be helping her. Parrish told me as a dominant wolf, he might be one of the only people who could keep her from losing all her humanity to her wolf.

My hand went to my throat of its own volition when I realized that was a moot point now. She was half shifted into her beast. Luckily for anyone who might be shopping this time of night in the tourist quarter, all her attention was on Layne.

Unluckily for me, there wasn't a sign of any shoppers ambling about anyway.

I was all alone with two feral werewolves staring into my shop.

"Sweet Jesus, Parrish, where in the hell are you?"

Another smart rap on the window pulled my attention back to the front.

"The sign," I said, pointing at the huge white poster board I'd taped to the door. "The shop is closed."

How many times had I said the same thing the last few weeks as horror after horror had visited me and I'd retreated to this one building as though it held the safety of a womb. How many times had this place cocooned me and saved me?

One more time, I hoped.

"Closed," I said and did my level best to turn around as though I was no one of consequence, just a woman doing her best to tidy up the area. A woman who did not see a werewolf in her lover's eyes.

I managed to make half a turn before the pounding began. This time, Layne used both hands and each blow made the window shake. I blinked at him stupidly, wondering why I was more bothered by the street behind him than I was the glass shuddering beneath his fists.

A splintering sound from the back of the shop gave me the first clue. I swung my head in the direction of the galley to the curtain beyond that led to my inner sanctum. Layne struck the window again, pulling my attention back to him and the empty street behind him.

Empty street. The young she-wolf was not there. That's what bothered me. I didn't need the next shuddering thunder of wood to tell me where she was. She was at the back door.

And me with no magic dog to protect me, no grimoire to blast an attacker, no amulet to vanish me out of sight.

Just a black wig and a torn pair of pants and a spunky lesbian werewolf God knew how far away, but no doubt speeding her way to the shop.

Too late, my brain rasped. She'd get here too damn late to help me. My brain speed-fed me images of a rabid wolf tearing my throat out. Or worse, turning me into a monster that couldn't control her hunger. I'd rather die than kill someone else.

Without thinking, I yanked out my cell phone and dialed Layne's phone. I knew he didn't have it in his pocket, but I was willing to bet Owen was monitoring it.

Another smashing sound from the back made me jump. Layne grinned on his side of the glass, and I was sure he heard it too. I dropped the phone as the noise rattled me and fell to my knees to sweep the floor in search of it.

I had no idea what Trish was beating on the door with, or even if she had found a battering ram. I had the feeling she was just shouldering herself against it, throwing all her weight with each thrust. It was a solid enough door, but I didn't think it could withstand the repeated pounding of a werewolf for long.

Nor did I think the window would hold against many more blows from Layne. Up to now, it seemed like he was toying with me, but I realized he was doing what wolves did. Distracting me while he set up his pack to surround their prey.

That realization made my throat tight. Layne was hunting me. Layne would kill me. I was as sure of that as I was that Parrish would not make it in time to keep either of those things from happening.

I couldn't just stand there. I couldn't run to the back and out the door. But I did have a pretty good storage room that had withstood a werewolf's frantic escape.

It was also the last place I wanted to run to. I'd be trapped there. Layne would eventually break through the glass and Trish would the door, and they'd both combine their efforts on the storage room door.

There was no way I could win that way.

A loud crash sounded alongside the splintering noise of wood. My back door had given way finally, and its collapse had probably taken out the small bookcase next to it. In that one instant, the question of me running for the storage room evaporated like steam. I'd be running toward danger now.

I kept a bat in the shop, behind the counter. I lunged for it as I rounded the display case and grabbed it by the handle. Only the sound of items falling to the floor or crashing against the wall alerted me to Trish's advance.

My heart pounded so fast I thought I would pass out. The already weak muscles in my legs threatened to seize up and refuse to fly me to the bathroom, which I'd already decided was my last resort and hope.

At least beneath the sink, I kept plenty of nasty cleaning supplies capable of blinding whatever crashed through the door to get me.

I didn't want to hurt Trish, but if she tried to eat me, it was going to be on.

I made it a couple of feet before I realized I had one more choice. The second floor attic. I hadn't been up there since I'd found my mother's trunks of ephemera, ever since I'd seen her shade watching me from the shadows.

Without giving it more than a second's thought, I ducked sideways mid-run and sped for the stairs. Trish had to make it through the apothecary gallery before she hit the staircase, and a large display shelf full of candles and cauldrons and crystals lorded over the space between them.

She might not see me, and if she did, I just might make it up several stairs before she caught sight of me.

Just when I made it to the bottom of the stairs, Trish burst through the gallery. Headed in the direction she'd last seen me, her eyes were cast toward the front of the shop. I would make it.

She was throttling forward so fast, heading for the front that she couldn't possibly have noticed me as I took the first three steps.

That was when Layne pounded on the glass from the front, and whatever he'd motioned to Trish, it made her swing her head my way.

I had one gut-wrenching peek at her face. The once beautiful features contorted in a half-shift. Her nose had lengthened, and her jaw took on the unnatural appearance of a lupine.

The seat of my leather pants grew warm, and I worried my bladder had let go the cup of coffee I'd had that morning.

I spun around, feeling for the steps with the backs of my heels as I held my hands out to her.

"Easy now," I said in a calming voice, the best one I could manage even if there was a tremor in it. "Easy. Remember me?" I patted my chest with my palm as I lifted my foot onto the tread above me.

The bat in one hand tapped the stairs as I leveraged myself against it to move up and back one step at a time. "I'm a friend. I tried to help you."

In response, her spine cracked as she twisted and shouldered her way through the confines of her torn shirt. It fell away, along with her bra.

Faint patches of peachy fuzz peppered her torso one second, and in the next, they grew to random clumps of fur. Several gashes across her chest showed blood, and it took a second for me to realize she was clawing at herself as she advanced.

Gone, I thought. She was so feral she couldn't stop even the violence against herself.

I lifted the bat, pointing the end at her.

"I don't want to hurt you," I said and took one more slow, painfully slow, step up. Judging by the six steps I'd gained, I wasn't going to make it to the next six. Or was it seven? Why didn't I know how many steps it took to get to the second floor?

She leveled her bright yellow gaze on me and lifted her half-muzzle, half-chin to the ceiling and howled. When she dragged her claws across her stomach, bringing fresh beads of blood to the surface, I nearly lost my footing. I staggered and caught myself only by dropping the bat.

It skittered down the stairs. I watched it go with an almost numb sort of fascination. A flash to my left stole my attention for half a second, but that brief flicker told me Layne was not at the window anymore.

Trish hesitated because she waited for her alpha. And now that alpha was no doubt heading for the broken down door.

Good sense should have bid me to turn and run. I ignored it. I was done running. Showing my back to a monster had got me nowhere in all this time. Despite the itch to move, I stood my ground, bracing my knees as I held myself rigid by clutching the railing.

All sound ceased to exist except for the thrumming of my heart in my ears. A roar broke through the shop, drawing Trish's attention, and in that second she shifted her gaze from me, a black shadow charged her from the side. An instant later, three large shapes grappled with each other below me.

I recognized them all, and I knew in that instant that it was too late for Trish. Abbi had reached Trish before Layne did. The dog's muzzle roamed Trish's belly as her paws held her down.

Trish thrashed side to side, trying to free herself but the dog was too heavy, too bulky for even a wolf to throw off, but I knew it was just a matter of time before the werewolf managed to twist out of the awkward position of being on her back.

She wouldn't have that time, though. Abbi buried her snout and teeth into one of the gashes Trish had inflicted on herself. Seconds later, the awful sound of flesh being torn reached my ears, and every little sound in the shop came to me then. Trish's howl of pain. Layne's roar of fury as he lunged for Abbi.

And the sound of Parrish's voice, hushed but powerful as she called out to Layne.

CHAPTER 14

P ARRISH WAS GOING TO die. That was it. It was that simple. She appeared at the bottom of the steps with her hands held out toward Layne, supplicating and vulnerable.

She held a chain and manacles in one hand and what looked like a cattle prod in the other. The chain clinked together as it dangled, and the rod reached for the ceiling as she held it aloft. The muscles in her arms knotted and knotted as she worked to keep her hands aloft.

Layne jerked his head in her direction, sniffing loudly. Like Trish, he was half-formed, a shape far more terrifying than a fully transformed wolf because he looked grotesque and unnatural.

I might have yelled at Parrish to run, but if I did, she ignored me. Instead, she advanced on Layne, whose nose twitched, whose claws curled into fists and bunched and unbunched against his thighs.

"I submit," she said in a breathless voice. "Whatever you need, I'll do for you, but you have to tell me, Layne. You have to say it."

One more step and Layne dropped his gaze to the woman just a few feet out of reach, who was all but hidden by the massive dog atop her. The revolting sounds of chewing and of flesh being torn carried on the air currents to my ears and I wanted badly to stop up the sound with my palms but I didn't dare move.

My stomach rebelled at the sounds, and I thought I might double over from the power of the nausea, but I held it together.

Layne could barely tear his eyes from it, and although I expected Parrish to take the opportunity to lunge for him, she merely took one more careful step toward him.

"Just tell me, Layne," she said. "Tell me what you want me to do and I'll do it."

He dragged his gaze away from Trish and Abbi, who was growling softly as her jaws clenched down tighter on Trish's neck. She gave a little shake and the young woman, still half shifted, shuddered. Bile rose up my throat and burned my cheeks.

As for Layne, he blinked at Parrish. Encouraged, she lifted her chin high enough to indicate she was submitting but not so high she couldn't keep her eye on him. One subtle turn of her head, and her throat arched, exposing a clear line of attack to him.

"I'm yours," she whispered. "But you have to tell me what you want."

I thought I understood what she was doing, calling out to the man inside the monster. If she could get him to speak, the man would have to come forth, and maybe then, she could reason with him. Maybe then she could save him.

I sank to my bottom on the step, unable to stand erect any longer. Whatever happened, I had no energy to fight it.

"I know you're in there, Layne," Parrish said. "And I know how you feel. It hurts. Your wolf is hurting."

As she took one more step, she came into full view. I noticed the pistol she had stuffed in the back of her jeans.

"I know your pain," she said. "I still feel mine all these decades later. She didn't deserve what happened to her. But violence won't solve anything. It won't bring her back. Nothing can."

I knew she wasn't talking about me or Layne as she faced off against him. Although I didn't know the circumstances or the history, I was willing to bet she was using her own experience to try to reach him.

Later, I might wonder over the woman Parrish loved who died and left her alone, but for now, it was about Layne, and if she was using her own pain to reach him, I knew he was farther away from sane than we'd feared.

"Come back before you can't," she went on, inching ever closer. "You don't have a Layne to help you. All you have is me, and I'm not a strong enough wolf to pull you back from that abyss once you step over it."

When she held out her hands, the chain and manacle dangled the length of her leg, catching my eye, but Layne ignored it in favor of watching Parrish's eyes. I expected he would know the exact moment she decided to make a run at him.

She swallowed as though she wanted to distract his gaze from hers. "Please, Layne. That moment will consume you. I won't be able to help you after that."

He shook his head as though to clear it in the short pause she left open to him. He swung his gaze toward the stairs, toward me, and I cringed at the look on his face. It wasn't Layne. No matter that some parts of him held onto the Layne I knew, it wasn't him.

Parrish knew it too. The moment he made eye contact with me, his shoulders went rigid. His lips curled back, and he dragged in a deep breath.

Faster than I'd have thought she would, she dropped the chains and the rod with a clang and a thud to the floor. With one single, smooth motion, she reached for the pistol.

He caught her movement and broke eye contact with me. Parrish raised the gun. It trembled for a second, then leveled out. She inhaled, then began to breathe out. I knew once she'd exhaled fully, the gun would fire.

Layne roared at the same time I shouted. Our voices blended together. Abbi lifted her snout from Trish's neck at the sound of it. She'd grown at least two sizes in the last few seconds even as Trish had begun to lose some of her wolfish features.

The young girl was beginning to show her beautiful features through that of the wolf.

Parrish placed her other hand atop the first, holding the gun steady.

"Don't, Parrish." I slid down three steps before my feet finally came under me. It was seconds, really. Maybe just a heartbeat, but I saw the instant she had fully exhaled. Her finger tensed.

As quick as that, Layne spun on his heel and bolted for the front of the shop. Parrish swore and ran after him, leaving me stranded on the stairs with Abbi and Trish and I wasn't sure how in the hell I was going to be able to mince my way past the carnage the dog had left of the poor woman.

And all that was depending on whether I could get to my feet at all. As it was, my legs were so weak they trembled, the knees knocking together as I reached for the staircase.

I felt the sag of every muscle protesting the command to move. Fatigue so acute, that I could have gone into a coma right there on the stairs.

I only vaguely heard the slamming of the front door and Parrish's loud curse. A loud thud echoed down the shop toward me, and I guessed she'd either stomped her foot or knocked over something from one of the shelves. I opted not to get up at all, then.

Instead, I dropped my head into my hands and let the tears come. They shuddered through me and tore at pieces of my stomach in ways that only a real ugly cry can do.

Parrish found me there moments later after she'd clomped her way back to the steps and growled at Abbi to get the hell out of the way. Her palm dropped onto my shoulder, and it was cold, not warm like usual.

"He's gone, Brie," she said, forgetting to use my new moniker. She was probably as worked up as I was, but I didn't, couldn't, lift my gaze to hers. I felt her eyes on the back of my neck as surely as if it were her fingers, stroking lightly.

"I tried," she said.

"I know."

The scent of vanilla swept over me as she settled next to me on the stair tread and wrapped her arm around my shoulder.

"You were going to shoot him," I whispered and lifted my head to stare at the treads between my knees. "You would have killed him to save me." My voice sounded ragged and flat to my ears as I processed it all.

It was a long moment before she answered and it was a quiet, careful comment.

"I love you," she said. "You know that. But it wasn't for you. It was for Layne. He wouldn't want to be the kind of wolf who killed innocents. I couldn't let that happen to him, even if he was so gone it wouldn't matter to him anymore. The true Layne, the man who shared his body with a wolf could never live through that guilt."

"You understand it," I said, looking sideways at her and seeing a pain in her eyes that went beyond that of nearly losing her alpha.

She ran her hand over the thumbnail painted a violent shade of purple. "All too well," she murmured. "Love can be a transcendent thing. It can also be a terrifying, awful thing."

With a click of her fingernails, she stuffed her hand beneath her armpit, hiding the violet color from view. "For the right woman, a man would do just about anything. And so would a gal like me."

Just the set of her jaw, and the wistful tone of her voice spoke volumes. I didn't want to pry, but I had to say something. The pain in her voice demanded it.

"She must have been something," I said and laid my palm on the back of her hand. "I'm sorry, Parrish."

She jerked her head up and for an instant her eyes were glassy with tears, then she blinked and shook her head and she was back to the same, tough girl.

"It was a long time ago," she said.

I thought of all the things she'd said to Layne, trying to get the man to push aside the pained anger of the wolf. "You know what he's going through," I said. "That's what you were trying to tell him."

"I was trying to tell him more than that, but the stupid bastard is hiding behind his wolf. He doesn't want to feel the fullness of his grief for you."

She gave me a long look that made me uncomfortable. I thought she'd leave it at that, since she never seemed interesting in talking about her past.

"It's a terrible pain," she said and dropped her gaze to stare at my hands as they hung over my thighs. "If I can't get the wolf to move aside, he might never come out again."

"Like Layne did for you." I guessed and knew I was right by the way the surprise leaped into her eyes.

"He pulled me out of my misery, yes," she said carefully. "But by then, I'd murdered lots of innocent people. It's not an easy thing to come back from. I'm harder than he is."

"Meaning if he does attack someone, he might never be able to come out from beneath the shame."

She took my hand closest to her and squeezed my fingers. "I mean if he kills someone, I will kill him myself. There is no coming back because he won't want to. I won't let him become what I was or try to live through it afterward."

Her voice was sharp with pain and I squeezed her hand back. "You'll get to him, Parrish," I said. "I know you will."

She shook her head. "I'm not strong the way he is. You don't know what it took to pull me from that horror."

"I don't need to know," I said. "Your secrets are yours to keep. No judgment here."

She dropped her gaze to stare at our hands. I pulled mine away, thinking she was uncomfortable, but when she kept looking at her nail, I knew her reaction wasn't discomfort and it had nothing to do with me.

"Her name was Violet," she murmured. Her hands started to tremble, but I was afraid to reach for them because I wasn't sure if she'd want the invasion when she felt so vulnerable.

Knowing her the way I did, I expected touching her right then might flip her switch. So I waited, remaining silent out of habit and practice. One thing a good fraud did was listen.

But this time, I did so with bated breath. I cared about Parrish. If she needed absolution, I'd find any way to give it, even if it meant just listening.

Eventually, she sucked in a breath, and the words came out in a ream like toilet tissue spiraling off its tubing.

"She was a hooker," she said. "Back at the turn of the century. I was eighteen. Ready to be married off to some dandy my parents thought suited me." She barked out a bitter laugh. "I kept putting it off and putting it off." She dropped her head back. "They couldn't figure out why. He was handsome. Rakish good looks. Full of alpha energy. Lots of money. So charismatic."

"But you were in love with a woman," I said.

"Not at first. I met Vi when the madam came to one of my father's parties. I didn't know she was gay. Not at first. I assumed like everyone else, she was man crazy. Baby crazy. Marriage crazy."

"But she wasn't."

She shook her head. "Vi's madam spotted me for what I was right away and took me aside. Told me I should come around for tea."

At that she laughed straight out, and I was glad she found some joy in the memory.

"That cagey old bat was set up right in the middle of town, and no one knew it was a brothel unless you were part of that world. I'd thought I was alone." She snorted. "I wasn't. I can tell you that much. They came from all over the state to that little brothel. She catered to a very elite clientele."

She caught my eye and winked. "The madam was pretty progressive. She was also very good to her whores. She gathered together all the gay men and women of the streets from all over Eastern US. She knew a woman who loved women wouldn't want to service a man, same thing for a male whore. She also knew there were more gay folks than society dared to admit. She made her money that way."

"So you met Violet there," I said.

She leaned back in her chair and clasped her hands behind her neck. "I kept up appearances, though," she said. "Let everyone think I was going along with the engagement. But the bastard knew something was off."

"He, your fiancée?"

"Mother fucking hair on the balls of a toad, that bastard. He knew something was up. He followed me for months, waited outside, prowled the property, scenting the air each time I came back out."

"Scenting?"

She nodded. "He smelled her on me. He knew what it meant."

"He was a werewolf." I didn't need her to answer, but she nodded.

"He turned me." She swallowed and dropped her hands to her lap. "And he killed her."

"Oh Parrish," I said. "I'm so sorry."

She waved the comment away and when she turned back to me, her expression was stones. "It's been over for a century or more. There's nothing to be sorry over. I just...well, I just wanted you to know what is torturing Layne so badly. That kind of love is rare."

I let that sit in the air for a long moment while the two of us gathered our thoughts or our courage or whatever it was we needed to climb back down the stairs and face the result of the last few moments. And in those moments a horrible thought occurred to me.

"Zacharia," I said with the thickness of disgust buttering my tone. "Please tell me the bastard that did that to your Violet wasn't Zach."

She barked out a laugh of surprise. "Oh good God, no. Zach isn't that sort of bastard at all."

She slapped her knees and stood. "But that's a story for another day. Right now, we should get you home." She blew out a loud sigh that rattled her throat as she gestured toward Trish, who lay very still on the floor. Abbi was nowhere to be seen. Again.

"And I suppose I'll have to call Owen to clean up the mess."

"No need," came a familiar masculine voice from the back room.

My hand flew to my wig as Owen stepped into the shop.

CHAPTER 15

I CRINGED AS OWEN strode forward, terrified he'd over heard Parrish and I discussing things. I pulled myself to a stand, ready to bolt up the stairs and shut myself in the attic if I had to.

"Nice job," he said to Parrish as he looked down at Trish's inert body. I thought I saw his mouth twitch, but he covered it with a whistle, the way a man might if he was impressed by something pretty horrible. Which the sight of Trish was. I couldn't bring myself to look in her direction.

"I can't say I'm unhappy to see you," Parrish said, moving aside as Owen approached Trish and leaned over to examine her. "Things got a bit hairy here. Layne broke in and—"

"I know," he said, interrupting her. "Some of the pack have him in hand now. We caught him as he ran out the front."

Parrish didn't miss a beat. She cocked her hip and gestured toward the dead feral wolf on the floor as though she didn't know Owen had been the one to make her. If she was worried he'd overheard anything, she didn't let on.

"You've been here all this time and didn't bother to come in and give us a hand here?" She planted one hand on her hip and used the other to gesture at Trish's body as she faced him, all pretense of submission gone from her features. She was pissed and obviously didn't have it in her to pretend otherwise.

Owen pulled a tissue from his pocket as he crouched next to Trish and poked at her neck with a tissue-covered finger.

"Not that it's any of your concern, but I haven't been here 'all this time'. We arrived with the van just as Layne was bolting out the front like his ass was on fire." He looked up at her. "What did you do to him, Parrish? I wanted you to corral him for me, not send him racing for lands unknown." He sent a fleeting look up the stairs at me but dismissed me just as quickly.

I breathed a quiet breath of relief. Still clinging to the railing, I decided it was best if I stayed where I was and let Parrish handle things. She seemed to have them under control.

"And exactly what happy happenstance do we owe that brought you and the enforcers here to Brie's shop at this time of day?" She narrowed her gaze at him, and if I'd had been on the other end of that look, I'd have cringed.

Owen flicked out the tissue and stood. He faced her with the same equanimity she gave him. Fear wasn't something I believe Owen ever felt, but in that moment, he gave off an air of guilt that was akin to fear. Fear of discovery. His lips compressed and he hunched inward, defensively. A twitch in Parrish's cheek told me she'd noticed it too.

"Happenstance had nothing to do with it, did it, Brie?" he said and turned to look up at me.

For a moment, all the air went out of the room. My pulse shoved out all other noise as it thrummed in my ears like a drum under water. He knew my name. He knew who I was beneath all the gloss and leather. I stammered out some sort of protest that I wasn't Brie, when Parrish spoke up, cutting me off mid-sentence.

"Brie is dead, Owen," she said. "I thought you got the memo."

A grin broke across his face, and he shifted his attention back to her as he stuffed the tissue into his jacket pocket. A single jerk of his head toward me, indicating me as he spoke.

"You'll have to forgive me. I forget her name, and it's such a callous and cold thing to do, I thought a little misplaced humor might disguise my ignorance."

He patted the wad of tissue flat against the fabric of his jacket as he inclined his head in my direction. "I presume it was you who called me from Brie's phone earlier. Calling you by her name seemed easier than the awkwardness of struggling to remember a name under the circumstances."

I shrugged. "So now, it's just as awkward but drawn out." I tried to smile as though it didn't matter, but my teeth caught my lip, and I felt like all I managed was a grimace.

"You think this is awkward?" He gestured around the floor and the young woman's body, her crooked arms and bloody skin where the dog had bit down. "You've a far sturdier stomach than most wolves I know. And a stronger desensitization to violence."

"I didn't mean that," I said.

Parrish laid her hand on the railing, sending me a warning look. Stay quiet, it said, and I clamped my mouth shut.

"She's in shock," she said. "She was even scared of me when I got here." Her hand ran up a few inches of the railing, smoothing it like she was trying to smooth the wrinkles of the discussion. "Cut her some slack."

He gestured up the steps at me. "Maybe you're right. I'm guessing when confronted with the ugly truth of what we can be, she freaked out." He stepped closer to Parrish and directed his next words to her. "The ugly truth of what you can be."

Parrish's nostrils flared at the suggestion in his words. "I'm not that woman anymore," she said. "I haven't been her in centuries."

He cocked his head sideways, studying her intently. He made a noncommittal sound deep in his throat as he rounded the body on the floor, inspecting it without touching it. After several moments, he turned his back on Trish's remains and addressed Parrish.

"How exactly did she die?" he asked as he jerked his thumb over his shoulder at Trish. "It wasn't Layne, that much I know. There isn't enough damage done to her, and she would have been in his control anyway. He'd have no reason to attack her if she was helping him coral his prey."

Parrish lifted one shoulder in a shrug. "That massive black dog of Brie's is what happened to her. Came out of nowhere and attacked the girl. Just in fucking time, too, I'd say." She cocked her hip and ran her nails over her shirt.

He made a thoughtful sound that I didn't like. One that needed a quick explanation.

"It must have come through the door," I said of the dog, trying to give him a reason to forget about the girl because if he kept asking questions, it would grow evident that something was amiss. Better to give him some information he could squirrel away and move on.

I lifted my chin in the direction he had come from. "The girl broke in through the back and left the door open. The dog must have come in that way."

I waved my hand in front of my face as though the memory was too much for me. I didn't have to do much acting. The cold wave of panic had subsided but now, I was left with the flush of adrenaline and if I didn't sit down or cool off, I was going to faint right there.

Except I couldn't. I wasn't about to show one sign of weakness to the predator in front of me.

He looked around to indicate the shop, empty of stray dogs. "Where did the beast go then?"

Parrish shoved her hands in her pockets. "Who the hell knows. The damn thing is like a ghost. Here one moment and gone the next. I'm beginning to think it's magic or something."

He had to know the dog was magic, because he was in the hotel room with me when Abbi and John Smith fought the coven back. But I knew he couldn't be certain Parrish did. I nearly applauded her quick thinking. Use the truth as much as possible when you wanted to fool someone. It was the fraud's credo.

If Parrish seemed to suspect the beast of magic, he might not realize she had more knowledge. He might think he knew more than she did.

Good. I was happy to keep him feeling superior right up until the moment I drove the knife in his back.

Owen toed the dead girl's foot. "I suppose we'll have to keep an eye out for the dog," he said. "Maybe it needs a home now that Brie is gone. Someone to feed it. Take care of it. I mean, it did do us a favor here." He turned a brilliant smile on me.

"A woman is dead," I said with ice in my voice for exactly how he regarded the wolves he created. "You call that a favor?"

Parrish leveled me with the kind of stink eye only she could give. "You don't know our world, Desirée. The woman is better off. Trust me."

I curled into myself, pulling a lock of hair from the wig down over my shoulder and fiddling with it. She was right. I needed to keep my mouth shut as much as possible where Owen was concerned.

I sank down onto the step, finally, all will to maintain strength gone.

He watched me, but he kept a careful, guarded control over his movements. When he turned back to Parrish, it was with a motion of dismissal for me. Relief made my knees weak.

"I never wanted you in the pack," he said in a flat voice. "You're a liability. One horrible tragedy and you could turn just like Layne did, and that would put the entire pack in danger."

"I didn't know there was any other kind of tragedy but horrible," she retorted, ignoring all the other ugly things he'd said. But she took a step backwards just the same. Her chin lifted in defiance almost without thought.

She wouldn't admit it, but he'd struck her where it hurt even if she wasn't inclined to show it. I knew what he was doing, and she should too, but her pain and shame wouldn't let her see it clearly. Offense is sometimes the best defense. She'd touched too close to his truth and he needed her off her footing.

He was one guilty motherfucker and cunning to boot. Now that I could see him for what he was, through the eyes of a stranger, it was much easier to read his body language, to hear his simpering falsehoods for what they were.

He chuckled at Parrish's comment, surprising me. "You're right there," he said. "The truth is, your reaction to Brie's death has surprised me. I know you cared about her. I was certain you'd be right there along with my son, killing and brutalizing the city, but here you are, rational and helpful as though you don't answer to him at all."

Only the smallest movement revealed how pleased she was to hear the surprised pride in his voice, and someone who didn't know her might have missed it. Owen didn't, though. And neither did I, even if it surprised me to hear. But while Owen was counting on it, I wasn't ready to be fooled. Not again.

I watched him with a keen eye, looking for betrayal of his thoughts through the smallest movements.

"It proves you are fit for pack life," he said in a softer voice that sounded so genuine I almost forgot the things he'd done to me. "I was wrong about you. You're strong. Strong enough to belong with us."

I clenched the railing as Parrish bowed her head. "I'm not strong enough," she said. "I couldn't bring him in."

Owen waved the matter away with a gesture. "Doesn't matter. We have him, and he will be cared for until he is better."

"That might be a while," Parrish mused aloud, and I caught the way she shifted her gaze from Owen to the girl on the floor.

"If it takes years, we'll be there for him." He bowed briefly in my direction to address me as I sat there, my knees knocking together, and my shoulder against the railing so I wouldn't flat out collapse. "It's because of you that my son is saved from harming anyone. I assure you, you have our deepest gratitude."

Oh, he was slick. I almost fell for the genuineness in his half-smile, the humility in the graceful nod.

"I didn't do much. Just hit the redial button," I said, trying to minimize my part in the story because damn him, he made doubt creep up the back of my neck and I knew the less he thought about me, the better.

His gaze flitted over me before he turned to Parrish again. "The team will take care of the dead girl," he said. "I'll send them back here after dark to avoid any unfortunate witnesses and questions. And I'll need you to come to the manse to help with Layne. I still think if anyone can reach him, it's you. I want you there with him as much as you can be."

She nodded. "I'll do what I can. I already called in sick. I expected it to take a couple weeks to bring him in."

He shifted his feet so they pointed in my direction. "Your friend should come too," he said.

The words urged me to take a step upward. "No," I said. "I can't do that."

He advanced, closing the distance to the stairs with two long strides. "Oh, but you will. This is pack business. I can't have you wandering around the city."

He didn't say divulging secrets and he didn't have to. That was implied.

"I don't wander," I said. "I go to work. I go home." I turned a brilliant smile on Parrish as a means to force the ruse. "I spend time with the best girl ever..."

"Be that as it may, you witnessed things no human should see. I hate to give you an impossible choice, but I will if I have to."

Parrish stepped between us, her hands held out waist level to both of us. "Owen, there's no need—"

"You want to remain in the pack, yes?" he said to her with a touch of threat in his voice. "You do what I say. She's dangerous to us. She can come to the manse or she can die."

CHAPTER 16

I COULD LIVE OR die, it seemed. Even Parrish was shocked into silence. I found my voice first.

"What happened to your gratitude?"

"You think any other mortal would have the choice?" he said. "That's my gratitude."

My eyes flicked to Parrish. The look on her face said it all. She'd known it would be the choice. It wasn't shock that had her silent. She expected it. She didn't like it, but she expected it. I blinked at her, for once feeling mistrust in her. How many other mortals had come up against the pack over the years and been conveniently disposed of?

"You're not serious," I said, using the leverage of the railing to pull myself to my feet. I shook. From my core to my fingers, I shook. The tremor in my voice made me sound too weak and yet I couldn't control it. I couldn't stop myself from arguing when I knew I should be silent.

"I'm a grown ass woman, Mr. Garder." I squared my shoulders, lifting my head high, pulling to myself the echo of a dozen clients over the years. "If you think I can't keep a secret, ask my family if I'm gay. Ask any of my co-workers if they think I'm a closeted lesbian or who my lover is. I assure you, Mr. Garder, I'm well versed in secrecy. Some of us have been brave enough to come out."

I shot Parrish an approving, proud smile. "But not all of us have that kind of courage. Even now, in this liberated, woke society, some of us still face hatred you can't imagine. You think your pack is in danger from me? I think my pack is in danger from you, Mr Garder. You think I'm a stranger to fear?" I barked out a laugh that sounded genuine because it was. I had an entire life of fear to pull from to lend authenticity to my tone. "I live in constant fear. Your kind isn't always kind to my kind."

He canted his head at me, and for a moment, I thought he would capitulate.

"Who are these co-workers?" he asked. "And who is your family? Flies on the wall and no more. You think you face hatred because you like to lay down with a woman?" He barked out the same sort of laugh I had, one of contempt and ill-humor. "Try being hunted and strung up by your wrists to a tree and disemboweled in front of your children. Try being forced to shift into your wolf so you can be skinned for your pelt, only to have it turn to flesh and skin as it comes off you. Try watching as your mother is raped and beaten while you are pinned to the ground by a filthy boot on your face. Try facing that sort of hatred. Try feeling that fear and then tell me you're no stranger to violence."

His lip curled back and the cords in his throat tightened as he delivered the words. I swallowed hard at the contempt and unconcealed hatred in his expression. When I looked to Parrish for help, I saw the same sort of pain in her expression, and it so surprised me that a small sound like a whimper escaped me.

"He's right, Desirée," she said, holding my gaze with compassion but determination. "We can't let you be alone until this is sorted."

I felt betrayed. "And what does 'sorted' mean, exactly?" I thought she'd try to argue to keep me out of the manse, not the opposite.

"I trust you," she said. "Sorted means until my alpha can too."

I turned to Owen, but he was already stepping over Trish's body, heading to the front of the shop. Presumably to hightail it to his stately manor where he would lock his son away. Because I've never been one to shut my mouth I called out after him, unable to help myself.

"And what if he never trusts me? What then?"

He paused, and in the moment it took for him to spin back around, his heels scuffing the wooden floorboards, I knew what he'd do in that instance. He'd kill me.

"You'll be at the manse tonight," he said over his shoulder. "I'm sure I'll feel much safer knowing where you are."

My knees went to water again and I sank to the step, my legs flung out in front of me, hanging over several treads. The edges dug into my calfs.

"What the fuck, Parrish?" I demanded. I felt as though everything in me had deflated and left weak spots like the blowouts in a balloon.

She lifted her finger to her lips. "You'll like it at the manse, Desirée. Think of it as a vacation. You'll stay with me, of course."

"The hell I will." Had she forgotten all the things we needed to do? How would we accomplish all that with Owen watching our every movement? "I have a life. A job." I didn't need to tell her that job was breaking the cult for good. Layne would have wanted that.

"Look," she said. "I was going to have to leave you for weeks so I could find Layne and help him out of the mess he's in. Now we have him. We know where he is and that he won't be able to harm anyone. I call that a win." She held up her finger to her mouth, suggesting she meant more than just the message the words conveyed of themselves. "You can help me with Brie's estate just like we planned. I need you, and Layne would want that."

Meaning what Layne would want, Owen would to. She was being careful. The man wasn't quite out of the shop. She knew he could hear. He'd expect a protest. He'd expect her to fall into line, but she was also telling me as well as she could in the moment that at least we also had an eye on Owen.

"But a property filled with werewolves," I said, meaning one werewolf in particular. The reason we had told him I was dead in the first place. Layne. If she managed to pull him out of his state, and I was there, wouldn't he see or smell through the disguise? It was too risky.

She shrugged, implying she knew exactly what I meant. "Layne will be in the safe room, out of range of harming anyone while he convalesces. There's no way he'll be able to get to you. And as for the other shifters?" She shrugged then. "The only one you'll be in danger of getting eaten by will be me."

I didn't expect the horrible joke under the circumstances, and it took me so by surprise, a chortle of laugher slipped free. Maybe we could make this work. We'd have to.

She hadn't got two steps toward me, her hand extended to help me to my feet when a loud curse came from the front of the shop. Owen. Swearing like a sailor.

"What in the fuck is all this? Fuck."

The bell over the door in the front rang almost at the same instant as he complained, so I knew someone had come in or gone out. Both Parrish and I headed for the gallery hall. I took pains to avoid Trish's body, stepping large over her shoulders and fleeing through the gallery like I thought she was going to jump up and bite my leg.

Parrish lifted one eyebrow at my reaction, but she gripped my elbow and helped me along when she saw how much of a struggle it was for me to move. Damn that stint in the hospital. It took more from me than a bit of time. I could swear there was a bit of atrophy going on.

Owen stood holding the door open as he kicked at several round balls of fur and feathers.

"Shit balls," Parrish said. "What the fuck is that?"

"Kittens," I said blandly as I eyed the forms Owen was still kicking through the open door to the sidewalk. "And birds and mice and oh my God, is that a rat?"

Owen directed a hard kick at something grey and filthy looking. It lifted several feet into the air and flew a yard before it landed in the middle of the street. A car ran over it with a thumping sound and I winced.

"I don't know what that witch was doing putting out so much food when there's vermin all over the city ready to take advantage. What was she thinking?" He grimaced and wiped his hands over his pants as though he'd touched something foul. He lifted his foot to inspect the bottom of his expensive loafers. "Fuck. I think I've got rat blood on me."

Parrish snickered, and he gave her a quelling look. She shrugged. "You'd think a little blood would get your heart racing, not your bile rising."

He held the door open, letting a draft of air finger its way into the shop. "If it smelled like blood, maybe," he said. "But it stinks."

I froze on my spot and looked at Parrish. She paused too. "What does it smell like?" she asked.

"Like rotten eggs and pizza."

Parrish's jaw seesawed back and forth. "You mean magic."

It was evident by the way his head jerked up and his eyes met hers that he hadn't given it a thought until just then, but he knew it for what it was. "It can't be magic," he said. "She's dead." His brow furrowed and he ran his hands down along his jacket, searching for something. "I have to call the boys. Make sure they double chain Layne."

While I stood rooted to my spot, letting the fact that a spell had been cast right there in my shop without my knowledge, Parrish approached him. She took her time, angling away from the place on the floor where the animals had lain.

"This wasn't Brie," she rasped out. "Someone else is casting magic. Someone who wants to get our attention."

He pulled the door closed, one hand clutching his cell phone and thumb-dialing. "Do you think she has power over death?" he said. "Can she be casting from beyond?"

He looked so earnest, I almost laughed. Except for how dangerous I knew he could be, I might have been inclined to pity him for the fear evidenced in his features.

Parrish planted her feet a half yard from him and peered down at the floor. "Brie was a witch, Owen. Witches are mortal for all their power. I don't think they have the sort of juju it takes to raise the dead."

"Fucking witches," he said and then held up his finger while he addressed whoever was on the other end of the line that he'd dialed. The orders were clear but succinct. Don't take chances. Get him home ASAP and lock him in the safe room with four guards round the clock.

After he'd disconnected, he lifted his gaze to Parrish, who was still peering at the floor. "You don't know witches like I do," he said. "Never put anything past them. If they can curse you from the grave, they'll do it."

He waited till she had dragged her eyes to his before he spoke again. "You and Desirée get this Brie thing cleaned up. The faster the better." He all but shuddered as he glanced out the door again. "Maybe if things are settled, she'll forget about us."

"I don't think she's doing anything from beyond," Parrish said but when his jaw clenched and went white, she nodded and said, "Of course. Desirée and I were actually going to the lawyer's before all this mess with Layne happened."

He wiped his hands on his kerchief and shoved it back in his pocket. "Get it done." He mimed someone shooting an arm with a syringe. "Zach gave us a triple dose to administer to Layne, so he should be out for a few hours at least. Then come to the manse, both of you."

She nodded and I ducked behind a shelving unit because the thought of Layne being triple dosed did something to my insides that left me trembling, and I didn't want Owen to see my reaction.

It was only when he left, that Parrish started grumbling.

"He's irrational when it comes to witches."

"But he has a point," I said. "Someone is deliberately leaving dead animals for us to find."

"Not just dead, magicked dead. Do you smell that?"

It was faint, but yes, I did smell it. No doubt her nose was more astute than mine. "Sulfur and thyme. Protection and healing."

She ran her toe over the floor she'd been studying. "And something else," she said. "Although he was too freaked out to notice."

I closed the distance between us to crouch where her foot was. Examining the wood, I saw what she'd smelled.

Dog hair. Black dog hair.

Chapter 17

I KNEW WHERE THE black fur came from as soon as I saw it, and the sight froze my heart. That Abbi's fur was mixed in with the dead animals made me nervous.

"It's hers," I said, lifting my gaze to Parrish's. "Do you think she's alright?"

Parrish snorted. "That bitch is probably better than most. She's certainly better off than the werewolf she took out with such extreme prejudice." A shudder ran through her as she glanced toward where Trish still lay, unmoving on the floor beneath the stairs.

"She wouldn't do that to you," I murmured. "She was protecting me."

Her hand rested against the glass of the door, and she pulled her gaze back to the floor and the tuft of black fur between her boots. She moved one boot toe away as though she was afraid it would leap onto her shoe.

"I'm pretty sure I could take her," she finally said, "but I'm also pretty sure it would be knock-down drag-em-out sort of fight." She leaned on the door, letting her hand fall to her side and be replaced by her shoulder. With one shove, she pushed the door open enough to crane her head outside, checking for Owen, I presumed.

When she leaned back in she said, "Don't get me wrong, I'm happy she's such a good defense, but that was some freaky, terrifying shit even for the likes of me."

I crossed my arms over my chest, feeling like I had to defend the dog for what she'd done in the face of Parrish's revulsion. "It wasn't that bad," I said. "She didn't tear her apart or anything." The anything I didn't want to say was that the dog hadn't actually consumed the girl's flesh. She'd just drained her, like a vampire might in a movie. "It was nothing like with Farrel."

Parrish's auburn eyebrows lifted into a disbelieving V-shape. "You are not a wolf," she said. "Being forced to submit so another animal can go for your jugular like that..." She shook herself free of whatever she was imagining. "I can't imagine a worse way to go. Well, unless it was death by chocolate. That's not a death anyone should suffer." She grinned at me with half a smile.

"I don't think I want to know," I said.

"You never will," she said, then heaved a long sigh that blew from her lips with a raspberry sound. "Alright. Owen and his cronies are gone. Layne is no doubt in transit and I don't see a single spy hanging about the street. No one in earshot anyway." She plucked a candle from the nearest shelf and tossed it back and forth.

"Your dog isn't dead," she said. "But I don't think that little picnic she spread for herself will lend her much magic for long. The girl was fledgling. She wouldn't have much old magic for the dog to draw. But I don't think your beast is coming apart at the seams, either."

I ran my boot over the tuft of hair, rolling it into a ball. When I lifted my boot away, the hair had gathered a light coat of dust. "You're sure?"

She crouched to nudge the fur with the top of the candle. "See there?" she said, indicating how the ball had gathered dust but wasn't wet or oily. "No blood. And it's the soft, insulating coat, not the outer fur."

My shoulders sagged in relief as I examined it against her words, and I felt the tension go out of my back. "That's good, then?"

"It's not anything except the suggestion it's just normal shedding. Although it's the wrong time of year to be losing her fur." She pushed the tuft along the floorboards with the candle toward me. "No doubt Trish grabbed a handful, and it came loose."

I looked over my shoulder at the poor girl and saw in my mind's eye the whole thing again. While I felt pity for Trish, it was hard to imagine what might have happened to me and not feel relieved that it was her on the floor and not me. Even so, I wouldn't have wished it on her.

"Do you think it's my fault?" I said, worrying my lip with my teeth as I tried to warm myself from the cold draft that had come in through the door. "I mean if Layne didn't think I was dead—"

"Layne's reaction is on Zach and me," she said, and gripped my shoulder with her steady hand. "We were the ones that ran with the idea of your death. And the girl was Owen's fault."

I lifted my eyes to hers and saw in her face true compassion. I nodded mutely, still not sure I didn't carry some burden of the girl's death. "We should cover her, shouldn't we? We can't just leave her lying like that."

She squeezed my shoulder gently. "I'll do it," she said. "The enforcers will come in a few hours." She checked her watch. "They'll come long after dusk, so it might be better to cover her." She held her hands out. "I need the keys to give to them."

I fished into my pocket and pulled them free. She took them from me, swirling them on one finger by the keyring.

"Now," she said. "We have things to do. You heard Owen. We need to get Brie's affairs in order. What do you say to burying her cremated remains with her mother? Won't cost much." Her mouth quirked up on one side in half a smile.

I squared my shoulders and determined I'd do what I always did regarding Trish. Bury the pain and keep moving. "Cheap sounds good to me," I said and dragged in a bracing breath. "We still have a few business hours left. We can start with the obituaries to find which funeral home took care of her mother."

"We'll need to stop by my apartment," she said, waving me out the door as she headed to the storage closet, probably for a sheet in the linen closet.

"You missing your flannel nightgown?"

She snorted at me over her shoulder. "Drawers," she said, waving her hand up and down in the air as though to encompass my body from head to heel. "I might go commando, but you, my dear, need a bit of dressing to keep up appearances."

It took half an hour to retrieve a bag full of cosmetics from her apartment that she could use to keep cos-playing me while we were at the manse, and another two hours to cull the obituaries at the library.

While the visit to her apartment was productive, the trip to the library netted nothing. Despite knowing the approximate date of my mother's death, according to the time frame the lawyer had contacted me, no single breadcrumb had been dropped in the papers to suggest who had handled her burial and internment.

In the end, with time running down, we decided to visit the lawyer himself, in the hopes he kept the information we needed. With my emails stored on the cloud, I could search out his email and enter the address in his signature into Parrish's GPS.

His office turned out to be in the middle of the city, a twenty-minute drive and a frustratingly far parking job away that left us a mere ten minutes to spare. The office took up half the floor, with whiskey-colored wood from floor to ceiling. The tin ceiling had been painted cream at some point, but it had worn in spots where the decorative embellishments rose from the surface. From the moment we exited the elevator, till the time we strode through the outer library that doubled as a waiting room, I smelled vanilla and orange.

It made me nostalgic for ice cream.

"I'm starving," I said, feeling the rumble in my stomach that reminded me I'd not eaten in hours.

Parrish paused long enough to run her finger over a few spines of books. "We'll get fries on the way home." She made a small grunt of approval as her finger rested on a Patricia Briggs novel.

"Yes," I said, suddenly feeling even hungrier. "With gravy and cheese curds."

She pulled her hand away from the bookshelf and held it up to me, palm facing out as though she wanted to push me away. "Please," she said. "No weird Canadian food dishes. My stomach can't take it."

"Doesn't matter," I grumbled. "They don't serve poutine here, anyway."

I followed her through the library/waiting room toward a huge wooden desk carved and appliqued with gargoyles and angels. Behind it, a buxom-looking brunette was all but buried behind a mountain of blue file folders. Her three monitors, ring lights, and multiple phones blue-toothed into one headset made her look like a spider in the middle of a web, with legs going in every direction as she kept things under her control.

Parrish made a half growl half purr deep in her throat at the sight of her. "If her ass is as half as big as those boobs, I'm going to need a bib."

I nudged her with my elbow. "Too late," I muttered. "You're already drooling."

"That's not why I need a bib," she retorted and I felt my eyes pop in sudden comprehension.

"OK," I said. "I forbid you to infer sexual things to me in public anymore."

"Who was inferring?" she said and pushed past me to barrel toward the very busy looking brunette.

She blustered over to the woman's desk. "You know," she said, "I do love a woman with power."

She didn't wait for the woman to look up, but sidled close enough to cock her hip against the desk. I noted she steered clear of the cherubic angel and aimed for the gargoyle. I couldn't help rolling my eyes at the suggestion of misogyny in her posture, and I expected the brunette to brush her off at the least. At the most, I figured she'd tell her to get the fuck away from her desk.

I shouldered Parrish out of the way, aware that my appearance made me look very little like the kind of woman who would be taken seriously by another woman. We women just mostly aren't built that way, and with Parrish's overly strong come on, I was pretty sure the brunette would assume the worst of me.

"I'm hoping to meet with Mr. Berg," I said, trying for an assertive tone to override what I knew would be a reaction of instinctual bias. I ran my gaze over the ordered chaos of her desk until I found her name plate. Ava Irving. "Ms. Irving, is it?" I said.

To my surprise, she smiled wide and rose from her chair. The seat cushion was padded and thick, with a velvet material that suggested Mr. Berg valued her. That bode well. I almost choked when she angled toward me to reach for my hand in greeting and showed off a booty that made Parrish swear beneath her breath.

"I wish I could fit you in," Ava said, "but he has someone with him at the moment, and I don't expect he'll be finished before he has to go home for dinner." She put her index finger along the side of her mouth as though she was revealing a secret. "His wife cooked tonight, and I told him if he is late, she will most likely serve him his balls next time. She doesn't do it often, so if he knows what's good for him--"

"He'll bring home a bottle of red to go with those nuts," Parrish said with a fake laugh that swiveled my head in her direction in surprise. I sent her a warning look, and she lifted one shoulder ever so slightly. What's it to you, she seemed to be saying.

A genuine laugh slipped through Ava's prim facade, and she nodded her head in agreement. "Right?" she said. "Because even smart enough to pass the Bar exam, he still can't manage to figure out that when a woman cooks, she wants it appreciated." She turned to me. "Can I book you in for an appointment? They're rare as hen's teeth these days, but it's not impossible."

"I know he's not expecting me, but my friend passed away this week and I need to find her mother's resting place. Your firm handled the details." I put my hand up to my mouth in echo of hers, anticipating that it would build enough rapport that she'd help. "She was cremated and wants to be buried with her mother."

The woman looked from me to Parrish. "If she's been cremated, then surely there's no rush." She started rifling through the mountain of folders and pulled out an agenda from the bottom. "He might have some time in the next month."

Parrish shoved me out of the way, hard enough that I felt the wig shift and a bit of air run over my forehead. With a glare in her direction, I stepped aside to reposition it, using the glass in one of the bookshelves. From behind me I heard Parrish murmuring and the girl titter. I caught sight of the two of them in the reflection, cozied up together by the desk.

Parrish sat on the one place on its surface clear of reams of paper. The brunette leaned in close, her breast so close to Parrish's shoulder that I expected the werewolf to subtly move in so that her shoulder would touch the fullest curve of it.

I expected some cheesy flirtation, but Parrish had her cell phone out and was scrolling through it. The secretary, leaning over the desk, was peering down at the screen and smiling.

She pointed at something she saw there. "Mine doesn't have that big a mask." Something caught her attention on the screen and she giggled again. "Oh my God, he's so sweet." She beamed up at Parrish and for a second, I felt as though the sun had fingered its way through the expensive blinds. "My rag doll has a cuter nose, though." She chuckled again and I was pretty sure I heard purring coming from Parrish's phone.

"Excuse me," I said, clearing my throat to get their attention. "But do you think we could discuss that appointment? I don't have a lot of time."

Ava smoothed down her expensive suit and backed away from Parrish to grab for her agenda again. She hoisted it to the air and let gravity flip the pages to show me how full they were.

"I really can't fit you in today," she said, glancing toward her boss's office door. "But if you come just before ten-thirty tomorrow, he blocks off twenty minutes for a morning constitutional every day, and it only ever takes him ten."

"Constitutional?" I said and Parrish elbowed me with a roll of her eyes.

"He visits the litter box."

I caught myself with my mouth open as I understood. Ava smiled with a single lifted black eyebrow and waggled it at me.

"Catch him in the hallway." She pointed out the door and toward the left where the library branched off. "Then just walk in with him. I'll see if I can find the papers to make it easy for him to help."

Parrish stuck out her hand. "We appreciate it."

Ava's lips pressed together as she smiled and nodded. I would have thanked her as well, but Parrish put her back to me, blocking Ava from view. She waved at me from behind her back and I took that to mean it was time for me to get the hell out of her way. I headed to the library and was browsing the shelves when she came through.

I waited till we were in the elevator before I poked her in the ribs. "You know, you're lucky she didn't decide to metoo you."

"Why would she do that?"

"Hello? You pretty much just steamrolled her with your sexist self. It was a revolting display."

She shrugged. "Oh, come on. You don't think I'd pull that sort of shit on a gal unless I knew she'd go for it do you?" She slipped her arm around my waist and tugged me close. "I'm not a Neanderthal or something. I do have centuries of experience at this. I have different faces of charm for every woman."

I choked on a laugh. "Some charm," I said. "You wooed her with a cat."

She sent me a smug look. "A pussy," she said, correcting me with a raised finger. "Call it foundation building."

"My God," I said. "You're incorrigible. What makes you think she'll go out with you because you showed her a few kittens. And what will you do when you have to admit you don't own a cat?"

"First," she said as we reached her car. "Haven't you heard of subliminal messaging?" She tapped the roof four times then pulled open the door so she could slide into the driver's seat. "Second," she said once I'd followed suit and we were both buckled in. "I don't foresee a confession being a necessity."

I snorted. "No kidding. The fact that you woo a girl with a picture of a pussy is every reason why you never get far enough to have to confess you don't have a cat." I shook my head.

She pulled out of the parking space with a jerk, and I gripped the roll bar, letting my body lean into the door. "And for your information, Miss knows-every-thing-about-wooing-a-chick," she said. "I got me that date, so shows what you know."

She said it like she wanted to stick her tongue out at me and I chuckled. "What are you? Ten?"

She checked her rear view and pulled out to shift lanes. "I like my naysayers to know when they're wrong, is all."

"Bully for you," I told her and let go the roll bar only to grip the roll bar as we accelerated into the lane. "So. Who's cat did you show her?" I asked.

She tapped the steering wheel with the index finger of both hands. Four times. "I have a few downloaded videos and pictures from social media." She cast a glance my way before returning her eyes to the street. "Don't even bother to give me the stink eye. I'm not interested in judgment."

"Don't worry," I said. "I'm the last one who should judge." I settled into the seat and let her drive. It was good to be ensconced in a vehicle where no one would be watching us. "But it's interesting to me that you premeditate wooing your dates with false impressions."

"Do you wear false eyelashes and makeup for a date? Do you wear a push up bra?"

"Not the same. I've already been asked. I want to look good so the date will think he's made a good decision."

She flipped on the blinker to turn left and waited for a break in traffic. "But you don't exactly go out in public wearing your sweat pants and pit-stained tee shirts either."

"That's just common courtesy. No one wants to be around someone who stinks like ripe cheese."

She laughed. "Sure. But it's also about ego, and whether you want to admit it or not, you want people to think well of you."

"Are you saying you fake having a cat so women will be more inclined to like you?"

"I'm saying when I finally make my move, I want them to think of me as a gal who enjoys a good little pussy."

"No more," I said. "There's no talking to you seriously." I dug my nails beneath the wig at the temple. "I can't wait to get this wig off." I scratched my skin. "You do wash it right? It doesn't have lice or fleas?"

Parrish looked over at me. "No fleas. Ticks, maybe." She smiled and yanked the visor down against the glare of the setting sun. "But don't get too comfortable. We've still got dinner to go before you can peel that hair off, and if I know Owen, he'll have the whole damn pack there sniffing around us waiting for that to happen."

CHAPTER 18

THE LAST TIME I'D been at the manse, I'd told Layne I'd betrayed him with Owen and run out on him. Now, as Parrish turned up the drive, all those memories came flooding back. From the moment I'd made the decision to push him out of my life in order to save his life, I'd expected to never see the inside again. Now, I was coming back for the same reason.

It felt like coming full circle, except this time, I had reason to be far more afraid.

So much more was riding on this return. I shifted in the seat, feeling every inch of my body tense as Parrish sought a good place to park her car in an area crawling with power vehicles and expensive cars of every make.

"Why so many cars?" I said, with my hand on the door as she careened into a spot with such an aggressive motion I was sure she'd scrape someone's paint job. "And why are we coming to this door?"

The entry in question wasn't one I remembered from my last visit. Layne had brought me through the guest suite, and later, I'd left through a back door as I'd hoofed my way out of his life for what I thought would be forever after.

Parrish put the car in park and cut the engine. "This is the pack wing. You stayed in the guest suite last time." She reached over to tug my wig into place after all the rooting around beneath it I'd been doing. "You're not exactly a guest now." Her delicate auburn eyebrows arched. "Alas, my dear Desirée, you are but a lowly pack member's girl toy."

A movement past one of the cars caught my eye and I sighed at the thought of facing heaven only knew how many wolf shifters. "I don't know if I can do it," I said. "I'll slip up somehow."

She grinned and shoved at my arm so I'd grab for the door handle. "Just don't talk. Hard to mess up when all you're doing is thinking about getting into my pants."

I rolled my eyes as she got out of the car and slammed the door. With a bracing breath, I did the same, pausing once outside to look around.

The pack wing must have stretched out for two blocks while the main manse sprawled the same amount in the other direction. From this vantage point, the breadth of the mansion was apparent. Owen must have paid a considerable amount of money to keep what looked like a quarter acre of grounds stretching out into the city, creating a suburban oasis with fountains and cedar trees. Late blooming flowers sent their fragrance over the air and that perfume mingled nicely with the herb garden close to the door.

The front of the manse had statuary, and I knew the garden where I'd left, owned several more. But here, the grounds were all natural, with bushes and the like perfect for wild game to wander.

"Beautiful, isn't it?" Parrish said as she paused to look out over the grounds with me.

"It's like we aren't even in the city."

She lifted one shoulder. "In a sense, we aren't. The pack owns several blocks in that direction, and keep the structures to a minimum so we can provide our wolves a bit of nature when they need it."

"But you don't live here," I said, turning to her with a curious glance. She lived deeper in the city, in a little apartment that smelled of mildew even if it was squeaky clean.

She made a subtle, almost dismissive movement of her head, but I saw the way she swallowed, the way she flicked her gaze toward the cedar trees and the bushes beyond and I knew she was jealous of all those who did live on pack land.

"You're not welcome," I said and didn't need her to confirm it to know that was exactly what the issue was. In that moment, I hated Owen even more than I thought I could. In all this time, he'd not made her welcome. He'd accepted his pack's mistreatment of her. Some alpha.

I wrapped my arm around her waist. "To hell with them. They aren't worthy of you."

She delicately extracted my arm from her torso and patted my hand before dropping it at my side. "I don't need pity, Desirée. I don't need anyone or anything." She shuffled one foot to the other. "I can manage. I've managed for centuries. It's Layne I worry about."

I nodded, sorry that she couldn't accept the comfort but understanding that she'd been pushing people away for almost two centuries. When you've been an outcast for as long as she'd been, trust would be difficult. Love even more so. "He's lucky to have you," I said and smiled. "Go do what you need to." I didn't want to say how worried I was too because I wasn't sure how many ears were within hearing distance, eagerly eavesdropping on the two of us.

She lifted her chin in the direction of the door. "I'm sure one of the pack will help you get settled before dinner."

I cocked my head at her. "Aren't you going to Layne?"

She dug into her pocket and extracted her phone as she nodded. "I have to make sure my boss is still fine with me being out for so long. You go on. I'll meet you at dinner."

I clutched my hands to my chest and nodded. I could do this; I had to. With a bracing breath, I spun in place and marched toward the door. Two brawny looking men stood just onside the entryway, talking but saying nothing. How I knew they were saying nothing came from the way both of them were far too animated to be really talking.

I stepped up to one of them and cocked my hip to the side. "Parrish told me someone would see me to our rooms."

The one on the left, the fellow wearing a blue tank muscle shirt and bandanna, stuck his hand out. "Charles," he said and jerked his thumb toward his companion. "This is Emmet." He looked me up and down but his gaze wasn't friendly. "Not sure what you have in those boots of yours."

I spread my arms wide to indicate I had no weapons on me. "I have dog-tired feet, is what I have," I said, unable to stop the sass after the long day. "Do you need to frisk me?"

He licked his lips and with a cant of his head, he said. "Would you like me to? Is Parrish not enough man for you?"

Emmet nudged him in the ribs hard enough to shove him sideways. Charles glared at him. "She asked," he grumbled.

Emmet, a foot taller than Charles, and wearing a black suit instead of workout clothes gave me a subtle bow. "He's a jackass. I'm sorry. He's just pissed we got called in to the pack wing when he wanted to work out." He extended his hand toward me. "If he'd bothered to dress for the occasion, he might have got a good meal out of the bargain, but his idea of dressing for dinner is to wear shoes."

I took Emmet's hand and shook it, inclining my head toward the long hallway that stretched out behind them. "I'm—" I stumbled over the introduction, and caught myself an instant before I said my real name. "Desirée," I said with what I hoped was just the right amount of sincerity. "I'm Desirée. I was helping Parrish when things...well, when things went south and now I'm here." I flapped my arms against my sides to infer that this was all so very overwhelming. I suppose I didn't have to act too hard, and I probably just sounded exactly like a girl who had discovered monsters existed and that she was dating one.

Emmett nodded. "We know. Owen filled us in." He shuffled one foot to the other. "I don't know how much you know about us, but we share this space when someone is in trouble. Owen takes care of all the essentials, our bills, our families, if one of us is in trouble." He pursed his lips momentarily, suggesting there was more he wanted to say but chose not to. "Like now, I suppose."

He dropped his gaze to his feet. "Layne isn't the sort of guy you met at that witch's shop," he murmured. "He's a good guy. A good man."

Charles murmured his agreement. "Whatever that witch did to him, we'll get him back," he said. "And then we'll get that fucking bitch back."

I couldn't help staring at him. "There's no such thing as witches," I said with a note of acid in my tone. I didn't like the way he'd said it and even if Owen had fostered a host of lies to cover up what he was really doing behind the scenes in his pack, I wasn't about to stand by and let someone bad mouth me to my face, even if they didn't know I was me.

Charles barked out a laugh. "You know what we are and you doubt the existence of witches. Girl, you need to wash those blinders."

Emmet rolled his eyes at Charles and offered his elbow. "Never mind him. I'll see you to your rooms. There are two other shifters staying here for the moment, and I'm in the room next to yours." He winked. "Charles is bunking in the shed because he's not litter box trained."

"Fuck you, Emmet," Charles said, but there wasn't any rancor in his tone that I could hear. Probably the two of them came as a good cop-bad cop pair.

"Will I meet the other men?" I asked.

"Don't worry. I'm here to make sure you're safe while Parrish is busy with Layne."

When I sucked in a breath, he hurried to cover his inference that I might not be safe. "It's not that you're in any real danger, but with Layne in his state, we're all on alert, especially with a human staying on the property. That's all." He tried to grin but it caught on his teeth. He averted his gaze and led me, silently, to a metal door with a handle in the middle. European style.

"This is it," he said and swept me with an assessing glance. "Dinner is at eight. Owen has already sent in a few dresses for you and a suit for Parrish in case she can get away."

He started to move away when I held him back by the elbow. I wanted to know what Owen had told these men that they hated me so much.

"Tell me, Emmet. What did the witch do to Layne?"

"She tried to kill him."

CHAPTER 19

I STOOD GAPING AFTER Emmet as he strode away. It was obvious the men in the pack respected Layne, and that Owen was doing his level best to put me, or at least the real me: Brie, under suspicion. With worries that Owen didn't really buy my disguise, I opened the door and sought for the light switch with my hand on the inside wall.

I was still groping around blindly when someone blustered up behind me, and I jolted into reaction as the panic took hold of me, I swung around with my elbow jutting out ahead of me. The pointy end of the bone met another hard surface with a thwack.

Parrish yowled in pain and swore loudly enough to shatter my eardrums. I cringed when I realized I'd walloped her in the nose.

"I'm so sorry," I said. "Holy shit, are you OK?"

She pinched the bridge of her nose while her eyes watered and tears pooled in the corners. "Nothing a little ice can't fix," she drawled and pushed me inside the room ahead of her. With her free hand, she flicked on the light switch I couldn't find and crossed the expansive room to flop onto the bed.

After she'd flung herself back and let one arm drape over the mattress did I dare approach her.

"You don't look OK," I said. "I didn't mean to, really, I—"

"It would take more than a weak elbow butt to my nose to hurt me significantly," she said. "It's Layne." She covered her face with the hand still holding her nose, but flipped the hand over so the back of it lay against her forehead. "He isn't even fully human all drugged up, and Zach has pumped him with enough meds to nearly put him in a coma. Fuck. It's not good."

I perched on the edge of the bed, almost afraid to ask. "It's not normal what you're seeing, then?"

She lifted her fingers up high enough that I could glimpse her eyes. They were red-rimmed as though she had been crying, but that could easily have been the blow to her nose. "Normal is not something I'd used to describe a wolf shifter at any time, but this...it's not like it was with me."

I must have moved, looked surprised or interested or shocked, because she groaned out loud as though I'd commanded her to spill her secrets. It came out like it might if someone dragged a secret from you.

"Yes," she hissed out. "I was a mess once too, just like you guessed. For half a century, I ripped and shredded my way through the city without letting the human woman out long enough to cage the beast inside. I doubt she would have wanted to cage the beast any-way. She was insane with grief, enraged the way a bear would be if a hornet bit its ass."

She pulled her hand away and rolled to her side, propping her head in her hand. She twisted her head in my direction. "You might think I had no sense of myself back then, and you'd be right. Almost. I was in there, behind the wolf's eyes. I saw what she did to women, to men, to kids for Jesus's sake."

She swallowed hard, and her gaze dropped momentarily to the mattress. She pursed her lips together while she gathered her thoughts or the right words to say, and I kept quiet. I didn't so much as move to touch her to ease the transition of memory to words. This was about her as much as Layne, and I felt as though she needed to see her way through it in order to help him.

For a long moment, she was silent. The muscles around the hollow of her throat were tight and I guessed she was struggling not to break down as the recollections took her. As badly as I wanted to comfort her, I knew she wouldn't accept it. So I waited, and I bit down on all the words I wanted to say to her, that I thought could make it all easier.

She flipped over onto her back again and laid her hands on her stomach. They balled into fists there. "The truth was, I didn't care what the wolf did. You can't know what it means for your wolf to be born in pain and grief. Without a leader to help you transition."

Her head tilted upwards as though she were aiming to see beyond the ceiling to the ether beyond. "Layne found me at my worst. I'm ashamed now as I've been for over a century, but the truth is what makes him my alpha. The truth is what makes him so important to me, why he was able to pull me out of the state I was in and let the poor simpering human peer past her grief to the possibility of healing."

I so badly wanted to prod her, but I was terrified to move or even swallow and break the trance that held her. Absolution was a terrifying thing, and it often required more courage than fighting a monster.

"I fought Layne, you know," she said and for a moment, her fingers splayed over her belly protectively then knotted into balls again. "He found me with my nose deep in the belly of some hooker I'd found alone in a dark alley. There was no worry of her surviving and being changed. There was no worry of anyone I attacked being changed. I was so complete in my consumption of my kills, there wasn't enough left to re-animate." She chuckled darkly. "He came to me in human form, even though it was the full moon and he could have easily torn my throat out. That wasn't Layne's way."

This time I couldn't remain silent. "What did he do?"

She sniffed out a bit of laughter. "He smacked me on the nose like a human would a puppy who'd soiled the carpet. Then he told me to back away and sit. Imagine it. A man facing a wolf just ordering it to sit like a good dog. I was incensed. I flew at him with my nose still bloody from the woman's bowels. Shit covered my snout. I roared at him and had him pinned beneath my paws before he could take a breath."

"Sweet Jesus," I breathed out.

"Yeah. I'm pretty impressive and I was a right beast then, but he didn't so much as quail. Predators like the chase, the hunt, the fear. He could have shifted right then and there, but he didn't. What he did, with me hanging over him, drool stringing its way down onto his cheeks, was stare up into my eyes, showing me the wolf in his. I think he expected me to back down, but it enraged me. It reminded me of the bastard who had made me and left me and killed the woman I loved, and in the second it took for me to clamp down on his eyes and face with my jaws, his hand came up to encircle my throat.

"His fingers dug beneath my fur to find my pulse and gripped the jugular between his finger and thumb. He held my life in his fingers just as I had his in my teeth.

I'd kill him and in his death throes he'd take me with him.

"But he didn't." She said this with a note of wonder in her voice. "He didn't." Her voice was tight, and I thought there was the hint of tears in it. "I wanted him to. Oh god, how I wanted it. But he wrapped his other arm around me and he forced me to roll over so that he was on top. Now, it was him looking down into my face. Me looking up at him. And his expression was so sorrowful, so compassionate that the woman inside the beast gasped at sight of it. She wept. She let go all the grief she couldn't release over her Violet."

Her voice went tight, and she gulped on her words. I almost reached for her, but her hands, fisted into her stomach, dug deeper into her belly and I knew she wasn't ready.

It took long moments for her to collect herself, and when she did, her voice was back to normal, gruff and sassy. "He forced me to shift back to my humanity. Don't ask me how he managed to do that, but he did. I lay beneath him, as a woman, naked and shivering and snotty from a big old ugly cry. He told me he'd been tracking me for months. I could barely speak for the residual wildness of the wolf. I don't think I spoke clearly for three days."

She rolled over and sighed. "I tried to kill myself many times after he pulled me into the pack. The guilt of the things I'd done was too much." She swung her legs over the side of the bed. "It's not so easy to commit suicide as a shifter who heals so efficiently." She laughed darkly. "I tried all the human ways instead of the right ones. After the last attempt, he promised to help me die if I gave him a quarter century of service. He needed me, he said."

"So you agreed."

"Damn straight, I did. I decided to spend the years fantasizing about death and told myself living with the guilt was my penance until then. But twenty-five years gave me other reasons to live. I didn't want to hurt him, and so they turned into thirty and fifty, and by the time the guilt was a tolerable memory, I had made my way through med school and began to pay him back."

She brought both hands to her chest and tapped her breastbone with her fingertips. "The woman you see before you is the brilliant, unfeeling, rehabilitated monster he was able to conjure from thin air." She grinned at me, but the grin faded quickly.

"Now it's him in that safe room, and I have no idea how to help him. I was a beast, yes, but never caught between my humanity and my wolf. I gave myself over completely. It's not the same for Layne. He's struggling with it and even though part of him is fighting, part of him wants to sink beneath the fire of vengeance."

"Maybe that's a good thing," I whispered. "Maybe the man can be reached."

She swung her gaze to look me direct in the eyes. "To be honest, Desirée," she said. "It would be easier to reach the monster." She sighed heavily and pushed herself to her feet. "At least Zach is here too and can sedate him if need be. Meantime, we'll feed him enough to make him puke when he wakes up so it slows him down, and then I go into the belly of the beast and try to tame him."

She scoured the room with her glance. "And speaking of food, we best change for dinner so I can fill my belly for the long nights ahead. Not sure when I'll get a chance to eat again."

I checked the time on my cell phone. "We have about half an hour, I think."

She dropped her feet to the floor and pushed herself upright. I stared at the wrinkles she'd left on the bed, working my way through all the things she'd told me, trying to imagine her at her worst and reconcile it with the woman in the here and now. My Parrish was not a monster. I wished she could see the humanity in herself, the goodness. I wished she could let go and trust and love.

I was still lost in thought when I heard her swear. I pivoted in her direction to see her standing in fronts of the closet. Her hand was on the door and she was glaring inside.

"What?"

She plucked out a navy suit and tie and shook it at me. "Owen's idea of a joke," she said then threw it to the floor. "Bastard doesn't have a clue."

She buried herself back in the closet. When she came out again, it was with two slinky looking dresses. One was gold lame and the other was scarlet red with a slit up the side that would expose a leg right to the butt cheek.

She started undressing and jerked her head at the gold lame. "That's your's," she said. "I'm taking the red number and ramming these gorgeous gams of mine right in his fucking face."

We dressed quickly, and she took a few minutes to adjust my wig and makeup. We hooked elbows, two conspirators ready to take on the entire coven and then some, and headed for the door.

She opened it up while I sidled out of the way, and I was all ready to follow her into the hallway when she jumped back, startled, and shoved me into the wall with a thud.

Rubbing the back of my head where it had struck, I leaned through the door to where she was bent over, scooping up what looked like a dead owl.

"What in the fuck, Brie?" she demanded and then clamped down on her lips as she realized she'd used my name. Three furtive looks up and down the hallway and behind her proved we were alone. She shoved me back into the room and closed the door behind her with the baby owl in her palm.

"What the hell is this?"

"How in the hell should I know?"

"A dead bird," she said. "A dead *owl*." She ran to the en suite bathroom and dumped the bird in the sink. "For shit sake, we can't afford harbingers at this point." She pointed at the bird as it lay crookedly in the basin.

"I didn't kill it," I said and leaned in to get a good look. "But you're right, it's dead." Dead for a long time was my guess. It was already stiff. "Do you think it's the same one as before?"

She sniffed the air and then leaned down next to me, staring into the basin. "Smell that?"

A wave of black moved in from the sides of my vision as I inhaled, not a threat of unconsciousness, but like too much blood was pooling out of my veins all at once. I swayed on my feet and she clutched at me.

"You smell it, don't you?" she said. "The magic?"

I nodded. "It's buzzing. Do you hear it?"

I couldn't stop myself from reaching out for the bird, where the buzzing and smell of strong magic were coming from.

And the moment my fingers touched its feathers, it jerked to life.

Chapter 20

WHAT SHOULD BY ALL rights have been a dead owl took flight. It flew into the suite and right through the bathroom door, where it careened around as though drunk. Instead of graceful flight, its wings didn't seem to draft well and it lost the air currents once or twice, threatening to spill it onto the floor. Several times, it caught itself before it smashed into the wall, screaming its fear as it went.

I'd always thought owls made hooting sounds, but this one had a noise that sounded midway between a chirp and a shriek, and it was so unholy that it made my hair stand on end beneath the black wig and hair net.

Parrish ducked as the tiny thing dove for her hair. "What in the great flying fuck is going on?"

I angled sideways as the owlet finally landed on the shower curtain and tried to perch with its claws caught in the rings. It slid sideways and backwards at the same time as the rings spun. Once it spread its wings to catch itself, it finally settled on the rod itself. It flapped its wings and shrieked at me as it scrabbled to find its footing.

With slow, deliberate movements, I eased my way over to the shower.

"Don't fucking touch it," Parrish hissed. "Don't even look at it for Jesus sake." She busied herself unfolding a bath towel and spreading it open. "We have to get rid of it."

My gaze darted to her wide-eyed face as she shook out the fabric in front of her. "You're going to scare it," I said and motioned at her to put the towel down.

"I think not," she said. "I'm going to toss this over that bird from hell and we're going to club it back into the coma it woke from." She shuddered as she eyed the bird.

I grabbed the edge of the towel. "You can try to catch it, but you will not kill it." I lifted my finger to Parrish's face. "Tell me you won't hurt it."

Parrish glared at me but shrugged her shoulders in assent. "Just don't come complaining to me when you find yourself six feet under."

"If it's a harbinger like you say, then it's not responsible for the actual death. And it would already have delivered its message."

"Too fucking late, then, is what you're saying."

I rolled my eyes and blew a strand of wig out of my face. "I'm saying what's done is done. Now we have to help the poor thing." I held my hand out to prevent Parrish from rushing the shower stall.

Parrish shook out the towel. "There's no way that bird was sleeping or hurt. It was fucking dead."

"I know," I said.

"Do you also know how a dead bird just happened to reanimate, too? Because from where I'm standing, it looked like you brought it back to life." She swung her gaze in my direction and I saw fear in her face. Fear of me or fear of the owl, I wasn't sure.

"I think maybe you're right," I said.

Her jaw seesawed back and forth. "The mouse," she said. "The cat."

I yanked up the dress as it slipped further down my breasts. "They both made the same buzzing sound," I said. "Did you hear it?"

She shook her head. "Just smelled the magic. Made my nose itch." She angled the towel so that it was out-stretched in front of the owl. "You think Honey or the cult is leaving these dead things to see if you're still alive? Testing for your magic?"

I snorted. "What magic?" I reeled back with the laugh of disbelief that slipped free. "I can't even tap into it unless I cut the runes or without dropping nearly dead from the effort."

I moved toward the wall so she would have more room to catch the owl.

Parrish gripped the corners tighter. "It's not impos-sible," she said. "Maybe Smith and the dog unlocked something during the coven's spell. Maybe you came back to life different. Maybe the cult did something to you."

I thought about that. I did feel different. Before, the magic had seemed a distant thing that I needed ritual and runes to access. Now, while my body was weak and recovering, I felt a bit more in tune to a power I didn't understand. The buzzing for instance. It was akin to static electricity in some ways, except drawing me closer, more like a magnetic pull.

"I don't think it's the cult," I said, trying to remember the things I'd read about them. "They sacrificed dogs not birds or mice or cats."

"But they could be testing your power."

"They don't know it's me." I was sure our ruse had worked. "Someone would have had to let them in on the secret and into the manse."

"Owen," Parrish said and jump-started when the owl shrieked at her. With a side eye, she edged toward the wall, obviously intent on going at the bird of prey from the side.

"Owen knows," she said. "He probably told Honey. Honey came in here and dropped the owl." She muttered a few choice words about how she felt about the witch and I leaned my back flat against the wall as the owl spread its wings again.

When it settled, I blew out a breath. "I don't think it's Owen," I told Parrish. "For one, he hadn't even seen Desirée when we found the mouse. And he was disgusted by the dead things on the shop's doorstep."

Parrish advanced on the bird, murmuring her agreement that maybe it wasn't Owen after all.

In return, the owl stared at us, and as it turned its head toward Parrish, she tossed the towel high in the air in its direction. I watched, breath caught as the soft fabric flapped open at the same time as the owl's wings. I thought it would take off, that the towel would miss and I ducked instinctively. My hands went to my head and I let go a little shriek.

But Parrish's aim had been true, and the owl had been too freaked out by its rejuvenation and was still too awkward to get out of the way in time. Parrish leaped for the bird and caught it by the legs beneath the towel. The bird shrieked at her from under the material.

"What now?" she said.

I shook my head. "I have no idea. Let it go?"

"I could eat it," she suggested.

"Let it go."

She breathed deeply and slowly. "Follow me, then. We'll dump it outside before we go to dinner."

I headed out of the room with her and followed her down the hallway, where she released the owl to the open air. Parrish took my hand and held it between us as the bird took flight and gained its grace. Watching it go, I realized I had the answer all along, and I'd just forgotten.

"Abbi," I said as we stood shoulder to shoulder on the flagstones of the back patio. "It was Abbi. I thought the cat was asleep but he wasn't. Abbi ate him. She needed its magic."

Parrish squeezed my hand. "What magic? The cat's magic wasn't its own. It was residual magic."

I shook my head. "Maybe Abbi caught him and killed him with magic, and laid him at my doorstep to find."

"You think your mother's familiar is bringing you dead things? Why?"

The air grew chilly, too chilly to be standing there in skimpy dresses and bare feet. And what we had to say should be said behind closed doors. There were too many ears here, listening. More of them inside. I dropped my voice as I clutched at her arm.

"Don't you see? It would explain why she was hurt. She'd used her magic to take his life because she didn't want it harmed. Wounds would be harder to come back from." I jerked my chin in the direction the owl had flown in. "If she'd broke its neck or wounded it in some way, and it got reanimated, it wouldn't be right."

Parrish shook her hand and peeled my hand away from her arm. "No," she said. "It can't be right. Why would the dog want you to raise something—as if you could."

"It would explain why she was hurt," I murmured, the thoughts swirling so fast, it was getting hard to pluck them from the spiral as they flew around my mind. "It took her magic to do it," I said. "It used her up and so she was suffering with the lack of it." I leveled Parrish with a look of certainty. "She'd used her magic to take his life and when I didn't do what I was supposed to, she took the magic back."

Parrish wrapped her arm over my shoulder and tugged me close as we headed back inside. "You think she's starting with small animals, testing your power?"

I closed my eyes, trying to focus, to see the images of the cat and the dog again, the mouse, the rats at my shop, the owl in the manse. "I thought it was just her scent on them that you were catching. You said it yourself. And her fur was there at the shop where the cat had been. Think about it, Parrish. What if she's killing all those small animals and bringing them to me to raise? What if she recovers her magic and tries again?"

Parrish backed away from me as though she was afraid of me. "What are you saying?"

"You said it yourself. Those dead animals smelled of magic. Hecate has power over the dead. Her blood flows in my veins, so maybe I have some residual power too."

"You mean necromancy?" Her lip curled back. "Unnatural. What's dead should stay dead."

She pulled away, finally, and left me standing on the cold flagstones as she headed for the doors. By the time she was yanking on the heavy ornate handle, I realized what the look on her face was. It had taken me several moments to recognize the disgust because

I didn't expect to see it in her face when she looked at me. But I knew that was what it was.

"Wait, I said as I hurried to catch up with her,"don't go."

She didn't bother to look over her shoulder at me, just piled through the door, the long slit in her skirt showing me a flash of leggy thigh. I ran in my bare feet all the way back to the room and caught her as the door was closing behind her.

"Parrish," I said. "It's still me." I laid my back against the door as it closed.

She spun to face me, and in her expression was something I couldn't quite measure. "What you're saying goes against all laws of nature," she rasped, her voice carefully low but filled with revulsion. "Bad enough we have witches doing horrible things to people, to you, to other shifters. But you, I thought you were innocent of all this. A victim."

I felt like she'd punched me in the stomach. My body even curled into itself as I studied her. "I'm no different than I was three minutes ago. I'm still the friend you saved. The woman you've laughed with, whose blood you took because you wanted to help me find out what was happening. You tested me. You know me."

"And that blood came back tainted," she whispered. "You're not human, Brie." She shook her head as she spoke and the fear in her voice lifted the hairs on my arms.

"You're not human either," I said.

She waggled her finger at me. "I'm made from magic; you're something completely different. Now I understand what those tests meant. Zach said you were changing. Those tests I got back aren't even your blood anymore. The lab asked me if I had sent them bad blood." She laughed abruptly. "Shit. I didn't know till right now that what you are is the worst kind of black witch."

"I never expected this from you," I said in a small voice. "I thought you'd be excited I'd figured it out." I pushed off from the door and took a step toward her. "All the pieces are finally coming together. I'm finally starting to see what it all means. After all this, I need you. I need a friend."

She shook her head and the swell of her bosom over the skimpy red satin bulged and let go as she lifted her hands, almost to ward me off. I froze, so filled with pain that I couldn't move if I tried.

"I can't," she said. "I can't do this with Layne. I can't deal with a necromancer on top of a black coven and magical dog and an alpha who is turning homeless youths so he can create his own little army. Jesus. Don't you get it? Our pack freed itself from black magic. It broke from a coven of witches who dabble in death, who used our magic for their own ends. They didn't just sacrifice us or our young ones. They called to Death, practicing their necromancy on us. The horrors they brought back."

She shuddered. "Don't you see? Owen was right. You are the witch who will kill Layne."

CHAPTER 21

BETRAYAL IS A BITCH. It always comes from the least expected quarter, the friend you trust, the lover you would die for. I stared at the woman who I'd thought would die for me, and I swallowed down a clump of pain that made cement of my throat. I didn't know what to say or how to defend myself.

"I would die for Layne," is what came out, and she nodded.

"I believe you," she said. "But would you take him with you? You're not the only one who knows a thing or two about Hecate. I did some reading of my own." She swept her arm toward the door. "Owen keeps a decent library. Much of it is first editions. Some are journals and diaries. He even has a grimoire in the collection. I read some of our pack's history. It's all there."

The air in the room had grown so chilly that hugging myself couldn't warm me up. "I know none of that, Parrish. You know me. I—"

"You're Hecate's fucking daughter," she spat out. "You said it yourself. You have her blood. The blood of a goddess with power over death, who uses dogs for her familiars." She jabbed at her chest and her dress gaped open, showing the fullest part of her bosom. "No dog," she said of herself. "But a pretty souped-up version if she wanted a new pet."

She barked out an acidic laugh. "Or better yet, why not an alpha wolf who is so in love he can't stand living as a human without her?"

"I would never hurt Layne. I would never use you as some enslaved familiar."

Her words hurt, but they were also so incredible that they freed my feet from their paralysis. I minced my way toward her, mindful of her pain and confusion. I thought of Sherry and her terror of her father's shade. I didn't want a repeat of that by a strong wolf shifter who could tear me limb from limb without a single weapon. I had to remind myself that Parrish was afraid, and she was hurt. That beneath it all, she knew me. She was a friend.

"I don't know what's happening to me," I murmured. "I don't know why my touch is able to raise a small animal or why my blood isn't my own anymore. But I do know I am me. I know I love you, Parrish. I know my life is better with you in it. You are my family. There isn't a thing in this world or any other that could tempt me to harm another living creature."

She eyed me warily, a sort of mania in her gaze. The way her chest was heaving echoed my own, and it took the dead silence of the room to discover my breath was coming in noisy gasps.

In a moment of inspiration, I pulled open the front of my dress, exposing my chest to her. I lifted my chin, angling my head to the side so my throat was exposed to her. My palm found the runes that only I could see and they settled there, over my heart, at the apex of the spread of them. With fluttering fingers, I thrummed out a beat, like my heart racing. I felt electricity dancing on my fingertips. The smell of jasmine and rosemary and just the faintest hint of sulfur rose around me.

"My magic, whatever it is, whatever source it comes from, in whatever shape it lives, is yours Parrish," I intoned. "It's Layne's and your pack's, and I swear my life will wane before I do any of you harm."

I felt the spell wrap around me as I finished. It wasn't Latin. It didn't require blood. It had intention though, and the ritual of language and promise and I knew by looking at her that she felt it too.

It took several long moments of us staring each other down for her to let the spell wash over her and give in to it. It was a spell of promise. If I'd have owned a pack, the spell would have taken her in. But I didn't. I wasn't a wolf. I was a witch. She was part of my coven. A peer. Not a subordinate.

She must have sensed it, finally, because she inched toward me, cautious.

"I'm sorry," she whispered. Her chest was heaving with hitching breaths, the same as mine. "I went crazy for a minute. I know better. I do."

She gripped me by the shoulders and held my gaze with hers so intently that the yellow of the wolf inside flashed. "I should be honored to be your familiar, should I ever die before you and you need me."

She grinned then, a bright split in her face that flashed white teeth at me. "Just don't chain me in the basement, OK?"

I breathed out all the strain and tension, and the room expanded again. I felt it inhale. I smiled back at her. I knew better than to belabor the point with Parrish. This was a huge step. Best we take the next one quickly.

"I'm starving, aren't you?"

She blew out a long breath. "I'm so fucking hungry I could eat a dog." Her arm draped over my shoulders and she guided me to the door.

We were several feet down the hallway before we realized we were still barefoot. She lifted her finger for me to wait and ran back to the room and collected sandals that were strangely the perfect size for both of us.

Ambling into the dining room, it was clear Owen had gathered the masses to dinner. All eyes ran over both of us in hungry glances. Parrish preened, and slithered to her seat, saving a space between her and Zach, who wolf whistled in her direction. She cut him with her eyes, but it was clear she enjoyed it.

"Fucking dogs thought I'd wear a damn suit to dinner." She ran her hand down her sides as she took her seat and sent a meaningful glance in Owen's direction. "Would you hide this body in a shapeless suit?"

Zach made some comment about her not being able to hide no matter what she wore, but it didn't seem to have anything to do with the clothes or her body, but rather her smart ass mouth, and she slapped him playfully on the arm. I noted he blushed as she struck him, and while she'd been prickly with him before, now she didn't glower at him. That was progress at least.

I sat on Parrish's other side, glad to see Emmet twirling a glass of wine next to me. "What did we miss?" I asked because it was clear we'd missed something important, judging by the scowl on Owen's face and the way Charles was staring down at his salad plate.

Emmet leaned in close, the smell of his aftershave wafting over me, something with peppermint and patchouli. "We were discussing why Zach isn't downstairs giving Layne another shot. Charles is insisting

Zach isn't doing his job and Owen told him to shut his gob. Pretty interesting stuff, really." He picked up his glass and tilted it toward me with a grin.

I pulled a glass of water closer. "Why would he want Layne to be drugged all the time?" I whispered this since I was afraid to catch Owen's attention.

He shrugged. "Zach doesn't think it's a good idea. He says Layne has already been out to long and should be allowed to wake up. He says Parrish can't do a thing for him in a drug-induced coma."

My heart hiccuped at the words. "He's in a coma?" I tried and failed to keep my voice level, but even I heard the worry in the tone. Luckily, Emmet either missed it or didn't care. He just responded with another spare lift of his shoulder.

"What would you call a sleep you can't come out of? And Zach says he gave Layne so much it would kill a regular man. Good thing werewolves are hardy, but he doesn't want to give him more. Can't say I disagree, but Charles is a different sort of wolf. He doesn't like Layne very much."

I caught the different wolf in question staring at us from across the table. I wanted terribly to tell him to screw off but instead, I lifted my water glass in his direction, saluting him silently before taking a sip.

It gave me the chance to think over what Emmet was telling me, and to glance around the table. In all, eight people sat with me, and an empty chair at the foot of the table, opposite Owen. I'd met Zach and Parrish of course. Emmet and Charles made five. The other three, a woman and two older men had begun an animated conversation with Owen that took his attention and gave me a chance to watch him. He seemed agitated, not the cool alpha male who'd come in to my shop.

I nudged Emmet with my elbow. "Who are the others?"

He leaned out over me just enough to make sure he knew who I was talking about. "That's Ana and her husband, James. Equally as rich as Layne. James is his third. A real ruthless wolf, which is why Owen employs him as lead enforcer. Ana is human like you are. She's his yin, his conscience. I don't think without her he'd be as genteel as he is."

He pulled back as he spoke in undertones, moving out of sight of those at the table he referred to and I ran my gaze over the man who was supposed to be genteel. James looked like he'd lived a hard life in the elements. He was older than Ana and wore his experiences in his face.

Emmet set his glass on the table and twirled it by the stem as he spoke beneath his breath. "And the other is Floyd. He's a worker bee. Soldier type. Does most of the really horrible stuff that James won't."

I pulled my hands down into my lap. If Owen had amassed the harder wolves of his pack here, he must not be certain Layne could come out of his mania. It didn't bode well. I stole a look at Parrish, who was arguing with Zach across the empty chair between them.

When a server came out with a platter of soups and gathered up the salad plates, I realized we'd missed part of the meal. Not that it mattered. My anxiety was red-lining and my appetite had decided to flatline to give it energy.

I was politely accepting a bowl of broth when a howl broke the tension that already clung to the air. The pain in it lifted the hair on my arms, and Parrish dropped her spoon with a clatter to the table. Everyone froze in the middle of whatever they were doing.

My eyes flashed to Owen, whose spine went ramrod straight. His throat muscles worked like he was struggling to speak. He turned to James.

"It's time," he said.

James got up, and at his movement, Parrish leaped to her feet.

"I don't need you," she said to him. Her voice was even and low, but the threat in it was palpable.

James smirked at her and she all but bared her teeth.

"I can handle it," she said and swung her gaze to Owen. If I didn't know her so well, I'd have guessed by the look on her face that she was pleading with him even if her voice was heavy with authority. "You gave me the task. Let me see to him."

James pushed away from the table, tossing his napkin down into his soup. "He nearly killed Charles when we got here," he said. "Zach had to shoot him up again, and you think you can take him?"

Her fingertips touched down on the tablecloth, steepled, and I could see she was doing it to keep her hands from shaking. "I won't need to take him," she said. "You males. You think violence solves everything."

He snorted. "And what do you think you can do for him that a man like Zach can't?"

Parrish's face blanched at the insult and she stuttered on the curse I knew she was trying to smother in face of Owen's direct glare. My fingers clenched on the napkin in my lap. I wanted to reach over and pat her leg in support, but I didn't dare move.

Zach's chair scraped back as he leaned backwards on it, his gaze a steel trap that captured James's despite the casual way he balanced on the chair legs.

"I fail to see how you would know what a man is capable of, James," he said. The way his chair teetered on its back legs, so inappropriate for a dinner party, just emphasized the insult in his words.

I waited, breath caught in my throat for what might happen next. Even Parrish gawked at Zach for a long moment while James's jaw went tight. His hand went beneath the table and I had the horrible feeling that he was reaching for a firearm like in the old Western movies.

Zach seemed to wait for a response with the rest of us, but when James merely brought his napkin back up to the table and tossed it on his plate, he turned to Parrish.

"Go see to him. It will be interesting to see him tear your throat out." He looked to Owen for reassurance, and when the alpha gave it with a curt nod, Parrish flew back from her seat and with a silent glare at James, spun on her heel.

She was already to the door by the time I caught my breath.

Owen watched her go with a pensive look on his face. "What of the she-wolf at the witch's shop?" he said to the table in general. "Have we made arrangements to gather her body and dispose of it?"

My hands clenched in my lap. Such callousness. I could barely keep my mouth shut. Zach must have sensed my discomfort because he leaned close and took my hand in his, pulling it onto his lap beneath the table.

"I'll be sure it's respectful," Zach whispered to me, then, much louder to Owen, said, "I should give her a once over before we commit her to ash. Make sure there isn't something odd we don't understand. She did bond to Layne, didn't she?" He placed his free elbow on the table and gestured toward his back, in the direction

Parrish had fled. "Are we sure he wasn't the one who turned her?"

Owen dismissed the comment with a fork pointed at James. "You'll have to arrange any of that with our enforcer. If he thinks we should worry, we will."

"I beg to argue," Zach said. "James doesn't have the expertise. You hired me so I could give my expert opinion. My opinion is that we shouldn't rush to ash her. Her body might have clues that can help us understand why Layne has gone feral."

Owen snorted, but it wasn't meant as an insult. More that he wished it was so simple. "Layne is feral because of the witch. We both know that. Hell. We all know it. It's his curse, God damn it. I knew she would be the death of him."

I squirmed in my chair as his gaze fell on me. I knew exactly why he didn't want any intrusion or inspection into Trish's death. He was afraid Zach would figure out he was the one who had turned that poor girl. Acting as though I knew nothing, as though I was the woman Parrish was dating instead of the witch he was talking about meant I couldn't look him in the eye. I knew I'd give myself away in that moment.

So I pulled my hand free of Zach's and reached for my water glass. When I noticed how much it trembled, I dropped my hand back to my lap, and was relieved when Owen's gaze moved on. When another pained howl, filled with rage and grief rose through the floor, he closed his eyes and drew a long breath.

"My son may not come out of this, and if he doesn't, I don't know how long we can leave him in this state."

He swallowed hard before continuing. "If he cannot be cured, I'll end him myself."

Chapter 22

MY BREATH STOPPED MOVING. Zach's hand clutched for mine again as the table went silent. Despite knowing better to leave silence alone, I forged into its breach.

"You can't be serious," I said as I addressed Owen. Every member of the table sucked in a breath as Owen leveled his hard stare at me. He pushed his plate away and folded his hands over the table as he leaned forward. Another peal of primitive guttural cries came from the basement, and he let each one of them roll over the room as though he wanted us all to hear exactly how much pain was in each note.

Only when the last of it faded out did he speak again.

"You think to question things you don't understand?" He narrowed his eyes at me, and handsome as he was, that one look made him look as feral as his son. "Please enlighten us with your mortal sensitivities that a pack of wolf shifters couldn't possibly understand. We would love to learn from you."

The scorn in his voice was nothing to the rigid posture, the thickness of contempt, but I wasn't going to be swayed. The thought that he'd murder his own son was too much.

I pulled my hand away from Zach, who struggled to keep it in his control. Be still, his actions said, but I couldn't. "You said he was cursed."

Owen's smoky eyebrow lifted. "I did. Do you understand curses by chance? Do we have a witch in our midst that we weren't aware of?" His open palm swept the air over the table. "Please, do, enlighten us."

Zach's knee butted into mine and I glared at him. "I'm sure it won't matter," he said, turning his eyes from mine back to Owen. "Parrish knows what's at stake. She'll do everything she can to reach him."

Owen snorted. "That butch wolf break through when his own father who knows him better cannot? The idea is ludicrous."

"We've tried everything else," he said. "The drugs are just a stop gap."

"You think I don't know that?" Owen shouted, his reserve abandoning him, and in that one instant, I believed he really did care about Layne. His grief stood out in every vein bulging from his forehead.

"Surely there's another way," I said despite the clenched hold Zach had on my knee. "There has to be something."

Owen rose from his chair and leaned on his steepled fingers. "Do you think I'd not try everything I can to save my own son?" He barked out a laugh. "You show your ignorance here. If I were you, I'd be careful not to show too much of it else the pack who houses you become nervous about your existence."

It was such a blatant threat that I clamped my mouth closed. The real Desirée would be a threat to their existence, and each of them knew that. Zach leaned toward me. "Maybe it's best you go back to your room," he said. "Wait for Parrish while we do what's best for our pack mate."

I lifted my gaze to his. I didn't want to leave. I wanted to follow Parrish to see Layne. I wanted to help. But

I knew the precarious position I was in. My vow to stay as silent as I could, to stay under the radar, was drifting away fast. If I didn't get some control of my emotions, Owen was sure to figure out the voice that sounded so familiar belonged to the witch he hated. If that happened, everything, including my life would be forfeit.

I sighed and nodded meekly. It would be a relief to get out from beneath all their studious glances.

"Would you like me to walk you to your room?" Zach said. "The manse can be a bit confusing if you're not familiar."

"Thank you," I said, meaning it. "I would like that."

Someone, James, I thought, made a comment about Parrish not being man enough to hold my interest as Zach took my elbow and led me from the room. I blew out a long breath, telling myself it didn't matter what they thought.

"You have to be careful," he whispered in my ear when we were a safe distance down the hall. "Owen is already suspicious. James is a prick and ready to remove any mortal who he thinks puts our existence at risk, and Charles and Emmet are just plain old-fashioned werewolves who understand the order of things and will do whatever they're told. That includes making a midnight visit to an unchaperoned mortal."

The inference was frightening.

"I'm sorry. I just couldn't stand hearing that," I said.

He tugged me close, slinging his arm over my shoulder so he could adjust my wig where it had moved. "You can believe what you want, but Owen loves Layne. He won't do anything final until there's no choice left."

I nodded silently. I was good at reading people, and I'd seen the truth of that in Owen's face. Whatever

I thought of Owen, whatever he'd done to me and a dozen other people in his service to the black coven, he loved his son.

When we reached the door to my room, Zach touched his fingers to his forehead in a mock salute and smiled, showing a dimple in his right cheek that I'd never noticed before.

"I'll leave you here," he said, opening my door for me like an old world gentleman. Not for the first time did I wonder how old he was.

"You and Parrish," I said in a leading tone, looking up at him as the door yawned open.

One eyebrow lifted over his careful gaze. "You want to know what happened between us," he said, and I nodded, ashamed to be poking my nose where it didn't belong. If it bothered him, he didn't show it. Just loosed a long-suffering sigh.

"I offered to marry her to solve a rather nasty problem she brought down on herself." He lifted his gaze, looking off to the side as though he was remembering. "She agreed so long as it was a shifter who married us, and he had to be Catholic."

"Her way of postponing the inevitable, I suppose," I guessed, and he nodded.

"So long as it looked like we were engaged and had this pesky issue getting the deed done, the problem stayed in the background and she was content. Werewolf priests are not easy to find in the pack world, and she knew it." He chuckled beneath his breath and shook his head in admiration. "She can be crafty when she needs to be."

He leaned his back against the door jamb, and I had the distinct impression that he didn't want to say more but was politely waiting for me to dismiss him.

I cast a look over my shoulder into the darkened room and felt a shiver run over my shoulders. Zach must have noticed and reached in without looking to switch on the light. The interior of the room flooded with a yellow glow, casting illumination over the mess Parrish and I had left of the room before we'd headed out for dinner. When he saw the cast off jeans and shirts and sneakers on the floor, he chuckled.

"I see her compulsive behaviors still haven't bled over to a manic streak of tidiness."

I blushed to see a pair of panties, mine, draped over the bed where I'd left them. "Not just her, I'm afraid." I steeled myself not to race into the room to shove them beneath a towel.

To distract him, I asked the question burning on my tongue. "So will you tell me if you ever found a priest?"

He ran a thumb over my chin and then showed me a stray bit of salad dressing my napkin had missed.

"You know the answer to that, I'm sure," he said. "I'm not the sort to give up easily. Our engagement lasted for three years before I found the right man, a dying priest who spent his whole life saving orphans from the streets and looking after them." He swiped the salad dressing against his trousers and pursed his lips thoughtfully. "I turned him," he blurted out.

At his confession, I heard my sharp intake of breath and tried not to show my shock that he'd do something drastic like that to a man of the cloth.

He crossed his arms over his chest. "I know what you're thinking, but my pack magic healed his cancer right then and there, and he lived through another generation, taking care of unwanted kids before he sought me out to end him. I can't be sorry for that decision."

It dawned on me that this was the thing Parrish held over him. He didn't need to tell me her reaction; it was obvious in how she treated him, that they didn't wed. "She called it off," I said. "And had to face the trouble she created. I bet she wasn't happy."

His head drooped and his shoulders, formerly rigid and square, now sagged. "Parrish's unhappiness isn't a new thing," he said. "It's nothing she hasn't been able to push through for the last century. I just wish she would forgive me."

"Because of the priest," I guessed. "She hated what you'd done to him."

He laughed out loud at the suggestion. "Oh my, no. She had the grace to admit I'd been as crafty as she was, and when the priest admitted he was happier being able to do God's work for another generation, she had a hard time hating me for that."

"Then what?" I asked. "What could you have done that made her so mad she'd not forgive you?"

His arms uncrossed as he laid his right hand over his heart and held it there. "Can't you guess what unpardonable sin I could commit to earn Parrish's undying anger?" He tapped his heart in a rhythmic beat. "I told her I loved her."

I caught my breath at his admission. It shouldn't have surprised me that he loved her. His behavior, his every action fairly shouted it. And he had a way of looking at her when he thought she wouldn't notice. If I'd been on my game, not so worried about Layne and all the coven business, I might have seen it too.

"It's hard loving someone who can't love you back," I said.

He said. "I've resigned myself to it. I know she can't see me that way, but I hold out hope that some day she'll at least forgive me." He smiled again and gestured toward the room. "Your bed awaits, my lady. I have to go check on our stubborn friend before she tears Layne a new one."

With a soft touch on the shoulder, I bid him goodnight and closed the door behind me.

Alone, I began picking up all the discarded clothes and stripped off my dress to fall into bed. I lay tossing and turning for at least an hour, worried about Parrish, worried about Layne, before exhaustion finally won out.

I only knew I was sleeping when I saw my mother.

CHAPTER 23

MY DEAD MOTHER SHOULD not have been standing in my room, yet there she was, back to me and she wore a Grecian style dress. Nothing about her should have told me it was my mother, but my subconscious knew. When I found myself walking behind her through a dark tunnel deep in the earth, I realized I was dreaming.

"She's taking you to see your father," Scarlett said from beside me.

I swung my head to the right, not at all confused that the young woman I'd hired as a shop clerk and who had been murdered by her ex-husband accompanied me down the long earthen tunnel we traversed. I was mostly concerned that she looked to be disintegrating, much as Abbi had been before she'd consumed the tomcat inside my shop. She carried a torch that cast light in hard angles around us. Our shadows loomed large on the walls. When I looked at her, I had a hard time seeing her face.

"My father's dead," I said to her.

She nodded toward my mother's figure as it wove around a sharp corner. "Don't lose her. It's dangerous down here."

"Am I dead?" I asked her as I stepped over a thick root, gnarled upwards, it seemed, to trip the unwary traveler.

"You were, but not now," she said. "Don't you remember?"

I sighed. "Sometimes, I do," I said although I had no idea what she was talking about. I didn't remember my near death, and I certainly didn't want to.

She sniffed and wiped at her nose. "Almost there," she said. "It's a shorter journey when you're not paying attention." She pointed ahead of us into the shadows.

A reddish sort of light glowed in the distance, breaking the gloom of the tunnel. "There," she said. "I can't go there or he'll own me." She paused and held the torch high over our heads. "She's the only one who can bargain with him. Don't let him see you or she'll end up having to choose between you."

I froze with my hand on my chest. I didn't want to go down that tunnel toward the light.

"I've been here before."

She cocked her head to the side. "Yes. When you died. You do remember."

"She wasn't here then," I said of my mother. I didn't want to remember, but flashes of those seconds, drawn out like lifetimes, started firing through my memory.

Scarlett pursed her lips and tilted her chin sympathetically. "You were dying, then," she said. "You're alive now. This isn't your journey; it's hers."

Her journey. My mother's. I wasn't dead. But that didn't mean I wanted to travel that tunnel again. That light. Something about that light...

A shove from behind propelled me forward and I tripped on another root, one so large I had to crawl over it just to find a place to put down both feet without being lopsided. Abbi appeared from the dark shadows and crept forward, her head hanging low, her eyes gleaming like lamplight. In the distance, a chorus of dogs barking drew my attention.

And that led to another step and another until I was so close to the red glow that it took up several yards of space in front of me. My mother stood there, just in reach. She wouldn't turn around.

I tried to call out to her, but in the moment my mouth opened, she stepped through the light and it blasted back at me, swallowing me whole.

I had to shield my eyes from the glare. When I pulled my hands away, I stood in what looked like a foyer, with a large map made of leather hanging on the wall ahead of me. My mother was gone. The red light had dimmed to something much more manageable, and in the recesses of my mind, I recalled my father telling me that red light preserves a person's night vision. Good thing, because it was dark as hell in the foyer but for that red glow all around.

I took a step closer to inspect the map, wondering the whole time why things were so viscerally realistic. I didn't remember walking in dreams or having such clear thoughts. Usually, they were high on emotions, low on logic.

On inspection, the map reminded me of one of the large mall guides, with large squares denoting areas like foyer, which was where I was, and bath suite, and bed suite, dungeon, gallery, and something called a menagerie. That one took up most of the left half of the map, and it seemed to be crisscrossed with numerous halls and dead ends.

Just as I noted something that looked like a brown spot that reminded me of a freckle and was leaning in to touch it, a noise from behind me caught my attention. My heart leapt up to my throat. Fear razored through me. Startled, I swung around.

Nothing. I cocked my head to the side. The noise came again, and I recognized it for what it was. Voices. Two of them. Arguing, I thought, and not from behind me but from somewhere to my left. A quick consult of the map told me they were either in the dungeon or the gallery. I shivered, hoping dungeon was a kitchy sort of label, much like the entire map was.

At first, I expected the dream to simply move me to the voices, and I waited, sensing that the lucidity of the vision would slip away at any moment. It didn't. I was left standing there, staring at the map and growing ever more certain that the brown spot really was a freckle.

Right about then, my mother's voice cut through the air. It had been years since I'd heard her voice, but I knew it was her. Everything in my core lit up at the timbre. Everything inside shrank me down to a kid again, both terrified and awed by the woman who had both nurtured and abandoned me.

"He's mine," she yelled, this time so loudly I couldn't doubt it was her. She sounded furious. The rage propelled me to the left, not thinking about the dungeon anymore, just wanting to go to her.

Racing down the hall, I barely noticed the dozens of round lights buried in the walls that peppered the space from top to bottom. They blinked on and off as I ran past, aiding me with enough light to see where I was going. Once or twice, a fog lifted from the floor in front of me.

"Ghosts," I murmured to myself as I realized, like you do in a dream, exactly what those fog banks represented even though I should have had no reason to think so.

The stream of mist began to take shape, and for a second as I ran past, I thought it might solidify. A flash of image breezed through my mind's eye and for an instant, I thought the fog would shape itself into a monk with a gas can, hefting the cannister over his head.

Terrified that the form would solidify and show me something my gut warned me I did not want to witness, I waved at it, forcing the mist to dissipate. As I did, I heard a groan. A snap crackled in the air as one of the bulbous lights flashed red then white then went out.

I froze. All the hairs on my arms and nape lifted as though electricity had whispered across them. I swallowed hard. I could try to fool myself all I wanted. This wasn't a dream.

Somehow, I'd fugue walked like I had all those weeks ago from my apartment to that run down, flophouse where the coven had left the remnants of their ritual sacrifices. Something told me I'd not truly 'walked' there either.

Whatever magic resided in my DNA, it allowed me to throw my soul somewhere, and pull my body along with it. The truth of it, as impossible as it was, made me hug myself because while I'd been simply unconscious when I'd traveled to the flophouse, I was at least somewhere on earth.

I had the feeling where I was now, couldn't be called earth in any sense.

Before my mind could go into full-blown panic, my mother shouted again. Her temper a raw thing in her voice, and this time, oh yes, this time I heard the other voice, and it flattened me against the wall. Not because

I recognized the voice, but because of the sheer power in it.

"This isn't like Persephone," the masculine voice drawled. "You have nothing to bargain with."

"I'm a fucking goddess," she said. "How many of those do you have in your menagerie? How many goddesses would offer themselves to you?"

The sound of my mother's voice drew me like a magnet, and I crept along the hall toward the sound of her voice. When the sound of low-throated male laughter met my ears, I froze. It was too close. Around one more turn, and I might be in full view. I might see everything.

The laughter drew itself out like a snake uncoiling from its skin, and it had the same effect on my flesh. Goosebumps raised to the surface. "You're not offering yourself to me," he said. "You think I'm foolish enough to fall for your bargains again?"

"But he's mine," she said. "I have power over death. I have the power to bring him back to me."

He laughed. "You used to have that power. You gave it up for the poor sod. Look at him. He's nothing. He's not worth the skin he's fleshed with."

"He's mine. That makes him valuable."

I peered around the corner, not truly being careful to stay out of sight. This was my dream, lucid or not, and I had no compunction about being caught. I wanted to SEE dammit and lurking in the dark hallway put too many barriers between me and the first glimpse I had of my father in decades.

What I saw shocked me. My father looked as he did in life, except he was thin and gaunt and sort of gray looking. He stood between my mother and a hulk-sized man with a barrel chest and muscled thighs. This man was beautiful all the way through. His hands could have crushed a small small dog, and I had no doubt looking at him, that he'd done such a thing in his time.

The man stood in front of a wall that stretched upwards for several floors, and it rose behind him with the same sorts of lights I'd seen in the hallway. Enough light brightened the room that I could make out what looked like veins of moving blackish water threading its way over the surface of the wall, connecting each orb.

As a dream vision, it was certainly unique, but what really caught my attention was the racks of weapons and leather and whips and chains that surrounded the room. One entire wall was devoted to devices that looked distinctly medieval and quite terrifying.

My mother squared her shoulders, and though she looked younger than I remembered and hollowed out by some emotion I couldn't name, she faced the man with courage and grit.

"I've done my duty by you for a millennium or more," she said. "I accompanied your beloved to and fro each year the same as always."

He glowered at her. "But not this last century," he said. "Oh no, she has not returned since you last walked her from my gates."

"One might say after a millennium, that the girl should know the route well."

His glower grew darker. "None but you can come and go in this realm with such ease as a stroll through the gate, and you are well aware of it."

She shrugged. "And I companioned her dutifully as I was wont, even past the time I was wont." She planted her feet on the floor, rooting them there as she faced him. "I tired of the task long before I ended it."

"For a man," he said. "You tired of it for your own beloved and left me bereft of mine."

"In all those centuries, I've not asked one soul's worth for my own that wasn't mine. I've taken only those who belonged to me before they crossed your threshold."

He canted his head at her. "One might argue that once they cross my threshold they belong to me and no other, regardless of who owned them when they lived."

My father crossed his arms over his chest and shivered visibly. His glance at my mother was a secretive one, filled with words he couldn't express. I read them clearly on his face even if my mother ignored them. Leave, they said. Save yourself. Let it be.

Exactly what he wanted to let be became clear when she stepped closer to the man.

"He's not worthless," she said. "He is mine. He will always be mine."

"Indeed," the man said, glancing at my father. "Maybe you're right after all. Perhaps he does have value." He dressed her down with a single look. "As a mortal, you're nothing, Hecate. But as a goddess who gave up her godhead for a mortal man. Well, that is unique." His smile slithered over his face like a serpent climbing an apple tree, and I knew right then who he was. Lucifer. Satan. God of the underworld.

I shuddered at the look he gave my father.

At once, his arm flicked toward my dad and in the instant his fingers let go a stream of sizzling light, my father dropped to his knees. He curled into a ball so tightly, his spine cracked. My mother let go a scream of fury and fear and ran for him.

By the time she reached his side, my father had transformed into a ball of light and was already streaming toward the wall behind the god of the underworld. An orb waiting there caught him and it glowed for a long moment with an eerie green light before it settled into a gentle glow like the others. The thready veins of light that joined his orb to hundreds of others pulsed and moved like the transit of blood through flesh.

"Goddesses are a dime a dozen," Lucifer said. "Mortal women and witches, even more common." He see-sawed his hand in front of his chest. "But a mortal man worth the power of a god? One she loved enough to relinquish it for? Now, that's a priceless totem indeed."

Understanding spread across her face. "It was you. You took him. He didn't just die in a freak accident." She laughed without humor. "You had your minions take him." She fell onto her backside as the comprehension stole her energy. "What did you promise them? Immortality?" She snorted. "You don't have that power."

She ran her palm over the floor in a circle, weaving her fingers in and out as she contemplated him. By the time she was finished, a Hecate's wheel was drawn in light on the tiles.

As though the symbol had delivered some message, Hecate's mouth dropped open in sudden discovery.

"Me," she said. "That's what you promised them. My power."

Lucifer shuffled his feet and blinked at her but said nothing to either confirm or deny. Not that it mattered. My mother dropped her head back and laughed. The sound made the hair on my neck strain for the heavens.

"We've had each other for a century, he and I," she said. "You've had your time to place your minions, and I've had time to place mine." She leveled him with a hateful gaze. "Do you think your poor pitiful witches are up to facing me?"

He lifted an eyebrow at her and for a moment, a glow of white light haloed his form. I almost caught the shape of black wings spreading out behind him. At the sight, my mother collapsed into herself. She wrapped her arms around her knees.

A single movement and he was next to her, towering over the small ball that remained of her flesh as she hugged herself tight. He put his hand down on her shoulder where she sat crouched where my father had been.

"Don't worry, Hecate. I'll only take him out to play on special accessions. I wouldn't want to break such a treasure, and then when you come, I'll pair you with him. Side by side for eternity." He swept his arm to encompass the racks of torture devices. "And we'll have such a lovely time together the three of us."

She whipped her head upward and glared at him with such rage I expected her magic to turn him to stone.

It didn't. She looked frail and helpless beneath his gaze. I clutched my throat in fear for her.

"You're wrong. My magic isn't dead," she said in a throaty voice. "I didn't just abandon my godhood with no thought to what might happen the day my mortal lover gave up his ghost. I shed my power." She cackled, manic with grief and desperation and just a hint of her former authority. Her grin equalled his in awe-inspiring terror and sent a wave of shivers over me that lifted each hair on end.

She lifted her gaze to his and then to the spot on the wall where my father had disappeared.

"You may keep him for a time, Lucifer. But mark me. I will gather my power from the places I stored it. Places neither you nor your wicked coven can reach. And when I get it back, all of Hell will tremble."

He snorted and waved her away. She evaporated right then and there and as I stuffed my fist into my mouth to cut off my cry for her, I realized it wouldn't matter if I screamed out loud.

Because I knew right then, what I had witnessed. My mother and Lucifer, bargaining for my father's soul, for his life. And it was that moment I knew I hadn't traveled to another realm with body and soul intact. I'd gone back to my mother's memory. Back in time.

And my mother had just lost possession of my father's soul. It was the moment she'd failed, and the moment everything changed.

CHAPTER 24

I WOKE TO THE sound of birdsong and the smell of coffee. At some point, someone had entered my room and opened the window to let in a whisper of breeze. Whoever had done that had left me a carafe and a large mug, a rather chunky looking thing that read: I whiten my coffee with the ashes of my enemies.

Parrish, I guessed. She'd come and gone while my body slumbered and my spirit projected to the underworld. I'd seen Lucifer or Hades. I'd seen my mother and my father and I knew the breaking of my mom's spirit.

I understood now what was at stake.

It was too much to contemplate when I was ravenous for justice for my parents. It was clear then, what the coven wanted. It was clear what my mother had done for me, for my father.

Those pictures I'd found of her and my father and her coven. They didn't age. We'd been right about that. They'd stayed the same because my mother was the goddess of witchcraft and necromancy, the goddess of death who had abandoned her biannual accompaniment of Persephone and in doing so, earned an enemy of Hades. She was the owner of magic and it was her magic that kept them all young.

The cult of Blackburn was his. They'd used my father to get to her.

But she'd been crafty, or she'd been premonitory. She'd stored her true power in places the coven couldn't reach. John Smith, a loyal acolyte meant to keep watch and act when the time came. Her familiar, Abbi, whom she'd imbued by magic with the souls and energies of dozens of dogs. Her grimoire and her amulet had protected me from them, shielding me from their black magic for years until some trigger had made them beacons to the cult instead.

But what had that trigger been? Was it her death? Had they taken her life in the hopes that doing so would gain them what they sought? They'd certainly used enough sacrifice, of even my mother's acolytes, in order to gain enough power to overcome the goddess.

Finding my mother's grave seemed even more important now. It wasn't just me breaking the cult and saving myself. My father's soul was at stake.

I wasn't even entirely sure I had it all right, but in my core, I knew I was close. The breadth of the mystery was overwhelming and at the same time energizing. I felt the compulsion to do it all and do it right now.

The trouble was, I didn't know where to begin.

I slung my legs over the side of the bed, not wanting to consider how my body had managed to travel with my spirit and stay here at the same time because just touching down on that concept made me dizzy. All I had to go on was one simple notion: the runes, the blood, the magic, all of it was coming from my mother's source. Wherever and in whatever she'd stored it, that source had to be close if it was capable of aiding me this way.

The hope I felt from believing in this one concept opened the tight buds that had formed but never bloomed in my chest.

I sighed as I stretched and swept the room with a glance, following the smell of coffee. I crossed the room to the large oval tray that sat on the bureau. A brown plastic carafe companioned a plate of cold buttered toast. One square was three quarters burned while the other quarter was pale and soft. At some point, Parrish had crept into the room and left it for me, but she'd obviously been in a hurry when she prepared it.

Three pots of different flavored jam formed a semi-circle around the plate of toast. She'd also left a dollop of peanut butter on a spoon off to the side.

As I went for a corner of toast, I noticed she had left a note and her debit card propped up on the other side of the carafe. Stuffing the triangle of bread between my teeth, I unfolded the paper. Her handwriting was large and looping with long tails, but it was also pinched together in tight knots. As complex as the writer.

I smiled at the tangible representation of the woman I'd come to think of as family, feeling the warmth of familiarity ease some of the worry and residual dread from the dream. Her assurances that she was going to be busy all day with Layne, but felt she was making progress eased even more worry. Zach had only needed to shoot him up twice with a weaker dose. She insisted I did what I needed to do in order help her close Brie's affairs while she was occupied. She'd already OK'd it with Owen.

I rolled my eyes at the thought that I needed Owen's permission to do my business, but at least it would keep me busy, and with Layne being in such trouble, maybe they wouldn't follow me everywhere. I read the last of the note where it said: *Be careful, Desirée. I love you* and crumpled the paper up into a wad when I interpreted what it really said through all those words.

Watch my back. The ruse was still very much necessary.

I sighed and headed to the closet to get dressed, thinking all the while about the strange dream. I had been right about my mom trying to resurrect my father, but I hadn't realized the price she'd paid to be with him in the first place.

At least, if I was right, the dream explained why the goddess Hecate wasn't able to do more than store her power as the woman, Kate, did all she could to protect her family. As I flipped through some of the clothes someone, probably Parrish, had thoughtfully hung in the closet, I considered what I knew of Hecate the goddess and Lucifer. The most important thing was the one she'd mentioned to the god of the underworld. Her companionship of Persephone to and from the underworld seemed to stop when my mother met my father.

That my dad was over a century old, granted some sort of long life by Hecate, the god, surprised me. But it was clear that the moment my mother gave up most of her magic to be with him, she stopped accompanying Persephone on her journey. My guess was the last trip left her outside the gates, and Hades was most mightily pissed at my mother for giving up the task.

So it seemed my real rival was Lucifer himself. Great. Bad enough I was fighting a black coven of witches capable or willing to sacrifice whoever they wanted to get what they wanted, but they were doing it with the express permission of the devil himself.

How terribly, horribly and terrifyingly cliché.

I ate the rest of the toast as I chugged two mugs of coffee, then pulled on a pair of stretch jeans that molded to my body with just enough bagginess to feel comfortable. I'd slept in the wig and it was a bit of a mess on the left side, so I did the best I could to rearrange it without taking it completely off. I had the feeling once I did that, I'd never get it back on straight. It had taken Parrish' expert hands to make it look natural in the first place.

The magnetic lashes went on easily enough, but the bits of fake skin and makeup that Parrish had used to create a different face than Brie's was beyond my scope. Big sunglasses and a kerchief would have to do. But just in case that wasn't enough, I found a low cut shirt and push up bra to ensure no one gave too much attention to my face.

Once I was ready, I took a deep, bracing breath, and telling myself this was all as much for Layne as it was for me, I hurried through the halls to the back entrance, dialing for a cab on my cell phone so I didn't waste a single second.

As luck would have it, I managed to hail a cab and get off pack lands without even running into a single shifter. I worried for a while that the absence of Zach or Emmet might indicate some bad news about Layne, but reasoned that if something had happened, I'd have heard from Parrish.

We were supposed to be at the lawyer's office by 10 so we could have the wiggle room we needed to catch him coming out from his morning constitutional. I knew I was cutting it close even with the cabbie's manic driving. I stood in the lobby, twisting my heel back and forth in the flat sandals I'd shoved on to make running around the city easier than the high heeled boots Parrish had given me the day before.

I didn't bother to cross the library to see if Ava was working behind her desk until ten thirty came and went and no one came out of the men's room. I found her sitting behind the mountain of folders, two pencils in her hair, and a phone against her ear. She noticed me immediately, and when she leaned a bit to the side, I realized she was looking for Parrish.

"She couldn't come," I said. "She had a family emergency to tend to."

The relief on her face spoke volumes. She spoke into the phone with a pleasant tone that sounded at once dismissive and kind. When she placed the phone on its cradle, she stared at it for a moment before sighing heavily and spinning around in her chair to face me.

"I hope it's not too bad," she said in a tight voice.

"She didn't call you, did she?" I asked and crossed the room to sit in one of the leather chairs in front of her desk. The arms had been worn smooth by hundreds of palms, and I found the groove of use a comfort.

Ava's gaze flicked to her monitor and away from me. "She was supposed to phone last night. I just assumed she'd changed her mind." Her shoulders curled inward just enough that I knew she had been brooding about the lack of communication. She wasn't the sort of woman who would want to be pitied, but I did want to ease her bewildered sadness over it.

"I'm sure she'll call as soon as she can," I said.

She gave a snort nod and pulled up to her desk, steepling her fingers together as she leaned on her elbows. "What can I do for you, then?" she asked. "You were here with her, I remember. Looking for some paperwork on a friend of hers. Are you sisters?"

She didn't think we were related, that was clear, and it took a moment for me to realize exactly why she was fishing. I almost chuckled out loud at my own stupidity. "Parrish and I are good friends," I said. "But we have very different tastes in partners." I got up to stretch my hand over her desk in the hopes she'd take it. "I'm Desirée. I'm certain she'll phone you when her business is taken care of. It was unexpected or she would have called as she said. She was very excited about the date."

Ava squirmed on her chair, but she did take my hand as she stood and pushed back from her desk again so she could stand. "I'm sorry," she said. "I haven't dated in so long I forget to feel confident around other women." She turned a bright smile on me that made her look quite stunning. "I'm afraid Mr. Berg isn't in today. He had a terrible bout with food poisoning."

I sighed heavily. "Maybe you can help. I'm looking for more information on who might have handled Kate MacAllister's affairs."

She narrowed her gaze. "All that information is confidential. I can't just give it out to anyone. You really should check with Mr. Berg."

"There really isn't time," I said, pressing on even though I knew it would get me nowhere. "Like I said, Parrish is busy and she asked me to take care of some of Brie's affairs. Her last wish was to be buried with her mother, but we don't know which cemetery to look in or who to contact to arrange that."

She pulled one of the pencils from her hair and used it to point at me then toward the library. "You are free to look through the library for the obituaries. That should be listed in the narrative."

"But that's just it. We tried that. We couldn't find an obit."

The tip of the pencil tapped the desk several times as she chewed that information over. After a few moments, she dropped it to the top of the desk and bent to open a drawer. When she pulled out a large yellow legal pad, she grabbed the pencil again and started scribbling on it, then slid it across the desk toward me.

"A list of the funeral directors in the city along with where they work. There aren't many. You might have better luck starting there." She tucked the pencil back into her hair, trapping it between her ear and her skull. "I'd start at the top and work my way down. I've put them in order of least expensive, and therefore, most used."

It was something, at least. I looked down at the list and thought I recognized the second one. Maybe my mother had used them for my father's funeral. Not that we'd had much of a service. A graveside send off and lots of histrionic tears. But I was pretty sure it was the same funeral home. I shot her a grateful smile because in all the stress of the last months, I'd not even considered just going to my father's grave. I knew it well enough, since mom and I had gone there plenty to gather grave dirt.

"Thanks," I said, meaning it. She'd done what she could for me, and truly, it saved me a bit of searching the web. The bonus was really the names. That would cut my research time down dramatically. It only made sense that my mother would use the same funeral home.

I turned to leave but she called out to me before I made it to the door. Looking back over my shoulder, I expected her to ask after Parrish again, but she surprised me.

"You know you're not the only one to come looking for information on Kate McAllister," she said. "That's not breaking confidentiality to say."

My throat clogged up. "Who else?" I said through tight lips.

"A man. Handsome. Salt and Pepper hair. Wore a very nice suit. And a woman. She was very sweet looking."

Honey, I thought. As saccharine as her name but far more deadly. She and Owen no doubt.

"May I ask when?"

She looked around her as tough she was worried someone was listening and would disapprove.

"Not breaking confidentiality," I reminded her.

"The man came about three years ago. We wouldn't give him anything either. And the woman just a few weeks ago."

My stomach felt like someone had dropped a cement block onto it. What Owen would want with my mother had to be the same thing Honey wanted.

The question was: what was it?

CHAPTER 25

I CAUGHT A CAB from the lawyer's to the cemetery fifteen minutes away in the bowels of the old part of the city. On the way, I asked him to drive through one of the bagel restaurants so I could buy a sandwich. I offered it to him for his lunch, and he seemed genuinely touched. The truth was: I wasn't hungry. What I needed was the paper bag.

I climbed out, feeling as though I'd reached some sort of invisible threshold. I couldn't help thinking as though I'd turned a corner, that things were going to look up. I paid the driver enough that he agreed to come back for me in an hour. I liked his kind face and hoped he was sincere.

The hour gave me enough of a leeway to trek across the cemetery grounds to my dad's grave, and it would leave enough time for anyone following me to see Parrish's lover scouting out a place to bury Brie's ashes. To everyone, it would look like Brie's life and affairs were being put to rest.

But I was really going for an entirely different reason. Ava had reminded me that my father had a grave and that the dirt from a loved one's resting place had power. Maybe my mother hadn't been able to raise him, but it wasn't because the earth that harbored him was powerless or that she was. It was because Lucifer had him imprisoned in his menagerie. I wasn't sure when she'd figured it out, but she did, and that visit to his realm took a lot out of her.

The cemetery looked how I remembered, and the child in me recalled each step she took. Five minutes past the gated Jewish section where the tombstones were peppered with pebbles and stones. Three minutes through headstones made of white marble with enough erosion to nearly erase the names of the deceased. The cemetery itself was the oldest in the city and some of the headstones had been planted above the deceased in the 1700s.

The sky above me clouded over as though the very heavens knew the somberness of the journey. A scarlet cardinal perched on the head of an angel as it wept for a newborn. Cedars stood sentry on the edge of the grounds, strung with solar lights that gathered energy for the coming night. The scent they threw off mingled with the leftover smell of bread and yeast that wafted up from the paper bag clutched in my fist.

When my father's tombstone came into view, my stomach dropped to my shoes. I'd not been to see his resting place for two decades, and all the old grief came rushing back. I'd not understood his death back then. My mother said he died in a freak accident, but I never knew him to ride a motorcycle. I'd accepted the information for what it was, not questioning it.

Now, I knew better. The cult of Blackburn had taken his life for Lucifer in return for power. I'd never be able to look at my father's grave and not know that now. He died so thirteen witches could live. So Honey could live, the bitch. She'd pay for it, I swore to myself.

As I neared the spot I knew he rested, a raven lifted off from one of the cedar trees. A black shadow moved within the bushes. My nerves jangled. It was midday, but I was glad I was here before dark. I wasn't sure I'd have the courage to come after the sun went down.

At first, as I drew closer, I thought his plot was overgrown with weeds that had grown high and then died and turned brown, but by the time I stood a few feet away, I knew what littered his spot.

Animals. Dead ones. Six to be exact. At least, the carcasses made one good reason for my knees to buckle when I was supposed to be no more to him than a custodian of the man's daughter's ashes. Anyone watching wouldn't question the shocked reaction.

I dropped to the turf as tears burned my eyes and blurred the forms of what looked like various vermin. My palms sought the grass, and I leaned on them, one hand on top of the empty paper bag.

"I'm sorry, Daddy," I whispered. "They shouldn't be here."

I lifted my gaze to the writing on his stone, and didn't need to see the letters to know what it said: Ewan McAllister. A man worthy of eternity.

I'd not known what it meant as a kid, but I did now.

I blew out a bracing breath as I sat back on my haunches and studied the bodies piled up on his plot. One skunk, a raccoon, and several dead puppies that looked newborn. My stomach rebelled, not at the smell because there wasn't any fragrance except the aroma of herbs and sulfur. I knew how they'd got there and that was the thing that made my stomach ache.

Abbi had caught them and killed them with her magic and brought them here. The ringing in my ears sounded so much like heartbeats under water that I cocked my head to the side to be sure I wasn't hearing my own heartbeat. My fingers itched to touch the puppies. Their eyes weren't even open yet.

"Poor things," I said, my eye roaming their tiny bodies. Black labs, they looked like, all round and fluffy. Three of them. Three. One of Hecate's sacred numbers.

I pulled the paper bag between my knees, out of the way and out of sight of anyone watching. I'd need to dig beneath the turf to get grave dirt. The last time I was here, the grave was fresh and my mother and I collected earth without trouble.

I scrabbled through the grass, tugging and digging in with my nails. Most of it lifted easily once I got a good edge to work with, and since grave dirt is always so nicely loose and clean of rocks and debris, I managed to scoop several handfuls into the bag before my fingers started hurting and the heel of my hand grew raw from digging.

By my reckoning, I had at least three garden spades full in the bag. I had no idea what I was going to do with it, not yet, but it was good insurance against Honey and her band of merry evil-doers.

I stuffed the bag into my jacket and decided that if anyone was indeed watching, they'd expect Parrish's lover to at least inform her of the dead vermin littering Brie's father's grave.

So I pulled out my phone and noticed three messages from Zach that I'd not heard ping me. I opened the first one just as the snap of a branch caught my attention.

"You should probably come back," it said. A strange enough message that I scrolled to the next, mildly curious, but another snapping noise drew my eye away from the phone screen. I could swear I saw something moving in the bushes. Cautious instead of curious now, I dropped my gaze to the screen, my senses on high alert. My body felt electric, like it was about to catch static.

The next message was cryptic, sent twenty minutes later. "Get the first ride back. Go straight to your room. I'll meet you there."

I stared at the message, thinking I was finished here anyway, but the cab wouldn't be around for another fifteen minutes. I chewed on my lip as another sound, this one closer, echoed through the air. This time it was from the bushes. I could just make out the outline of a bulky black form. Abbi, I thought. The dog was watching me.

The hairs raised on the back of my neck. The cryptic messages and her appearance put my nerves to jangling. I laid my palm on the grass to push myself to my feet and when I did, I felt a jolt go through me. I yanked my hand back to my chest and stared at the ground.

No, not the ground, at the dead animals. The buzzing, the electricity. I knew those sensations. The scent of magic rose around me. My fingers were already moving toward the nearest newborn puppy. Its nose looked wet. Now that I looked more closely, I thought it must have died very recently.

I reached out to touch it and gasped at the jolt that went through my hands and slammed into my chest. I flipped my hands over. They were filthy from the digging, yes, but they were also cut and bleeding too. The abrasive work of digging with my hands had torn into my skin here and there. A smear of blood mixed with the black soil.

I blinked as my vision blurred, trying to clear the shadows creeping into my vision. A roar started behind my ears like the sound of surf after a wind storm. Dizziness shivered through me and I had to prop myself on my hands, my head hanging between my shoulders.

I was catching my breath when a tiny sound met my ear. The smallest of movements caught my eye, and I lifted my gaze toward the earth in front of me. It took several seconds for me to realize one of the pups, the one I'd touched, had started to twitch. Its movements in the sod made a rustling sort of sound.

My sharp intake of breath burned my lungs as confusion swam in the currents of my mind. I reached for it out of instinct, thinking to warm it, and when I touched the soft black ear, the little thing jerked to life.

It foraged for me, smelling me on the air, its eyes still shut. I pulled it close, gathering it beneath my jacket and tucking it against my chest. It snuggled there, warm and undulating while I stared numbly ahead of me. Two more puppies. Could I do the same thing? Was it a fluke? Was this tiny thing not really dead at all?

I couldn't stop myself. Two more times, I laid my palms on the newborns and two more times the jolt and dizziness blistered through me. I gathered them all together beneath my jacket with a sense of elation and awe. I looked at the other poor animals, the raccoon and the skunk and decided to try for the biggest. A test of sorts.

I swallowed hard. The sensation of those pups mewling beneath my coat, burrowing into my armpits and up toward my neck to find the most warmth, clearly was not imaginary. I did raise them. All three couldn't have been asleep. But if they were, it was plain that the other two animals were not. The raccoon showed sign of decay. Its fur had come off in places and whatever luster it had in life had long abandoned it.

I sniffed, testing the air for rot, but smelled only the magic. I looked up over the headstone toward the bushes. Abbi had come all the way out of the tree line and stood between two graves. Her head was slung low, her eyes gleaming red as they watched me.

"You want me to try this, don't you?" I whispered. "You brought them here to me."

As if she could hear me, she shuffled her front paws. I took that to mean yes.

But did I dare? I was already breathing hard from the magic I'd used to raise the pups. The buzzing at the back of my ears had become more high pitched, like a gear revving too high. One of the puppies broke free of my collar and pushed its wet nose into my neck. It tickled.

"Fuck it," I said and reached toward the raccoon.

I almost touched down when my phone buzzed again. Like an anticlimactic scene in a movie, I let go a long breath and sat back again on my haunches. Maybe it was a good thing the phone interrupted me. The magic always took so much from me and the last thing I wanted was to find myself passed out in a graveyard.

I dug the cell out from my pocket, fully expecting Zach to be prodding me again and figuring I'd fire off a text saying I was on my way. I brushed my hand against my jacket so I wouldn't get the screen filthy or bloody and swiped open the screen.

Abbie barked as I did so. She never barked. I'd heard her growl and I'd heard her whine, but never yet had I heard her bark. I looked up to see she'd come closer. Instead of being on the tree line, she had crept forward by several plots. She ducked her head the way a dog does when she's caught sight of something she didn't expect, the primitive movement designed to alert her pack.

That one movement sent shivers through me. Zach wanting me home. Abbi watching me. Her barking. The hairs on my neck raising in alarm. It could only mean one thing. Someone was behind me. Someone was watching me.

With a surreptitious glance over my shoulder, I casually brushed the grass in front of me as though I was clearing away debris. My throat knotted with nerves. As far as I could see, I was alone in the cemetery, and I pulled my hand back to help balance myself and the load of puppies in my coat while I answered the message.

My hand connected with fur right about the same time my gaze fell on my screen again.

I saw the words for three entire seconds before the magic swelled on the horizon of my being like a tsunami gathering.

"Parrish is hurt. Get your ass over here."

But reading it did no good, because one second after seeing the message, the tsunami swept over me.

CHAPTER 26

I WAS DROWNING IN magic. Instead of passing out the way I'd done in the past, I was keenly aware of every ripple of power beneath my skin. I felt it coursing through my veins with a scalding heat that surged upward to my skin. As the magic coursed through me, I felt every prickle, every ache, and every jolt.

It was like sitting in an electric chair without the release of death.

One thought ran through my mind during the whole of those agonizing moments. This wasn't my power.

I understood why it had been too much for a mortal body. The magic came from the power of a goddess. No wonder I couldn't contain it. No wonder I couldn't direct it all those times I'd tried. All those attempts to use the magic, all those times I'd mistakenly tapped into it. It wasn't mine and so it was foreign, an alien substance my body didn't know how to manage.

And it was growing. That was as certain as the sight of the sky above me, the ground below as I writhed on the grass. I panted as the power finally ebbed, my chest heaving and tearing my lungs into shreds. A fist went round my heart and squeezed. I wasn't sure I'd survive the pressure even if I got through the throttling of the power.

I might have blacked out once or twice. I was vaguely aware that the puppies had escaped the confines of my jacket and were mewling around me like baby cats. I hallucinated the raccoon's yellow eyes piercing my gaze. Its face bare of whiskers, it hissed at me through a mouth half decayed, and then leaped on my chest. Its claws dug into my clothes and through them, my skin.

The howl of a wolf echoed across the air and next I knew, the raccoon went sailing over my head. I flung my arms over my face, terrified beyond any sense, letting instinct take my limbs when reason had abandoned me.

In the next instant the fragrance of sulfur and jasmine wafted over me in drafts of hot air. I blinked out from the depths of my fear and dug backwards into the earth with my fingers. My nails dug deep as I clutched at reality, trying to tie myself to this realm. Dizziness threatened to steal me away. I fought it. I fought the power. I might have yelled.

Something touched down on my neck and I did scream then. The sound tore through me from the depths of my marrow. I lost contact with the earth as my hands flew to whatever had me by the throat. Black, whatever it was. Black and filthy and matted with blood.

Whatever reason I had left betrayed me. Kicking and striking out, each blow I delivered landed on solid muscle. The thing from the underworld, I thought. The thing that had tried to steal me before. The thing Scarlett had been afraid of. It was here. In this realm.

Just when I gathered enough air to shriek, enough energy to deliver one final blow, teeth bit down into my neck.

My back arched in pain. My shoulders dug into the earth below me. I gaped and sucked at air like a landed fish. Fur tangled in my fingers as I grappled the thing that held me. I no sooner registered the feel of it then I knew what it was that held me locked in its teeth.

Abbi.

The dog that had protected me and warned me all these weeks had finally turned on me. Betrayal, hot and searing, flooded through me, driving away the terror.

In a heartbeat, all that evaporated.

I fell still.

As a new adult, I'd gone to a water park in the hot summer and picked a ride with a long yellow tunnel that was fully encased. Even at the speed I'd shot down the slide, it had taken an eternity to see the light at the end before I splashed into the pool as the reward. This moment was very much like that. Time stretched out like a long string of hot mozzarella. I had the feeling that I lay there like a landed fish with my eyes bugging out as they stared at the heavens, my arms flung out sideways as the dog pierced my skin.

I expected to die.

I didn't expect to see my mother again.

I barely recognized her, and in the instant I knew it was her, I feared I'd find myself in Lucifer's Boudoir again, begging for my father's soul.

I must have moaned because the dog's grip tightened on my throat. My arms fell away in surrender and the clutch loosened. A hum went through me. Peace flooded my solar plexus. A circuit of sorts had been connected, and it hummed through my veins in elation.

So this was what it was like to feel whole again, I thought. I let my body go slack. The humming intensified. She wasn't trying to kill me. She was trying to communicate.

And the images she sent me robbed me of the peace even if the connection inoculated me against the pain. With a numb sort of awareness, I heard chanting coming from somewhere in the darkness that waited for me. One moment, I was bathed in golden light, feeling the height of possibility, the next I was slammed down into a dank cellar, the cobwebs of magic tangling in my limbs.

I cried out in fury. The chanting swelled, making my skin feel raw. A glance downward revealed my nudity. My skin looked old and haggard. It clung to my bones like tattered rags on a clothesline.

Rage crept up my throat and formed a knot at my larynx. Bitches. They thought to take my power right there in the confines of a disgusting cellar without pomp or ceremony. Their Hecate wheel drawn with a crude hand in salt instead of blood. No sacred sacrifice of pups or horseflesh.

A young woman drew my eye as she came toward me. The knife in her hand was already blooded. Open wounds seeped from between her breasts.

"Your blood is useless, witch," I said to her in a voice that wasn't my own, but sounded terrifyingly familiar. "I find it sour and unpalatable."

She ignored me as she drew the blade across her palm. "Hecate, we bind you," she intoned, and I laughed, a black sound that should gather my power around me like a black mist.

"Better than you have tried," I told her. "Come closer. Paint that sour blood on my skin. See what true power really looks like."

Candles guttered to my right as a draft moved through the cellar. The shadows of the others came into view. Old skin, old faces. Mortal bodies. I barked out another laugh. "Fools," I said to them, lifting my chin defiantly. "You think I'm unprepared for your attack?"

With a mere thought, I let the black shroud of my power pulse around me. It met the magic of the coven and tangled within it, but it freed me from their restraints as their magic battled my own. It was weaker than it should have been stored in the blood that ran in my veins, a residue of what was left to me.

"You should have killed me when you had the chance," I said to the young witch, who had dropped to her knees beside a molded bronze box marked with all the trappings of my power. Molded into its sides were images of dogs howling and chasing hares. Horses in full rear and gallop. A serpent coiled itself around the edges of the box, finding the corners with its tail and shedding its skin along the bottom. Beautiful and hand-crafted, I eyed it suspiciously.

Whether she was aware or not, she was feeding me with her magic. I haven't felt so alive in a century.

"You should have been more careful, witch," I said to her. "What remnants of power I have in this mortal body is awakened by your spell casting."

I grinned at her even though my lips felt as though they're curling back off my teeth in revulsion. "Like calls to like, does it not? My magic wants to answer yours."

She threw herself forward, prostrate on the filthy floor covered in spider excrement and beetle carcasses. Like Salome, she undulated as she called out to her master for his help to battle my magic and hold it at bay while her coven did what it could to steal what it couldn't before.

"Your magic feeds me, witch," I say, and I felt the binds slip, finally. The elation of magic's electricity charging the room tasted like a fine wine on my palate. I drew in a breath, dropping my head back, stretching out my arms to gather it all to me.

Like a man starved and thirsting for water, I strained for the power she and her coven gave off like perfume. It tasted of brimstone and pitch, the stink of Lucifer's magic. Even so, I welcomed it.

The young witch pulled back like the tide releasing the beach. She drew herself up, pointing the knife blade at her heart.

"Do it, witch," I dare you. "You call to my magic, thinking I will raise you?" I snorted even as I sensed the power gathering around me. I nearly had a fully bloated orb of it within reach of my outstretched arms. One more burst of power, one more incantation and it would swell to within the scope of my reach. "Lucifer is greedy. He won't let you give me one particle of energy to allow me to do that."

She canted her head at me as she pricked her breast. Blood trickled from the wound.

I didn't feel the blade cut into me from behind until I tried to laugh and discovered it came out in a gargle.

My hands flew to my throat. She'd tricked me, the bitch. Her whole damn coven tricked me and as I strained to keep her in my gaze, I fell to my knees. Our eyes were at the same level, and I could peer right into her black heart through her eyes.

She grinned.

"Mother, return to us whole that we might give you to eternity. That we might wear your mantle. That we might become as one with the gods through your blood."

They've called me here to steal what they think has the fullness of my power. Fools. The mortal body I wore slumped to the floor. That blood they wanted soaked my ribs. Cold crept over me with clammy feet as she flipped open the cover of the trunk.

"It's not yours," I told her, but the words burbled through the fluid coating my lips. I wasn't sure she or her sisters even realized what they've done. "It's not mine, either, not anymore." I said with a laugh that made me cough. I couldn't breathe with the way my lungs were filling up.

With one last sharp inhale, I held onto the air that found its way into my lungs. My palm dropped forward into the pool leaked out onto the dirt and dust, and I used it to prop myself up as best I could. With a trembling finger, I etched the final symbols into the dirt for the spell I began all those years ago, a spell cast in birthing blood and carried to term by this moment.

Runes for time, for protection, for transference, and memory. Runes for binding and communicating and reanimation. Seven runes for my daughter, all creating a time bomb of sorts. A spell that on my death imparts the last of my power to the blood of my kin. A spell triggered by blood, a smattering of it on my book of spells, my photos, my amulet, all things she will find in her time, her magic—my magic—will awaken. Seven vessels, holding my essence.

I was barely aware of the coven as it crept forward, thinking they've ended me, thinking to steal my power. I hardly noticed when one of them lifted my foot and dragged me by the ankle toward that blasted trunk. But when the air I held in my lungs finally leaked through my lips, and I burned with the last of the air, I knew that when Brie finds my blood and it called to her, she'd be that cudgel I couldn't be.

And then all Hell will break loose.

CHAPTER 27

THE CABBIE FOUND ME weak and incoherent. All I could do was lie there and look up at his concerned face. He checked my vitals and made satisfied noises, so I supposed that although I couldn't form a coherent sentence, I was far from dead. Shock, he probably thought, a notion that bore out when he spoke to me.

"I'll get you in the car and get you warmed up." He hefted me beneath my shoulders.

"Damn lucky I found you," he said. "You were so adamant you'd be back that I came looking for you. Just in time it looks like. You pissed yourself. And your wig is nothing but a skunk's hat now." He jerked his chin in the direction of my father's grave. Following his gesture, I caught sight of Parrish's splendid cosplay wig lying on top of the dead skunk. I grimaced. I didn't think she'd want it back now.

The raccoon was long gone, and so were the puppies. I tried to tell myself they'd not gone mewling around the cemetery, easy pickings for ravens or owls, that Abbi had found a way to assimilate them. She was gone, that was for sure. So maybe it was possible.

I tracked my gaze back to the cab driver's face, inhaling to put some strength into my legs. From below him, I could see his nose wrinkle as he took in a breath. "I don't know what the hell you were doing here, but you stink." He looked down at me as he wrestled me against his chest. "Did someone throw rotten eggs at you or something?"

I swayed in his clutch and managed to get my footing, albeit tentative and weak. His grip on me helped, and I leaned against him, grateful for the kindness that set him on the search for me. I could have lain there for hours before I regained my senses.

"Time?" I asked.

"What's that?" His brow furrowed and wrinkles bracketed his eyes. I repeated my question, this time concentrating on enunciation. It took a few moments of him wrangling me, slipping his arm beneath mine to wrap over my back, before he understood.

"Oh, time." He muscled me along with him, and my feet dragged as much as they moved. He was grunting a lot. "I waited for you for ten minutes before I decided something must have happened and you weren't just late. Took me almost an hour to find you."

Each step, I was regaining my strength, but it was slow going. His patience never wavered and he didn't grumble about the money he was losing, trying to help a seemingly incontinent mad woman out of a pickle. Instead, he rambled on as though this was an everyday occurrence. I told myself I'd take some of the money that I'd earned from exorcising the death mask and make sure he got it as reward.

"You're doing better," he remarked by the time we made it to the cab. "I thought for a while, I was going to have to take you to the hospital." He propped me up beside the cab as he worked on the handle with one arm holding me up. When he slid his gaze over me, I made an effort to smile.

"I'm feeling better," I said and was surprised it came out coherent. My shoulders sagged in relief as his head bobbed.

"No hospital, then?" he asked.

I shook my head and gave him Owen's address. I felt sick that I'd been out so long while Parrish was hurt. "I need to get home."

He tapped his forehead with his fingers. "Sure thing. But don't let me see your picture on the news tomorrow or in the obits."

I slid into the back seat and rested my head on the backrest as he closed the door. He tapped the hood and I squeezed my eyes shut to hold back the tears. Parrish would have done that four times. Worry made me fidget in the seat as the cab pulled out of the parking area.

I wasn't sure why I gave one last look behind my shoulder. Maybe I was looking for Abbi or the puppies as I tried to work through the events she had shown me. There was so much to unpack and I knew it would take me a while to do so.

Whatever it was, the tingling at the base of my nape or the need to see my mother's familiar, or the haunting feeling that my father might be standing at his graveside, I did catch sight of something, and it caused goosebumps to rise on my arms.

"Honey," I said as I noted the swing of hair and stoic gaze of the woman watching us beside one of the crypts.

"What's that?" the driver asked.

I shivered involuntarily and turned around, hanging my head out of sight. "Nothing," I mumbled.

Had she watched us mincing our way across the grass? If she'd been close enough to watch the entire event unfold as Abbi held me pinned on my father's grave, she'd know it was me even if the wig had stayed on.

The wig. I groaned out loud. I was heading to Owen's manse sans wig. I pulled my phone out, breathless with nerves and sent Zach a message, telling him I was coming and asking about Parrish. The phone rang.

He didn't waste time with niceties. "She's not able to shift to heal," he said. "She'd be fine if she could shift. I don't know what he did to her, but it's not just physical." The pain that seeped through the technology reached me in the cab and a fist closed around my heart.

Not just physical meant there was absolutely physical wounds. I didn't dare ask how bad. I wasn't sure I was ready to hear it. I could be brave, but not that brave.

"I'm in a cab," I said, indicating I couldn't say much. "Is she in hospital."

"You sound weird," he said.

I swallowed down the hard lump that had formed. Weird was a vague term. It could mean anything. "I'm worried about her."

"Both of us are," he said. "She's in bad shape. But that's not what I meant. Are you alright?"

I ran my fingers over my forehead, drawing the thumb toward them as I put pressure on the place that had begun to ache. "A headache," I said. He didn't need to know what had happened at the cemetery. Not right then. Too much was at stake with Layne and Parrish. "It's nothing. Just tell me you've got her safe. That you're looking after her."

"She's in the emergency wing here at the manse."

I didn't like the thickness of his tone or the way it sounded like a huge 'but' should have been tagged to the end. Sagging against the back of the seat, I let my head roll to look out the window as the buildings sped by. Horns sounded outside the vehicle as traffic pushed and shoved its way through rush hour.

"I'm so tired I don't even look like me," I said in the hopes he'd understand.

"I'm alone," he said. "Unless you count Parrish."

I nodded mutely. "I want to see her," I told him. "But I don't know how."

"Just come. You should be here. The emergency wing is small, in the basement. It has its own entrance but it won't matter. I told you I was alone. Everyone else is with Owen."

The strangeness in his voice worried me. I tapped my credit card on the taxi's payment machine and thanked him profusely. He blushed. An older gentleman who still had a sense of old world genteelness. I couldn't stop myself from squeezing his hand.

"You're sure you're fine?" he said.

I nodded. "I feel much stronger now. Probably just my low sugar. I'll be better once I eat." It was enough to brush off his concern.

I wasn't lying. Except for a pulsing sort of headache at the back of my neck, I felt more energized than I had in weeks. A tingle not unlike tinnitus hummed behind my ears.

I got out and followed Zach's directions through the back of the manse into the elevator that went one way only. He was right when he said he was alone. My footfalls echoed back at me with every step in an eerie ricochet. And with every step, my throat grew tighter.

I stood in front of an iron door that looked like a bank vault.

"You weren't kidding," I said when he opened the door. "The place is a ghost town."

The lines around his eyes deepened as he gave me a tight, humorless grin. "No one cares about her," he said. "I didn't think you'd have any trouble. The emergency is all about Layne." He cast a look over his shoulder into the interior of the room. "If she lives or dies is of no consequence to them."

I tracked his gaze to the single bed in the room. Without consciously taking in the surroundings, I knew the space was sterile. I knew the windowless interior held all the trappings of an operating room. What I didn't know was how bad I'd react when my gaze fell on the form lying atop one of the three stretchers lined up along the wall.

Zach caught me before I fell.

"It's hard, I know," he said as he wrapped his arm around my waist and held me aloft so easily I might have been a feather pillow. He peered down at me. "You'll be fine. Even if she doesn't respond, she can hear you."

Meaning be careful. Remain positive.

I nodded and swallowed down the nerves. For Parrish's sake, I needed to stay calm. But it was hard. She looked so frail. The multiple wounds on her arms, the bruising on her cheek and neck, she looked a mess.

"Most of the damage is internal," he whispered when he noticed the direction of my gaze. "By the time I got to them, he had her by the throat and was just pinning her to the floor. To be honest, I'm not sure it would have been so bad if she hadn't fought him. Emmet said it was almost as though he was forcing her to submit but she wouldn't."

He shook his head and sighed. "But at least you're here for her. She'll be grateful."

I pressed my palm into his chest to push off and gather my own strength.

"I can manage," I said and he gave me a short nod.

I approached the stretcher the way I might if I was approaching a cobra. When I lay my fingers on her wrist, one of the only places I felt safe to touch, her hand twitched. A hiss of relief escaped me, but I knew it was temporary at best. Even I knew it was bad. Deathly bad.

"I'm here," I whispered. "It's me. You're in good care."

I knew she knew that. She might have history with Zach but she'd have to know he cared about her, that he would do his best to help.

"What happened down there, Parrish? What the hell happened?" I didn't mean to demand information from her or sound so hopelessly angry, but I was a chaos of emotions and the threat of them overrunning my sanity was too close to hold back. Zach moved beside me, and luckily, the ache of tightness in my throat kept me from saying more.

"I keep telling her to shift but she won't," he said. "It's not a power over her that I exert, but I tried today. Damn it all, I tried."

I looked down at her. It was hard to believe shifting could take away all the damage to her body.

"Parrish," I whispered. "You're being too fucking stubborn just because it's Zach asking it of you. Shift already. Damn you. I need you. Shift."

Her throat moved as she swallowed. Her fingers closed over mine.

"Please," I said. "I can't lose you too."

Zach tapped the monitor attached to her chest four times. "I was hoping she'd listen to you," he said as his fingers roamed from the monitor to the pulse in her throat. "But if she won't, she must not want to heal. No one but her alpha can force her to shift if she doesn't want to."

I pivoted to stare at him. "Her alpha can force her to shift?"

He snorted out a laugh. "Fat chance of that happening. We'll be losing both of them at this rate." He threaded his fingers through hers and held her hand. "I told her I loved her," he said and then I recognized the pain in his voice. If he'd let it slip through, I knew it was bad. "I thought maybe that would put the piss and vinegar back in her spine, but she just lies there. I can't do any more for her than I have."

I tracked his gaze back to her face. The cheeks were swollen and bruised. She had a cut beneath her left eye. Her red hair in spots was clotted with blood. It was so hard to believe Layne had done this to her.

"Can Owen do anything?"

"Owen *is* doing something," he said. "He's called the pack together to discuss the final measures." He nodded in Parrish's direction. "At first, I thought he asked her to work on Layne because it didn't matter to him if she lived or died. But now, I'm realizing it was his last hope." A dark timbre carried through his voice. "I think he knows he can't save Layne and I don't think he has the heart to keep him chained." He swung his gaze to mine.

"I'm pretty sure they're voting to put him down."

CHAPTER 28

OWEN WAS PURE EVIL. Any man who would kill his own son had to have a chunk of black coal for a heart.

I pulled away from the bed. "How can he even consider such a thing?" I reeled toward the door of the ward.

"Brie," Zach said, catching my arm. "It's not his decision alone. He has to consider the pack."

I spun on him, tearing my arm from his grip and rubbing the wrist where the pressure had been too tight. "You're OK with this? You condone it?"

"It's the pack way. He's a danger to everyone. No shifter would want to be chained or imprisoned until he wastes away. Layne wouldn't want that."

"Layne would want us to fight for him," I said.

He shook his head. "You're wrong. Layne wouldn't want to live with the knowledge he'd hurt someone." His voice carried a note of anger that made me look over at Parrish. "He would hate knowing what he'd done, what we'd let him do."

"You're letting him die because you're angry at him. Because of what he did to Parrish." My voice broke and it took a moment to collect myself. "I am sick to death over what's happened. I don't want to lose her, but I can't just let you all kill him."

"You have no say in the matter," he said. "The pack will vote. It will be done."

"And if he can save Parrish?" I asked. "If he can force her to shift?"

He reached for my hands and held them against his waist. "Don't you think I've thought of that? But if he isn't himself, if he did this to her in the first place, how could he?"

My eye drifted to where Parrish lay. "What if I can reach him when she couldn't?" I asked. "You said it was like he was trying to force her to submit but she wouldn't. What if there's some piece of himself still in there?"

"What if not?" he responded. "We'd end up with three dead pack members instead of two."

His comment took me aback. "I'm not pack," I said. "No one will care. Take me to him."

He shook his head.

"Take me there," I demanded. "We don't have time to lose. Do you want to save her? At least give me the chance. I'll stay clear. Just give me the chance."

The lump in his throat plunged and rose then he bobbed his head. "We best be quick," he said. "These things can take a while or they can be decided very quick." He let go one hand and led me with the other to the door. "We keep the safe room on the same level as the ward in case of emergency." His voice broke. "In this case, I'm very glad of it."

It occurred to me that all along we'd been within yards of Layne but I'd heard nothing. When Zach yanked open the door and looked back at me, he must have seen my confusion.

"He's heavily sedated," he explained. "In case. Well. In case."

I didn't need him to say that he was sedated in case someone needed to approach him to deliver the death blow, and I didn't ask how it would happen. Because it wouldn't happen. Not if I could help it.

Layne looked nothing like the man I loved. The wolf was what greeted my gaze. It lay stretched out on his side with his chest rising and falling in irregular rhythm. Layne as his wolf half was huge. I'd only seen it once, when he'd shown me what he was, and I'd been in such shock, I'd not truly registered exactly how both magnificent and terrifying he was.

Blood still gathered in puddles around him and spattered the walls. The cot had been upturned and the legs torn off and flung, in twisted pretzel shapes out of his reach.

"Sweet Jesus," I said.

At my voice, Layne looked up and his eyes rested on my face. He squinted. Cocked his head to the side. I touched my cheeks, feeling for the prosthetics Parrish had glued there the day before. My fingers brushed against the frayed and lifting edges of them.

"We need a Jesus-sized miracle right now," Zach drawled and closed the door behind us. He nodded at the legs. "He did that before he transformed. When Parrish..." he hesitated, probably gathering his thoughts. "When Parrish told him he needed to be a man already and take control."

We both stood just inside the room, out of reach of the chains that held Layne to the wall of the cell. I took in the whole of the area, noting where the cot lay and the drying stains of blood. When I approached, I didn't want to trip over or slip in anything if I needed to run.

"What are you doing?" Zach said as he caught my arm when I took a step deeper into the room.

"What do you think?" I asked. "What I came here to do."

I pulled free and inched closer to the wolf as it lay there watching me with a wary, almost knowing eye. I ran my hand through my hair as I approached, thinking to brush it free and finding the netting holding my locks tight to my head to fit the wig. With an impatient movement, I yanked it off and tossed it aside.

The wolf's head lowered and his front paws slid out in front of him.

"Layne," I said. "It's me."

Even as my fingers moved to my cheeks and peeled away the prosthetics, the wolf had heaved himself to his feet. Zach's sharp intake of breath behind me almost made me freeze, but I was all in now. I recalled that before, my scent had been covered by alcohol and various oils, but I'd not put anything on that morning. My own pheromones were all the perfume I wore.

"I'm sorry," I said. "I lied about it all. I lied about me and your father. There was nothing between us."

I paused just out of reach. The wolf shuddered as it tried to remain standing.

"Parrish needs you," I said. "She needs her alpha."

Layne's wolfish head dropped. His hackles went up. A low growl rumbled through the air as his nostrils flared.

I swallowed nervously. Zach entreated me to back up. "It's foolish, Brie. Let it go. He's gone."

I answered without taking my eyes off Layne's. "That's why you're here," I said. "If he hurts me, I deserve it, but make sure you finish him quickly."

With my breath caught in my throat, I took one more step. This one would put me within a hair's reach of those massive paws. The claws dug into the floor.

Layne blinked, swinging his gaze from me to Zach and then back to me again.

"I won't let them hurt you," I said and peeled away the shirt, exposing the runes I knew were there, runes he couldn't see except for the scars I'd inflicted on myself trying to access them. "If I have to bring all the magic I own to bear, I won't let them hurt you."

I drew in one last, bracing breath and took that last step. Zach called out to me, but it was too late. I was already in striking distance.

Before I could stop myself, I dropped to my knees beside Layne. I trembled with fear as those yellow eyes looked into mine. Something flickered behind them. His jaw dropped.

"If by some miracle you still love me, Layne, then come to me."

As if the wolf needed to be sure, he swung his muzzle toward me and forced his nose beneath my chin. Instinct alone let me lift it, exposing my throat. Electricity sizzled through the air as my terror bowed to the love I felt for the man. Whatever happened, I knew Zach would finish him quickly and humanely.

I felt the air around me suck toward Layne as he drew in a long inhalation. My arms moved on their own, wrapping around the wolf's neck, my fingers tangling in his fur. Even though I embraced him so tightly my fingers barely reached each other enough to thread together.

I was aware of Zach inches behind me. The wolf beneath me shuddered violently and then the distinct sound of cracking and popping met my ears. I felt the shifting of muscle and bone beneath my arms. Zach yanked me away.

I fell on my backside, my hands striking the cold tile. Zach gripped me beneath the armpits and helped me crab my way out of reach.

"He's changing. It will be painful. Your touch will just make it worse." The wonder and excitement in his voice was unmistakable. "You fucking did it, Brie. He's changing."

At that, he rushed forward with a blanket and by the time he tossed it over Layne's shoulders, the wolf was gone.

"We've got you, man," Zach said. "Holy fuck, we've got you. Jesus, man, that was too fast. You're going to hurt for weeks."

Layne pushed him aside and flung the blanket off his back. "Brie," he said, reaching for me.

I hesitated, not wanting to hurt him.

"Come to me, Brie."

I went. He gathered me against his naked skin and when it shivered and trembled, I tried to let go.

"No," he said, his voice a growl. "I want the pain of your touch. I want *you*." He buried his face in my neck, this time as a man and I felt his tears sliding down my collarbone.

I vaguely heard Zach's retreat and the door closing, and for long moments, we remained glued to one another by his sweat and fluid and blood. I might have whispered secrets to him as we clung to each other. If I explained my death and rebirth and the reason for it all, it might not have been in coherent sentences. He listened and tensed and squeezed me tighter, and then he cupped the side of my face and kissed me long and hard, with the abandon of joy that he'd discovered the greatest of gifts.

Then, like the alpha he was, he pushed me away and stood on legs that had to be quaking with weakness.

"It's time to bring Parrish back," he said and completely naked strode to the door. He rapped four times and before he pulled his fist away, Zach had opened the door.

"Our stubborn wolf is playing dead is she?" he said to Zach, pushing him aside. "Let's see what I can do about that. Take Brie out of here."

He looked down at me with fire in his gaze. "My father hurt you," he said to me. "That won't happen again."

CHAPTER 29

I WORE A SIMPLE black dress to my funeral. Parrish and I and Zach and Layne all stood at my father's graveside and buried an empty urn at the head of the grave.

Parrish stood in the middle of Layne and I, holding our hands. I didn't think her swaying on her feet was a complete act for the benefit of beta pack spies. Neither was Layne's. Since Zach had taken me to his apartment after we'd left the manse, Layne and Parrish had to fill us in on what happened once Layne strode down the hall to see her.

That they were both burying a witch beneath an autumn sky filled with mackerel clouds was a testament to the magic of an alpha wolf shifter. And it spoke volumes about the personal strength of the man himself. To hear him tell it, he'd simply lain his hand on her chest and told her to let her wolf heal her.

Her recollection was much different. Her transformation to her wolf was an arduous task. It hurt her. She cried out and swore and sweat, and Layne mercilessly drove her through it because he knew it had to be done. Weak and spent himself from the drugs and the rehabilitation, he'd given her of his own magic what he could to help ease what pain he could. By the end of it, they were both curled into fetal positions on the floor, whole and human, but not without the evidence of wear and tear.

They both wore the wear and tear like sheets as they stood with me at my grave.

Zach told me that when the pack finalized their vote and descended to the cellar hours later, they were both still lying on the cold tiles, clammy and shivering. Everyone assumed he'd broken free of his prison and went to her to finish the job he'd started and that with her submission, he regained his humanity.

If Owen felt Layne's cold rage and wooden response beneath his crushing embrace, he showed no indication. Instead, his relief was palpable enough that the entire pack heaved a collective sigh. As Parrish told it, daggers were sharpening beneath Layne's eyes but Owen acted as though they would be used to skewer juicy morsels of steak for a pack buffet.

No one questioned the miracle. Layne would bide his time, and when that time was ripe, he'd make his father pay for his betrayal.

That's why as I sprinkled dry earth over an empty urn, burying myself, I still wore the disguise with a brand new wig. It was the reason Parrish played the grieving friend and Layne, the mourning ex. It was the reason we'd done all we could to make the burial look authentic.

"Do you think they'll fall for it?" Zach whispered and Parrish snorted.

"People see what they want," she said.

Zach made the sign of the cross over his chest as the 'minister' intoned a prayer and said Amen. "Let's hope they want to see Brie dead."

"Watch it," Parrish growled beneath her breath at him.

"I didn't say *I* wanted her dead," he muttered. "Besides, what are you going to do to me anyway? You can barely stand up."

"Don't tempt me," she said.

I had the feeling the bickering would continue, and I just didn't have the head for it right then. Sensing my unease, Layne cut them both off with a quiet curse. Both of them went still and rigid, but my shoulders sagged in relief. When he squeezed my hand, I squeezed right back.

We'd not had much time to plan, but luckily, it didn't take much time to arrange the details.

My funeral was a small affair, noted in the obituaries as a tragic suicide. We'd hired a homeless man and bought him a suit so he could act as minister, offering a blessing. He came cheap, a bottle of rum and fifty bucks, but Layne stuffed another couple hundred in the pockets. The old sod might want to eat at some point, he'd said. The matter of keeping him just sober enough to deliver the rites without looking too unnatural was managed by housing him in a motel for the morning.

I lifted my gaze to the man as he read from a script we'd stuffed into the Bible he held. His eyes had a rheumy glaze to them, but I doubted anyone looking on from some strategic spot in the cemetery would notice. The grounds were relatively clear, and Parrish didn't know any of the people visiting graves around us. Then, we couldn't be sure how many new werewolves Owen had made and turned into a second pack so he could do the coven's bidding, so we were taking no chances.

A few strangers lingered over various graves, and I eyed them with a fatigued but cautious glance. I'd learned not to put anything past the cult, and although

I was sure Honey had spotted me getting into the cab two days earlier, I still held out hope that she wasn't entirely sure it was me. One more reason for the funeral.

The sharp report of a book snapping closed drew my attention back to the minister. He was beginning to blink too quickly. Beads of perspiration had collected on his brow.

"We should finish up soon," I said to Layne. "He's looking a little peaked."

Layne said nothing but his glance at Zach caused the doctor to gesture at the minister. The old gent wasted no time cutting the graveside eulogy short. A single nod from Layne and he backed away several feet before turning his back to us and hurrying from the cemetery.

Parrish let out a long sigh. "Thank God that's over," she said as she pivoted to face me, dropping my hand and brushing aside a long strand of black hair from my forehead. It was a gentle touch, compassionate, and I knew she wasn't just doing it for show.

"It's far from over," I said, gripping Layne's hand even tighter, aware I shouldn't be when the woman who was supposed to be my lover stood right there with us.

As though Layne read my thoughts, he pulled his hand from mine, but laid it over my shoulder and tugged me close in a friendly gesture. He smelled of vanilla and aftershave and when his lips dipped to my cheek on the side Zach blocked from view, they lingered long on my skin.

"It may not be over, but you have us," he whispered, and I couldn't help turning my gaze to his. "And the only thing that will separate you from me again is your true death or mine."

Zach's eye trailed to Parrish's face as Layne made that declaration, but her gaze was off in the bushes somewhere. She hadn't stopped surveying the grave-yard since we'd entered. Layne was the same, except his eye abandoned his surveillance once or twice to catch my eye. The three of them surrounded me almost without thought, as though I'd compelled them to me. They were mine, my pack, although I wasn't a werewolf nor did I want to be.

I was something else completely, and they were will-ing to accept me and what I was, the same as I was willing to accept them. But if they thought they were there to protect me from the coven, they were wrong. So very wrong.

"I'm hiding for now," I said as I caught sight of move-ment from the corner of my eye. I turned to see a familiar woman striding across the grass. "But mark my words," I said as I lifted my hand in greeting to Ava, who I'd purposely notified of the service, even if I did give her a time twenty minutes later than we planned for.

"What in the hell, Brie." Parrish shuffled to the side when she saw her. "What is she doing here? She's going to blow your cover, you fool." She backed into me and reached back for my hand again, all nerves and des-peration. I just wasn't sure either of them was for my welfare at all.

I gripped her fingers and squeezed. "She was wor-ried about you." I gave her a shove forward as Ava approached close enough that the grin on her face as she saw Parrish was hard to miss. "And besides. I'm done being afraid."

Layne kissed my temple with soft lips. "I doubt you were ever afraid," he said.

I pulled away so I could see his face, the hardness of his jaw, the yellow of his eyes, the bruises beneath his cheekbones that made his profile look so harsh because he'd lost weight and everything in him had drawn inward.

"I'm not wearing this damn disguise because I'm afraid," I said, loud enough, clear enough that all three of them would hear my truth. "I'm dressed like this so I can fit the rest of the spell into place. This is a ruse. One designed to make them think I'm afraid. I just need the time to pull together the spell my mother cast and created and put in place the moment my father died."

Layne canted his head at me, pride deepening the lines that bracketed his eyes as he regarded me. "You're going after them?" he said. "You're going to finish this."

I dropped my head back, letting the strands of the black wig hang away from my face and exposing the skin to the air and the mist that had begun to gather. I was Hecate's daughter, demigod, child of magic.

"They have my mother's bones in a box," I said. "They think they can hold her and raise her and steal her magic. They have her grimoire, her amulet. They've taken her photo. But they don't have all of her. They haven't mastered command of John Smith or my mother's familiar. And they don't know the true secret of the seventh vessel."

"You're saying you've found the final vessel?" Parrish said, her eyebrows squirreled together. "You know where the last of her power is."

I chuckled out loud because of course I did. They all knew. "You're looking at it," I said. "My blood isn't my own anymore. You said it Zach. It's transformed. It's not human. It's the blood of a god. That's the truth of it. My mother stored her essence in seven vessels while she was still alive. Her bones, her mortal body was just what remained of it. I'm going to find her bones, and I'm going to do what I was meant to do, what the cult is trying to keep me from doing. I'm going to raise my mother from the dead."

I heard their sharp intakes of breath, the gasps, the curses even, but what they didn't know, that I did, was that in order to raise my mother, all those parts had to reintegrate. The dog, the loyal follower, grimoire, amulet, photo, and me, all of us had to join to animate those bones and bring her back to life. We all had to do our part and that meant that once we reintegrated and Hecate raised, she'd vanquish the cult once and for all, but the rest of us, the vessels, we'd be empty.

And I'd never known an empty vessel to be useful. And once used up, what would happen then?

I didn't need to read the whole story to know the end.

But for now, it was pleasant just to be. To watch Parrish cross the manicured grass to meet a woman who would never be her Violet, but who would, I was sure, give her some peace.

Layne tugged me close, giving Parrish the space to withdraw as Ava drew nearer. "Show her what you got, Parrish."

"Yeah, Parrish," I said, with an indulgent tone swelling in my voice, thickening my throat. "Go give her hell."

-The End (for now)

Dearest Reader,

Thanks so much for believing in this series and getting this far. I'm so humbled by your support. As you can see, we are nowhere near done. I am feverishly working on *Mortal Magic*. If you don't want to miss the rest of the story, do go check out the next book. It's called Mortal Magic.

If you don't want to miss any updates, and are looking for a quick read to fill in the gaps, you can grab a free copy of ***Savior*** from my website.

About Author

Thea is a NEW YORK TIMES and USA TODAY Bestselling Author. She used to have a black lab at her feet when she wrote, warming up the calves. It can be cold in rural Nova Scotia. Now it's just a cuppa tea keeping her warm.

Whether she's finding ways to lure Isabella Hush into the Shadow Bazaar or throwing the switch on a new monster, her urban fantasy pulses with dark themes and action-packed intrigue. Her characters are always deeply wounded creatures struggling for redemption. The romance is slow-burn but worth it, and the humor just might have a touch of Canadiana.

As a fan of Dannika Dark and Patricia Briggs, she hopes you enjoy slipping into the skin of her characters as much as she enjoy theirs.

Hang out with her on the socials:

ACKNOWLEDGMENTS

Debra Martin is an author I admire, and I want to give special mention to her for all the hours she has put in to help me make this story clean. She found several inconsistencies in the overall plot that inevitably creep in when you write a story over several months. If you enjoy romance and fantasy, do look her up on the internet and pick up a book or two.

In addition, I have several loyal readers who occupy special places in my writer's heart. Some of them, like Caroline Jenkins always take the time to find my little oopsies and sometimes my big ones. She is also incredible at encouraging me along the way. An author needs readers like that.

Then there's readers like Crystal Crystal Amason, who isn't just a reader, she's a sponsor, and you don't get more loyal than that. She is the first reader to make me feel like my tales were worth reading. Thank you, Crystal. I hope I can continue to write stories you enjoy.

To my other patrons who prefer to remain anonymous, I thank you. You know who you are.

I really appreciate you all.

-thea-

www.ingramcontent.com/pod-product-compliance
Lightning Source LLC
Chambersburg PA
CBHW020652120726

47906CB00001B/230